THE
INSANE
TRAIN

ALSO BY SHELDON RUSSELL

Dreams to Dust
Empire
Requiem at Dawn
The Savage Trail
The Yard Dog

THE
INSANE
TRAIN

SHELDON RUSSELL

MINOTAUR BOOKS ☪ NEW YORK

THE INSANE TRAIN. Copyright © 2010 by Sheldon Russell. All rights reserved. Printed in the United States of America. For information, address St. Martin's Press, 175 Fifth Avenue, New York, N.Y. 10010.

www.minotaurbooks.com

Library of Congress Cataloging-in-Publication Data

Russell, Sheldon.
   The insane train / Sheldon Russell. — 1st. ed.
      p. cm.
   ISBN 978-0-312-56671-5
   1. Mentally ill—Fiction.   2. Railroad trains—Fiction.   3. Murder—
Fiction.   4. Revenge—Fiction.   I. Title.
   PS3568.U777I57 2010
   813'.54—dc22

                                2010032672

First Edition: November 2010

10 9 8 7 6 5 4 3 2 1

To Nancy, who brightens my days

ACKNOWLEDGMENTS

WHEN WRITING, IT'S easy to be enticed down unintended paths, to become lost in one's imaginary world. At such times, I'm grateful for the collaborative aspect of writing. At hand are clear-minded professionals who are capable of guiding me back home. I'd like to acknowledge my editor, Daniela Rapp, at Minotaur Books and my agents, Michael and Susan Morgan Farris. In addition I would like to acknowledge all the other team members at St. Martin's who helped root out my errors. They made the work the best it could be.

PROLOGUE

Nurse Andrea Delven looked out the upstairs window of the women's quarters at the Baldwin Insane Asylum in Barstow, California. Her feet ached, and the evening shift had only just begun. Over its course, the war in Germany had drained away almost all available help, leaving her with long and demanding hours.

When she spotted a light across the way in the boys' ward, she paused. At first she thought it flickered, like a lamp or a candle might. But inmates were not permitted matches, not even for their cigarettes.

She finished rounds and returned to the window to stand in the cool breeze. The smell of smoke drifted in. The Mexicans who worked section gang for the railroad often built campfires in the desert nights.

Andrea clicked the lights on and off to signal bedtime. She waited and then clicked them again, her third try that evening to settle in the patients. Earlier, Bess Henson had refused to get undressed, and, when Andrea had insisted, Bess pulled all her bedding onto the floor.

Back at the nurses' station, Andrea prepared meds for Esther Ringwood, a dementia patient. Esther claimed her meds turned her stool green, and that taking them made her vulnerable to malaria and other dreaded diseases. Twice now Andrea had found Esther's meds in the toilet. Last week she'd discovered a pill hidden in Esther's ear canal.

The smell of smoke that came through the window was even stronger now. Sometimes the Mexicans burned old ties that had been replaced along the tracks. The creosote in them made a hot fire, but the smell drifted for miles in the wind. On a hot day in Barstow even the desert sun could release the pungent odor from out of the ties.

Andrea settled back with a cola. She preferred the night shift. There were fewer bosses and less confusion. The women's ward, which also housed the younger girls, was generally the easiest to control. There was still the potential for trouble under the right circumstances, though typically her patients were more annoying than violent.

Frankie Yager, the orderly over in the boys' ward, had been hired shortly after Doctor Bria Helms's arrival at Baldwin. Though Frankie was not a nurse by any stretch, his physical presence served well in controlling the male adolescents, many of whom were diagnosed idiots and defectives. Even though by legal definition they were children, and seperated from the older men for their own protection, the males in Frankie's ward could blow out of control with the slightest provocation.

A breeze swept in and stirred the curtains. Andrea rubbed at her eyes, which now burned from the smoke.

At least she didn't work in the security ward, the lockdown unit for the criminally insane, which sat on the far side of the compound. Having committed heinous crimes, the inmates there were secured day and night. Even so, duty in the security ward was the most dangerous assignment at the Baldwin Insane Asylum.

Employees in that ward were not permitted weapons to protect themselves, though their lives were in jeopardy each time they entered. A panic button mounted on the wall constituted the single lifeline for the employees.

Females, save for Doctor Helms herself, were rarely permitted in the security ward. On a few occasions, Andrea had assisted Doctor Helms, but even now Andrea's scalp tightened at the thought of it.

Andrea rose to close the window and glanced over at the boys' ward across the way. She looked again, and her breath caught. Flames licked up the curtains, and smoke seeped from around the upstairs windows.

"Oh my God," she said.

As she headed next door, she grabbed Esther, who had gotten out of bed to go to the bathroom. The tail of her house robe had caught in her panties, and her false teeth were still in her hand.

Esther squealed as Andrea pulled her out the door and onto the lawn. The flames already lapped under the eaves of the boys' ward. Embers drifted upward and settled back down onto the cedar shingles. A cry rose up from behind the flames upstairs, and Andrea's mouth went hot. There were boys trapped up there.

She dragged Esther to the fire bell, which was mounted on a post in the center of the compound, and rang it once before shoving the rope into Esther's hand.

"Ring it!" she shouted, pulling Esther's arm down. "Like this. Ring it, Esther! Ring it!"

Esther commenced ringing the bell with wide swings of her body, filling the night with alarm. Smoke boiled in a black cloud over the compound. Flames crackled into the night, and the wails of the trapped boys lifted like a dirge from out of the fire.

Andrea raced for the outside stairway leading up to the top floor of the boys' quarters, her heart thudding in her chest. From behind her, the fire bell pealed. At the bottom of the stairs, she paused long enough to look back. Where was that bastard Frankie? Where was anyone?

She took the steps two at a time, only to hesitate at the exit door at the top. Heat seeped from around its frame, and the building trembled with flames.

She looked down to see Doctor Baldwin and Doctor Helms racing across the compound toward her. Frankie Yager now stood at the bottom of the stairway, pointing, yelling something up to her. She looked over to see flames now licking at the roof of the women's ward as well.

Andrea, determined to get to the boys, took hold of the doorknob, and pain shot up her arm as her palm liquefied under its heat. Gritting her teeth, she shoved open the door with her shoulder. Flames roared out, sucking away her breath. Her lips swelled, and she smelled the stink of burned hair and flesh.

She could see the boys inside, their bodies dancing and writhing in the inferno, their hands lifted over their heads. She held her arms against the flames and tried to move in, but the heat drove her back. Again she tried, but the firestorm flared and crackled about her, igniting the wooden landing under her feet.

She beat the flames from her clothing and stumbled back down the stairs to where the others were waiting. Above them, windows shattered from the heat, and glass tinkled down. The flames howled with new breath.

Doctor Baldwin pulled Andrea back as the old wooden structure of the boys' quarters heaved and moved. And with a great sigh, it collapsed in upon itself.

In the dawn light Andrea watched the firemen extinguish the last of the embers. The women's ward had been spared, though the roof was badly damaged. But the boys' ward now lay in ashes, and thirty lives had vanished forever.

1

THE RAILROAD SECURITY agent Hook Runyon slipped on his arm prosthesis before sitting down in his caboose to read the Needles paper. "Boys Die in Barstow Asylum Fire," the headlines read. He pushed the paper aside and poured a cup of coffee. There was nothing like starting a new day with coffee and a dose of human tragedy.

But he'd no sooner sat down when he heard Pap Gonzales, the Santa Fe section foreman, pull in with the motorcar. Pap was the section foreman here in Needles, California. His real name was Papan, though everyone called him Pap, including his wife and kids. They'd scheduled an early start to beat the desert heat. According to Pap, someone had been switch tampering at one of the crossings.

Hook dumped his cup and went out to meet him. Pap looked at his watch as Hook fished out a cigarette. Hook offered him one, but Pap declined. Soon they were clattering down the track. It was early and far too noisy for conversation, so they rode in silence into the desert morning.

When they arrived at the crossing, Pap coasted to a stop and shut off the motor. Hook got out and walked up and down the track. He hiked his foot up on the motorcar and then lit up another cigarette.

"I can't see that it has been tampered with," he said, looking up at Pap through the smoke.

"Someone's tried to lever it over," Pap said.

"There's nothing left of the switch point, Pap. That's a section-gang problem, not security. I'm tired of running out every time a car jumps track. Why don't you fix these damn switches before someone gets killed?"

"We've had a war on, Hook, been fighting Germans, or maybe you don't remember. I haven't had men enough to keep the main line open much less patch up siding switches."

"She's worn thin as a razor," Hook said. "I'd suggest you boys replace it or shut it down."

Pap pushed back his hat. "Albuquerque's been screaming about a washout for a week, but I'll just tell them I got orders from the Santa Fe yard dog to shut down the line so's he doesn't have to be bothered."

"That ought do it," Hook said, climbing onto the motorcar. "Everybody knows how much pull I have around here."

Pap cranked the engine of the motorcar and waited as she popped into life. Hooked liked riding the open car, though on a hot day in the Mojave, which was damn near every day, the wind could take off a man's hide.

The wheels chattered and growled as the car gathered up speed. When the Needles depot came into view, Pap idled back.

"Want to go to your caboose, Hook?" he asked, over the clatter of the wheels.

"Yard office," Hook said, pointing ahead. "Need to check in. Can you wait for me?"

Pap looked at his watch and shook his head. "Don't be long. Main line ain't the place to be sitting when the Chief comes through."

The Santa Fe Chief was powered by a diesel electromotive engine. The electric giants had begun to impact the railroad. They were more efficient, more reliable, and could travel a hell of a lot more miles without maintenance. But even the advancement in equipment could not offset the reduction in manpower when thousands of men went off to war. The result was a railroad struggling to maintain its system.

Hook checked in at the yard office and found a note in his box saying Eddie Preston, his boss out of Division, wanted him to call.

He dialed the number with his prosthesis and lit a cigarette. Eddie never called unless he had a problem, and the problem for the last month had been Hook himself.

While in hot pursuit of a bum outside Flagstaff one night, Hook had abandoned the company truck. He caught the bum, and everything would have been fine, except for one small detail. He'd failed to get the tail end of the truck off the crossing. A west-bound freighter tore off the bumper and dragged it a quarter mile down line. They said it looked like the Fourth of July.

Eddie had been pretty unreasonable about the whole situation and filed Hook's third Brownie for the year. He transferred Hook from Oklahoma to Needles, pointing out that the Mojave was just the place to keep a man prone to trouble on the straight and narrow. Hook had been awaiting the results of the Disciplinary Review Board ever since.

When Eddie came on the line, Hook doused his cigarette. "Eddie, this is Hook Runyon."

"Where you been, Runyon? Why haven't you called?"

"Pap's been having problems with some switches," he said, "and it's hard to phone from the middle of the Mojave."

"I got a call from Topeka," Eddie said. "There's a situation in Barstow."

"What kind of situation?"

"I want you to catch the Chief in the morning. Contact a Doctor Theo Baldwin at the Baldwin Insane Asylum."

"Insane asylum? Are you nuts, Eddie?"

"That ain't funny, Runyon."

"What do they want?" Hook asked.

"There's been a fire, people killed. Their facility is damaged, so they are in need of moving a lot of people and all at once. Call me when you've got the details."

It must have been the same fire he'd seen in the newspaper headline. Hook adjusted the harness for his prosthesis. The damn thing hung on him like a horse collar. He could hear Eddie breathing on the other end of the line.

"Has the disciplinary board met?" Hook asked.

"Not yet."

"I was chasing the bastard in the middle of the night, Eddie. How could I know the damn truck hadn't cleared the track? Anyone could have made the mistake."

"Except it was you, Runyon, the third mistake this year."

"But I got a commendation for busting that Nazi case in the Alva POW camp, didn't I? That ought to count for something."

"It does. Without it you wouldn't even be getting a hearing. Call me when you get Barstow lined out. Topeka's on my ass."

Pap had gone to sleep on the motorcar, and Hook kicked the bottom of his foot.

"Take me up to the caboose, will you, Pap? I got to catch the Chief to Barstow tomorrow."

Pap gave the crank a couple hard turns, and the motor struggled to life.

"Barstow?" he said over the top of the engine.

"Something going on at the insane asylum," Hook said.

Pap didn't say anything until he brought the car to a stop at the caboose.

"You're going to the insane asylum in Barstow?" he asked.

Hook climbed off. "Just keep it to yourself, Pap. I take enough ribbing from you bastards as it is."

"Oh, sure, sure," Pap said. "I won't tell a soul."

"Come pick me up in the morning, Pap. Maybe you could take care of Mixer while I'm gone. He loves going out with the crew."

Mixer fell into the category of mutt, an English shepherd and something or the other. The two things Mixer loved most in the world were fighting and eating, in that order.

"Damn it, Hook, you know it's against the rules to take a dog out on the line."

"That's kind of the point, isn't it, Pap? I enforce the rules, and I figure this to be a safety issue. One of your men might stir up a snake while he's sleeping under a bridge, or you might get waylaid by banditos. That dog could save your life."

Pap grinned, choked the engine a couple times, cranked her over, and rolled off down the track.

Mixer met Hook at the door. He wound through his legs and then went to the cabinet to beg for food. Hook had found him beat up and half-starved in the yards and brought him back to the caboose wrapped in his coat. Hook had fed him cornbread and milk and dabbed iodine on his wounds. Within a week Mixer had cleaned him out of food and never once since showed the least inclination to leave.

Though at times a nuisance, Mixer had arrived at a lonely time in Hook's life, filling a pretty big hole. After Hook was sent to Needles, Reina had returned to Rhode Island. At first they had written letters, a commitment that had faded over time. As the months passed, the letters dwindled and the frenzy cooled, though neither had been willing to admit it.

Reina had been there for him in dangerous times in the past. They had loved and made love, and that could never be lost. But memories can fade from flames to embers and then grow cold beneath the ash. The last time they'd talked, they'd reached out to each other, never quite touching.

Hook shoved aside a pile of books in order to get the closet door open. Desperate for more room, Hook had talked his ole pal Runt Wallace into storing his book collection while he was gone.

But a man suffering from book madness had little chance of a cure. Only six months had passed, and already the caboose creaked under the weight of his new titles. With a little luck, he'd manage some book hunting in Barstow. While not the literary heart of the world, at least it would be new and different.

He dug out a change of clothes and hung them on the safety rail that ran down the center of the caboose ceiling. The old steamers had a weak power stroke on takeoff, so the engineers would back up and then throttle forward to bump her ahead. By the time the slack hit the caboose forty cars down line, a man could accelerate from zero to ten miles an hour in one second. On more than one occasion, the handrail had saved him from being propelled across the caboose like a cannonball.

A jug of Runt Wallace's forty-year-old shine still sat in the closet. One day, given the right occasion, he'd dip in. For now, he had enough trouble to keep him busy. Eddie didn't need much of a reason to send another Brownie his way, and finding a job for a one-arm yard dog would be tough indeed.

That night, after he'd polished his shoes, he hung his prosthesis over the chair and went to bed early to read a little of Bradbury's *Dark Carnival*. When the coyotes tuned up out on the desert, Mixer growled.

"Go to sleep," Hook said, turning out the light. "You can't take on the whole world. Damn dog."

Hook gathered up his pillow and listened to the coyotes. He didn't know what awaited him at Baldwin Insane Asylum. But he did know that when Eddie called on an assignment, it would be neither good nor easy.

2

Hook SAT STRAIGHT up. The blackness of the
early morning hours filled the caboose like a still pool. No more
than a sliver of moonlight cast through the cupola window and
onto the floor. He'd heard something, something that had brought
him out of a deep sleep. He turned his ear into the silence. Perhaps
his imagination had gone wild, the foreboding that could rise up
unbidden in the night hours. Perhaps Mixer had sought out the
water dish, as he sometimes did, or perhaps the wind had swept in
from the desert.

He lay back and closed his eyes. Mixer's soft snore came from
the back corner of the caboose where Hook kept the throw rug.
Hook wondered if he'd latched the door, taken the basic precaution
against intruders. He'd been known to forget, particularly when
he'd had a drink or two or had become too comfortable with his
surroundings, a foolish mistake for someone well schooled in the
depravity of man. Who knew better than a railroad yard dog that
crime respected neither time nor place, that evil thrived on

complacency and overconfidence and sought out weakness like a pack wolf?

He turned on his side and stared into the darkness. In that moment he sensed the cool of the night air entering the caboose. He could just make out the shadow of someone standing in the doorway. His heart tripped in his ears as he searched the blackness for his sidearm. The crash of the ashtray onto the floor brought Mixer out of his slumber. His yaps resounded in the confines of the caboose, and Hook's adrenaline rushed through him like hot wax. He groped for the kerosene lantern, nearly spilling the chimney onto the floor with the back of his hand.

By the time he'd managed to light the lantern, Mixer's barking had turned frantic. He stood yelping at the closed door, his ears laid back, his tail swishing to and fro. Hook grabbed his shoes and slipped them on.

"Some guard dog," he said. "Come on. He can't be far."

He stepped into the cool desert air. A thumbnail moon hung low in the western sky as it made way for sunrise. Hook eased down onto the track and checked under the caboose. He'd caught many a hobo hiding under cars and had picked up more than his share of body parts because of it. Escaping from under a moving boxcar could be deceptively difficult. Even a steamer could bump forward fast enough to trap a man before he could roll out.

He spotted something lying in the bedrock, and he bent to examine it.

"Lug wrench," he said to Mixer, who waited at his side. "A goddang bo."

Hobos used lug wrenches to break the seals on boxcars or for a number of other things, including cracking someone's skull. Hobos were opportunists, half-starved coyotes who would steal the brakeman's lunch right out of his caboose if the opportunity presented itself.

"Go find him," Hook said.

Mixer spun off into the morning to work out the myriad smells that occupied his world. And when a yelp went up down line, Hook knew that Mixer had picked up the scent. Hook moved as fast as he dared in the dawn light. Ahead, the track curved off for its run into the desert. Mixer barked a series of hot yelps.

As Hook made the bend, he could see a shunting boiler with a short load sitting on the siding. The engine purred like a gigantic cat, and heat waves rose out of her stack in the morning air. The cab was empty, the engineer probably having gone to the yard office to wait clearance.

At that moment, both Hook and Mixer spotted the bo peeking from around the open door of the last boxcar. Mixer yelped and bawled and spun in a circle. Hook waited for the man's face to disappear back into the darkness of the car. He leaped across the tracks and ran along the right of way out of view of the bo. With a little luck, he could come in from behind without being spotted.

Gasping for breath, he crawled under the boxcar, and his stomach tightened. He could smell the heat of the engine drifting down line and the pungent odor of creosote. When it came to boxcar wheels and iron rails, bodies lost with some regularity.

Sunrise lit the sky in a blaze. Just then the pitched whistle of a diesel engine rose up in the distance. The shunting boiler responded with two short blasts, and sweat broke on Hook's forehead. The engineer must have been asleep in the cab while he waited on the east-bound to clear.

Hook knew that he didn't have long to make his move. As soon as the diesel cleared, the shunting boiler would pull out and drag him down line. They'd have to mail him back to Division in an envelope.

He reached for his weapon to make his move. "Damn it!" he said. He'd forgotten his weapon, and his prosthesis, and his pants.

Too late now. He reached up, grabbed the door handle, and swung his leg into the car just as the east-bound made the bend.

The shunting boiler lay in on her whistle and released her brakes. Unable to pull himself up without his prosthesis, Hook hung from the doorway like a opossum in a tree.

The freighter screamed by Hook just as the shunting boiler took up slack, lurching forward. Exhausted, Hook struggled to pull himself the rest of the way in. As they gathered up speed, the bo rushed from the darkness of the boxcar and leaped over Hook's head.

Hook managed to roll in, and he turned to look back. Mixer had the bo by the sleeve, and they were locked in tug of war between the two trains. Hook considered jumping, but by then the clack of the wheels had turned to a hum. He'd just have to wait until they reached the wigwag crossing, where the train would slow.

He leaned back against the door of the boxcar to catch his breath. No man should start his day like this, but then it could have been worse. That bo had plenty of opportunity to do him in, but he hadn't. Hook hoped Mixer granted the bo the same reprieve.

The morning sun shot through the beams of the railroad trestle overhead, and birds winged through the blue as Seth Durand examined the torn sleeve of his shirt.

He had planned to be in Barstow by now, but when that un-locked caboose presented itself, he couldn't resist. He'd barely es-caped with his life from that madman and his wild dog. After that, he'd waited at the edge of Needles for the next west-bound, but it turned out to be a diesel that blasted through at breakneck speed, leaving him with a face full of dirt. He hated the diesel, the way she whined and moaned, the way her whistle shot through a man like a knife. She was hard to board and even harder to ride.

So he'd camped in to wait for a hog, an old steamer with a load of freight pulling the grade, if one ever came again. But then his plans hadn't amounted to much since his discharge from Balboa in

San Diego. The nightmares had dwindled in the last year, but their intensity could still lock him up like a frozen engine.

He took a deep breath and rubbed at the stubble on his chin. The scar that ran the length of his face twitched in the cold morning air. A German Mauser bullet had plowed a three-inch furrow across his face. The wound turned septic after he lay three days in a wet foxhole. The scar distorted his jaw and drooped his eye like a broken window shade. That combined with six months of terror on the front lines, and he had spiraled out of control. A year in the hospital at Balboa had healed the wound but not the terror.

When he'd been discharged, he bummed to Barstow, where some of his buddies from Balboa were. He'd found them living under a bridge, drinking too much, and reliving days that no longer mattered to anyone but them.

On a Sunday morning while the town slept, he'd walked to the switchyards and hopped a train back to Tulsa. Though his wife had written, she'd not seen the wound, neither the one across his face nor the one in his soul.

He'd sat on the front porch of the house until the sun broke before picking up his duffle and catching the first freighter out.

Nearly back to Barstow, his uncertainty had resurfaced. His decisions turned and banked and turned again like the birds above the trestle. Did his judgments any longer make sense? Did he even care?

A cold wave eased through the canyon, and he slipped on his army fatigue jacket. The sour of his own body had steeped his clothes. Not bathing ranked high on the list of hobo misery. On occasion he'd managed a hot shower in a YMCA or a spit bath in a gas-station bathroom. Once, he'd showered at the Albuquerque rail yards. Without clothes, hobos and section-gang workers looked pretty much alike.

He dug through his duffle and set his store of goods on a rock, a can of pork and beans, a tin of Spam, and a half pound of coffee.

He'd hoped for more fare from that caboose. But for now he opened the beans. Three years in the army had diminished his taste for Spam.

He gathered up driftwood that had snagged around the trestle pier. A fire would feel good. The cool night had wormed into his bones. Building a fire always invited danger, particularly in the still desert air. A good yard dog could smell smoke ten miles off, and he figured they'd be looking for him now for sure. But he wanted that cup of coffee.

He kept the fire small and hot to reduce the smoke and moved in close to the flames. The top half of the beans he ate cold and nestled the remainder in the coals to heat.

He'd just poured his coffee when he heard the putt-putt of a motorcar coming down line. After dumping his coffee onto the fire, he dragged sand over the coals with his foot. He closed his things into his duffle, and he crouched in the pile of driftwood, barely breathing.

The popcar drew to a stop atop the trestle, and men talked above the clatter of the motor. When the motorcar chugged away, he took a deep breath. He waited until he could no longer hear the clack of wheels, and then he waited some more just to make certain.

Afterward, he ate the Spam, too afraid for another fire, and listened for the whistle of a steamer. She would be soft and mellow and with a life all her own. First sound of a steam engine, he'd pack his gear and climb the grade, wait there for a grainer or a hopper to come down line. With luck, he'd hike up and settle in for the last leg into Barstow.

As he waited in the morning sunrise, he thought about home and his wife and the scar that had severed his life. He thought about the dead he'd left behind in Germany and the starkness of battle. Most of all he thought about the coffee spilled on the fire beneath the trestle.

3

At THE NEEDLES depot, Hook picked up his bag and looked down the tracks. Pap lifted Mixer onto the motorcar.

"How long you going to be gone, Hook?" he asked.

"Eddie Preston didn't give out a hell of a lot of information," Hook said.

"I can't be taking care of this mutt forever," Pap said. "Son of a bitch fights everything that comes along."

"That's what guard dogs do, Pap."

Pap lit a cigarette. "And eat," he said. "He ate Jess Wilson's hat the other day."

"He thought it died," Hook said. "It sure as hell smelled like it."

Pap flipped his cigarette onto the gravel. "I better get back," he said. "Section gang thinks a shovel handle is for leaning on when the boss is gone."

Hook could hear the Chief coming down the stretch, her diesel engines howling.

"Keep an eye on my caboose, Pap. That hobo under the trestle might take a notion to help himself."

"How do you know it was a hobo? Could have been a raccoon."

"Raccoons don't cook coffee, least none that I ever encountered. I would have run him in had I the time. But Eddie's in an uproar over this deal, and he's just itching to can me.

"Tell the car toad to keep a watch out, especially when he's inspecting the boxcars. Tramps favor the boxcars when they are crossing the Mojave. Call security out of Winslow if you need to. They owe me one."

"Can't be too careful," Pap said. "Never know when a looney will pop up. The east-bound hot footer told the depot agent he saw a man hanging from a boxcar door early this morning."

"That so?" Hook said.

"Said he was wearing nothing but his boxer shorts."

Hook glanced over at Pap. "Engineers would lie to their own sweet mothers."

"Thing is, he said this feller only had one arm. Now there's a rarity for you, ain't it?"

Pap grinned, cranked the popcar, and rolled off down the track. Mixer, his ears flapping in the wind, watched Hook until he disappeared round the bend.

The Chief's whistle blew, and black diesel smoke boiled onto the horizon. Her red and yellow war bonnet shone in the sun. She sported a blackout shield over her light, and her silver passenger cars rolled into the station as quietly and softly as a Cadillac.

The conductor stepped out onto the platform, his uniform spotless and his shoes polished like obsidian glass.

Hook showed the conductor his pass and then his badge.

"We got no trouble on the Chief, Mr. Runyon, unless you count crying babies."

"Just hitching to Barstow," Hook said. "Maybe take a nap along the way."

The conductor smiled and touched his hat bill. "Better make it a quick one, Mr. Runyon. This here train tops a hundred miles an hour on the straightaway. Sometimes she don't touch the track at all. We ran over a cat's tail coming out of Tucumcari, and he didn't even squall."

"Thanks," Hook said. "Let me know if those babies get out of hand."

Hook made his way down the aisle and slid into an inside seat. The passenger car smelled of wood and upholstery. The Chief also had a Cochiti galley car that served up the best gourmet meals in the country and an observation car for viewing the scenery.

She blew her whistle and eased out of the yards, gathering speed up the alley. Getting on the Chief had the feel of luxury, like stepping into a sumptuous hotel. Her passengers, many of them celebrities out of Los Angeles, were known for favoring her extravagances. For a yard dog who lived in a caboose, the experience defied explanation.

An hour out of Needles and he snored quietly on his bleached-white pillow. He awoke to the dinner chime and rubbed the sleep from his face. Hook always ate on the Chief, hungry or not, a meal with linen napkins, Mimbreno china, and crystal glass, all while the countryside whizzed by like a silent movie.

He ordered rare steak, asparagus tips, baked potato, and caramelized carrots. A black man in a uniform as white as a cloud served it up. For dessert, Hook ordered apple pie, which arrived floating in butter and cinnamon, topped with a dipper of vanilla ice cream that melted down the sides like an avalanche.

After that, he went to the observation car, where he drank a cup of black coffee and smoked a cigarette. The whole meal cost him a week's pay, but he didn't care. To ride on the Chief and not go to the diner might well send a man straight to hell.

When Barstow came into view, the Chief throttled down and slid in alongside the depot deck. From his window, Hook could see the domed turrets and archways of Casa del Desierto, which looked like a gleaming castle against the setting sun.

Once inside the depot, he showed the operator his badge. The operator studied it and then looked at Hook's prosthesis.

"What's the trouble, Mr. Runyon?" he asked.

"I need to go to the Baldwin Insane Asylum in the morning," Hook said.

"Me, too," he said. "The goddang yard master's driving me crazy."

"Is it far?"

"It ain't never far to the nutty if you work for the railroad," he said.

"It's company business. I'll need a vehicle, something you can spare for a few days."

"Getting there ain't a problem," he said. "It's getting out."

"When you're through having your little joke . . ." Hook said.

The operator rolled his shoulders. "Well, I don't know. There's the yard truck down at the supply shed. You'll have to check with them."

"Thanks."

"I hear tell that fire about wiped Baldwin out."

"Don't know much about it yet," Hook said. "Is there a spare in the sleeping rooms?"

The operator checked his crew change schedule. "Will be at six. Linens won't be changed out until seven, though."

"Works for me," Hook said. "How far to the supply shed?"

"Just down the track about a block."

"I'll tell them out to Baldwin to be expecting you," Hook said.

The operator grinned. "Least I get paid in this looney," he said.

Hook left his luggage behind the counter and hiked down line to supply. The desert evening chilled about him, and he stretched out his legs.

He wondered what the Baldwin Insane Asylum had in store.

Trains drew troubled people like flies, so he'd dealt with his share of mentals over the years, but never an entire insane asylum.

The supply clerk grumbled something about having no vehicle when he needed it and asked Hook for his badge.

"Sign here," the clerk said, turning around his clipboard. "And don't push that old truck. There's a goddang rod knocking."

The yard lights had blinked on by the time Hook located the truck. He walked around it and shook his head. The latch had been jimmied, and someone had drilled a hole in the frame and secured the door shut with a piece of wire. Empty boxes had been left in the back, along with an old journal jack the size of a blacksmith anvil.

As he climbed in, a west-bound steamer rolled into the yards for a drink and fuel. Hook could smell the heat from her firebox. She bumped and rattled as a dozen empty boxcars gathered up slack. Behind them, a line of flatcars carried Sherman tanks and army jeeps. The old steamer hissed and sighed as she settled in.

Just then he spotted a shadow slipping along on the far side of a flatcar. Might have been the switchman, but he hadn't seen a lantern. He eased the door open and knelt down to wait and watch.

When he saw it again, someone dashing from car to car, he slipped through the darkness and dropped down close to the wheel journal, the heat from the brake warm against his arm. The engine blew off pressure, and a steam cloud boiled about the yard light.

First, he heard footsteps in the gravel, and then he heard someone grunting as they hoisted up on the grab iron. Hook waited for him to drop down before stepping in and clipping him hard across the ear.

The man snorted once and then crumpled into the gravel. After planting his knee on his neck, Hook cuffed him up. Back at the supply shack, he set him in a chair and waited for him to come around. His chin bled from the gravel, and soot from the engine clung in his brows. A deep scar, still red and newly healed, cut at an angle across his face and into his eye. His shirt sleeve was torn away.

"What's your name?" Hook asked, lighting a cigarette.

The man shrugged and then looked up, his eyes reflecting the wear of the rails.

"Does that matter?"

"It matters."

"Seth Durand," he said.

"You been bumming under the trestle at Needles?" Hook asked.

"How you know that?"

"Smelled your coffee this morning," Hook said.

"That motorcar that came through early?" he asked.

"What happened to your shirt, Seth?"

Seth turned his hand and looked at it. "Caught it in the grab iron," he said. "Damn near dragged me to death."

"You been in the army?"

"Forty-fifth out of Oklahoma."

"Don't you know better than to hitch a flatcar across the desert?"

"I aimed for an open side door on that boxcar back there," he said. "But she spit me out, so I grabbed what came next, which turned out to be a flatcar."

"A man riding a flatcar into the Mojave ought plan ahead," Hook said.

"First I fried and then I froze," he said. "And then I just hoped one or the other would hurry up and happen before the sand scoured off all my hide.

"When I pitched my duffle on, it rolled off the other side. I should have jumped off with it."

"No guarantees when you ride the rails, son. Last summer a bo got locked in a boxcar over to Needles. They sided him off at Pampa. When I found him, he'd dried up no bigger than a Sunday pot roast."

"You reckon you could loosen up the cuffs?" he asked.

"You aren't figuring on running, are you? This hook I'm wearing doesn't slow me down a bit."

"I'm too wore out to run," he said.

Hook took off the cuffs and put them into his pocket.

"You AWOL, Seth?"

Seth shook his head. "Medical. I spent some time in Balboa. They tried to patch up this mug. It didn't work out so well."

"Where you headed?" Hook asked.

"Here," he said. "Course, I hadn't figured on winding up in the slammer."

"Where have you been?"

Seth rubbed at his wrists. "Tulsa," he said. "Went home to see my wife."

Hook squashed out his cigarette. "Why didn't you stay?"

Seth shrugged. "This face is not something a woman wants to wake up to."

"Where did you get that scar, Seth?"

"You ask pretty straight questions," he said.

Hook nodded. "You *are* under arrest. Maybe you ought to be a little more forthcoming."

"Germany," he said. "A Mauser bullet. When I came to, I'd been laying in the mud for three days. My face looked like this."

"It's against the law to hop trains, Seth," Hook said.

"I'm ugly, not stupid," he said.

"You got funds?"

"I'll have a comp check on the first."

"You have a place to stay?"

"Yeah," he said. "You going to run me in?"

"What about work, Seth?"

"There ain't none to be had," he said.

Hook walked to the door. "I might have a few days for you."

Seth stood. "A few days?"

"I got no time right now to run in bums," he said. "Don't let me catch you in the yards again, Seth. The second time around, I'm not so forgiving."

Seth looked down at his clothes. "A few days doing what?"

Hook reached for his billfold and peeled off a five spot. "Do you know the Baldwin Insane Asylum?"

"More or less," he said.

"Well, get yourself some clean clothes. Meet me at the depot in the morning. And figure on taking a bath if you want to ride in the front with me."

Hook lay on top of the covers in the sleeping room at the depot and listened to the callboy waking crews next door. When they'd gone, he checked his watch in the light coming through the window from the yards.

He turned on his side and could see his stump against the whiteness of the pillow. He should have run that bo in. Weakness in a yard dog could be smelled out a hundred miles away, but he knew the price the boy had paid. He knew the pain that he bore.

4

Hook watched from his window until he saw Seth coming down the tracks. He met him at the front door of the Harvey House.

"Hungry?" Hook asked. "We have time for a little breakfast."

Seth, clean shaven and sporting a new shirt, said, "Naw, it's a bit fancy for the likes of me."

Though his ears were peeling with sunburn, a night's rest and a bath had taken ten years off of him.

"I'm buying," Hook said. "But I figure to get my money's worth out of you before it's done."

A Harvey girl, looking like a nun in her black-and-white uniform, took their orders, trying hard not to stare at Hook's prosthesis or Seth's scarred face. Hook ordered two eggs sunny-side up, flapjacks, country ham, and black coffee, times two.

When they were finished, Seth pushed his plate back. "Mighty fine eating," he said. "Who do I have to kill?"

"Nothing so simple as that," Hook said. "I need some help for a few days, someone who knows his way around. A one-arm driver like myself can be a little dangerous."

"Look, Hook, I appreciate what you're doing here, but I've been getting along on my own for a good long while now."

"I'll tell you straight up, Seth, I got no time for whiners one way or the other. I have one arm, so I just use the other one best I can. You got your face tore up a little, so smile more. Either way, if I pay money, I expect you to work. Do you want it or not?"

"I need the work," he said.

"Come on then. They ought to have things up and running at the asylum by now."

From the driveway of the Baldwin Insane Asylum, Hook and Seth could see the heap of ash that had once been a building. The facility across the way, while still standing, had a canvas stretched over one end where the roof had given way. A tent had been erected to the side.

Seth pulled into the lot and shut down the pickup. Hook rolled down his window and lit a cigarette.

"There's folks over there," Seth said. "Under those trees."

Hook flipped up the visor. A couple dozen people were gathered in the shade of the elms that encircled the compound. Nearby, a pile of freshly dug earth had been dozed into a heap.

"I'm going over," Hook said.

"What do you want me to do?" Seth asked.

"Stay with the truck. I don't know how long this will take."

Some of the people were crying, their handkerchiefs pressed to their faces. Hook realized that he'd come upon a funeral in progress, with people standing at the precipice of a mass grave.

He looked down at the dozens of bodies wrapped in white sheets, stacked like cordwood in the ditch. The smell of cold ashes hung thick in the morning.

On the other side of the ditch, a woman took off her glasses and dabbed at her eyes with bandaged hands.

The person next to her stood still and rigid with arms folded. At first Hook thought her a man, the angular cut of the jaw, until she turned to expose the tail of her dress from under the coat.

At the head of the open grave, a man in his late fifties bowed his head.

"God take these poor lost souls into Your care," he said, his voice cracking. "Their miseries have ended on this earth. May they now bask in Your glory. Amen."

He picked up a handful of dirt and tossed it into the grave. The others in turn did the same, and when all had done so, the dozer fired up its engine, splitting apart the silence. As it shoved earth into the grave, Hook approached the man who now stood with his back to the crowd.

"Excuse me," Hook said.

"Yes," the man said, turning.

"My name's Hook Runyon, law enforcement with the Santa Fe. I've been asked to come."

"I'm Doctor Theo Baldwin," he said. "I'm glad you're here. Would you mind waiting for me for a few minutes?"

"Not at all," Hook said.

Doctor Baldwin worked the crowd, shaking hands, letting his arm linger on a shoulder, pulling someone in for a hug. When he'd finished, he motioned for the woman in the black suit to come over.

"Mr. Runyon, isn't it?" he asked.

"That's right."

"This is Doctor Bria Helms, our associate psychiatrist here at Baldwin."

She shook Hook's hand with a firm grip.

"Mr. Runyon," she said.

"Could you come to my office, Mr. Runyon?" Baldwin asked. "We can talk privately there."

Hook followed them across the compound. Doctor Baldwin pointed him into a chair before settling in behind his desk. Doctor Helms stood at the window watching the dozer level the last of the dirt.

"You've arrived at a very difficult moment," Baldwin said.

"So it seems. Perhaps you could fill me in."

"We had a fire in the boys' ward. There were over thirty deaths. Tragic," he said. "Just tragic."

"But a mass burial?" Hook said.

Baldwin glanced over at Doctor Helms, who said, "You must think it callous, Mr. Runyon, but the fact is that most of the bodies could not be identified. Very few had relatives willing to claim them in any case. We didn't have much choice."

"Do you know what caused the fire?" Hook asked.

Doctor Helms sat down then and crossed her legs. They were thin but shapely.

"We believe it to have started in the attendant's room near the front door," she said. "Most likely poor wiring. The structure was wooden and quite old. The fire spread rapidly."

"The boys were unsupervised?" Hook asked.

Doctor Helms dropped her chin and focused her black eyes on him.

"Frankie Yager, the orderly, was making his rounds in the downstairs ward when it happened. When he realized a fire had started, he ran to fetch Doctor Baldwin and me. In the meantime, Andrea spotted the flames from the women's ward. She tried desperately to save them."

"The girl with the bandaged hands?" Hook asked.

"That's correct. Our nurse. She has suffered painful burns on her hands."

"But I'm not clear what you want with the railroad, Doctor Baldwin?" Hook asked.

Doctor Baldwin pushed back his chair. His undershirt peeked through where the buttons on his shirt parted over his stomach.

"We've a desperate situation here as you can imagine, Mr. Runyon, one that we can't sustain. With one building burned and another damaged, we have had to house some of the inmates in tents. The security ward for the criminally insane was spared, thank God. I don't know how we would have managed."

He pulled at his chin. His eyes were round and sad and filled with water.

"We've had considerable pressure from the community to move to a secure location. There are over fifty inmates remaining, and it's been impossible to locate a facility in the area that will serve so many. So far no lawsuits have been filed, but there's been pressure from the governor's office."

"I'm sorry for your troubles, Doctor Baldwin, but what is it exactly you need from us?"

"I've had plans to open another asylum for some time now. I knew that many troubled soldiers would be returning from the war someday. When an old abandoned military fort in Oklahoma came up for sale from the federal government, I purchased it at a rather reasonable price."

"You still own the property?"

"That's correct."

"And you want to move these patients there by train?"

"Our situation here is dire," he said.

"This could be an expensive proposition, Doctor Baldwin. And the problems in such a move could be considerable."

Doctor Helms stood. "As it turns out, Doctor Baldwin had the foresight to insure the buildings here. There should be sufficient funds to make the move. But this is the least of the difficulties, I'm afraid."

"Oh?"

"You see, the security ward houses extremely dangerous men, Mr. Runyon, men who have committed the most egregious crimes. To complicate matters, the law prohibits the use of weapons in their management."

Doctor Baldwin rose from his chair. "These inmates are mentally ill, Mr. Runyon. They are not evil, not in the way most people think of evil. They have been determined by the courts not to be responsible for their crimes. As such, they are considered to be patients and to have all the protections that come with that. In the end, it is believed they have the potential to be cured."

Doctor Helms said, "Whatever one's philosophical position on this issue, the security risk is considerable, given the violent nature of these inmates."

"How many patients are we talking about?" Hook asked.

"Of those who would require constant security, twenty," Baldwin said.

"But don't you have employees who work with these men?" Hook asked.

"That's just it," Doctor Baldwin said. "The employees are locals. It's highly unlikely that many of them will be willing to move themselves and their families across the country for what is a difficult job under the best of circumstances."

Hook stood. "Let me get this right. You want to transfer fifty mentally-ill patients from California to Oklahoma. Twenty of them have committed violent crimes. There are no employees to assist, and, even if there were, they couldn't carry weapons to protect themselves?"

Doctor Helms said, "There is another matter."

"And what could that possibly be?" Hook asked.

"This transfer must happen soon, or things are going to deteriorate. We are already having difficulty keeping the inmates under control. And, just in case you haven't thought about it, we have no idea what to expect at the other end of the line. That facility has been empty for some time."

"I see."

Doctor Helms stood and looked at her watch. "If you have nothing else for me, Doctor Baldwin, I really must be going."

When Hook got back to the pickup, Seth had disappeared. Hook searched out the parking lot, but no Seth, so he went over to where the dozer driver worked at cleaning the blade with a shovel.

"Yeah," he said, leaning on his shovel handle. "Baldwin security picked him up about half hour ago. He yelped like a goddang she wolf."

"Where?" Hook asked.

"Security shack over there, providing they ain't killed him by now."

Seth looked up through his brows when Hook stepped into the security shack. Sweat had popped on his forehead from struggling with the straitjacket he now wore.

The guard turned. "Who are you?" he asked.

Hook pulled his badge. "Santa Fe bull."

"You turning yourself in for treatment?" he said, grinning. "Never knew a bull who wasn't crazy."

"Get me out of this thing," Seth said. "I think I'm going to explode."

"I know this man is a little unusual," Hook said, "but he's my driver."

The security guard looked at Seth and then back at Hook.

"We figured he might have gotten loose from the security ward. We're running shorthanded around here."

Hook shook his head. "I'm not saying he shouldn't be in there. I'm just saying he currently isn't."

"Goddang it," Seth said.

The guard untied Seth's straitjacket. "It's a little hard to tell which side of the fence a man ought be on sometimes," he said.

"Understandable mistake," Hook said. "One time I arrested a man taking a leak off the Cimarron Bridge over to Belva. Had him cuffed and loaded before I recognized him as the divisional supervisor.

"Got a Brownie for that one, though they took it off later. He wouldn't admit to whizzing off the bridge like a schoolboy."

As they made their way back to the pickup, Seth rubbed at his arms.

"It's a poor son of a bitch can't tell a war hero when he sees one," he said.

"Drive to your place first," Hook said. "I'll take the truck back to supply before the clerk blows his boiler."

"I'm not staying at a *place* exactly," Seth said, pulling out onto the road.

"You sleeping on the streets?"

"We've got a jungle under the Fourth Street Bridge. They keep a pot cooking. Most of the boys are short of work like myself."

"You show up in the morning? I could use a little more help."

"I ain't sitting in no goddang pickup truck in an insane asylum," Seth said.

As they drove down Main, Hook told him about what he'd found out from Baldwin. At the bridge, Seth pulled over.

"They burned up?" he asked.

"And then they dozed them under," Hook said. "Guess they had no choice."

"What are they going to do?"

"They want the inmates moved to a new location, but there's a shortage of help.

"Listen," he said, turning to Seth. "I'm looking for rare books while I'm here. Happen to know where any are?"

Seth got out and leaned back in. "Books are rare all over this town," he said. "But there's a used bookstore up on Fourth, or you might find something down at the Salvation Army thrift. I've seen boxes of old books down there."

"Thanks," Hook said.

"What you going to do about Baldwin?" Seth asked.

"Guess Division will be letting me know that soon enough. See you tomorrow," Hook said.

Hook called Eddie from the depot. Eddie picked up before Hook could get his cigarette lit. Hook set out the details, then lit up and waited for Eddie's response.

"This is the problem," Eddie said. "Every engine in the system is booked or in the shed."

"About twenty of these inmates are violent, Eddie, the kind that would eat your beating heart. There's no private security willing to make the trip. Baldwin's in a big rush on this, too. Half his buildings burned, and he's having trouble keeping it all gathered up. My advice is to stick with hauling the mail."

"I'm getting heat from Topeka," Eddie said. "There's some political shit going on. What if we brought in the Pinkertons?"

"The union hates those bastards, Eddie. You know that, and the Pinks aren't going to do something like this without being armed."

"See if you can round up some local help," Eddie said. "We could make it worth their while."

"Where the hell am I supposed to get that kind of help around here? And what will Baldwin do for help after he gets there?"

"That ain't our problem."

Hook pecked out an SOS on the desktop with his prosthesis. The operator in Albuquerque had taught it to him.

"That's not all," he said.

"Not all of what?" Eddie asked.

"Baldwin doesn't have a clue how that fire started."

"What does that mean?"

"It could have been arson for all we know. I'm not keen to be riding around with fifty mentals and an arsonist on the loose."

"You have evidence of that?"

"It's just a feeling."

"Don't start with the feeling shit, Hook. You're there to do a job. Stick to it."

Hook paused. "You heard from the disciplinary board?"

"They said the truck thing had cost the company plenty. It's the Rule G violation for intoxication that's the problem."

"I'd had a few drinks the night before, Eddie. A man can't have a few drinks?"

"Rule G is a Railroad Association rule. The committee asked for a report from the night foreman out of Flagstaff. If it comes in bad for you, it's out of my hands."

That night Hook lay in his bunk in the sleeping rooms at the depot and listened to the east-bound Chief roll in. He thought about the Baldwin Insane Asylum fire, the trapped boys, the burned bodies now lying in a common grave.

There were just too many unanswered questions. Eddie Preston be damn, he had to know what he was getting into before climbing aboard a train with fifty mental patients in tow.

5

ANDREA STUDIED THE blisters in the palms of her hands before smearing them with salve and then wrapping them with gauze. She looked in the mirror that hung on the tent pole. She'd slept little enough last night, the pain throbbing with every beat of her heart. She'd lain awake unable to shake the images of the fire, the screams, the smells, the figures dancing in the terrible flames.

It had all happened so quickly. If only Frankie Yager had gone upstairs instead of searching for Baldwin and Helms. Maybe he could have gotten the boys out before the place had turned into an inferno. But then he'd done what he thought best, she supposed, and second-guessing now served little purpose.

The blisters extended between her fingers, making it nearly impossible for her to use her hands. She could barely perform the simplest task with her left hand. Esther had tied her shoes for her and helped her make beds. Even though it went against her nature, Andrea had let a lot of the details on the ward slide.

As she tightened the knot with her teeth, she thought about the one-arm man she'd seen talking to Doctor Baldwin after the funeral. He'd held his head high. Whether from courage or defiance, she didn't know. Either way, she could only empathize with the difficulties of making it through the world with one arm.

On top of everything else, Doctor Helms had moved the female patients into the tent so that the survivors from the boys' ward could be secured in what remained of her building.

Her own patients had roamed half the night in the tent. A fight broke out between Esther and Bess Henson over where they were to sleep. And then Andrea caught Esther eating a bug she'd captured in the grass, and Lucy Stewart, who suffered Stereotypy Habit Disorder, had to be restrained after repeatedly pounding her head against the tent pole.

Upon Lucy's confinement to Baldwin, her child had been surrendered to the custody of the state, and she had taken to carrying a rag doll everywhere she went. Over the years, the doll had become the sole source of comfort for Lucy when pressures mounted.

Unfortunately, the doll had been abandoned in the fray, and Lucy was inconsolable. So, in spite of Andrea's weariness, she had stayed on in order to search for the doll. Fortunately, she'd found it, somewhat worse for wear, under a pile of burned shingles that had fallen from the roof of the women's ward.

Across the way, Frankie Yager played his Frankie Laine records at full volume. He claimed to have been named after Frankie Laine himself and to have actually met him one time at a bar in Minnesota.

Yager had come to Baldwin shortly after Doctor Helms assumed the associate director's position. He controlled his ward through reward and punishment, mostly punishment. To cross him could result in retaliation. Even the most intractable boys feared Yager, and the staff had come to resent his bullying as well.

"Nurse Andrea," Rachael said from behind her. "Esther found another bug."

Andrea looked at Rachael in the mirror. Rachael's intelligence was limited, and, like a child, she took great pleasure in tattling on others.

"Did you take it away from her?"

She shook her head. "No."

"Why not?"

"She ate it," she said.

"Oh, dear."

"And Ruth pulled her pants down so the boys in the building could see," she said.

"Can't you stop her. You're my helper, aren't you?"

"I told her not to, Nurse Andrea. She said for me to go to hell."

"Alright. I'll take care of it."

Sometimes Andrea didn't know why she stayed with this job. Mental illness had a way of spilling over, of contaminating everyone around it.

She'd always dreamed of becoming a doctor. But after the breakup of her engagement, she'd faltered, and for a while drifted from one thing to another. Commitment to anything had somehow been diminished by the collapse of the relationship.

In the end, she'd settled for nursing, taking her internship with the nuns, but she could never master the specter of blood and death, could not separate herself or stand aside from the suffering of others. An inconvenience for most, a fatal flaw for a nurse.

When she heard that a woman psychiatrist had been hired at Baldwin, she'd applied for the psychiatric nurse's position. To her surprise she'd discovered that not only did she like the inmates, but she had a propensity for the work. Her empathy served her well with people who too often had been neglected by society and family.

Andrea had found Helms competent but aloof and not prone to abiding fools, while Doctor Baldwin, with his bear hugs and boisterous laughter, went out of his way to lighten what could sometimes be a dreary atmosphere.

When she looked up, she saw Doctor Helms working her way through the cots toward her. Even though tall and bent, Helms walked with a clipped gate more common of shorter people.

"Nurse Delven," she said. "May I speak with you?"

"Yes, Doctor," Andrea said.

"It has come to my attention that Ruth is causing a stir among the male inmates."

"I'll check on it, Doctor Helms, but it's difficult to control her when we're out in the open like this."

"Ruth is an exhibitionist and simply can't be left unattended."

"I asked Esther to monitor her, but she forgets. And there's no place to isolate Ruth. We *are* in a tent."

"See that she's kept under control, but that's not what I came to talk about," she said.

"Oh?"

"It's clear that this institution cannot continue to function as it stands. Some adjustments are being made."

"Adjustments?"

"Doctor Baldwin has acquired an old military fort that he believes can serve as a new facility."

"A fort?"

"In Oklahoma, a leftover from the territorial days, it seems."

"Excuse me?"

"I know," she said. "It came as a shock to all of us."

"You are planning to move all these inmates to Oklahoma?" Andrea asked.

"There are few alternatives," she said.

"But how?"

Doctor Helms pushed her glasses back up on her nose, where they promptly slid back to their former resting place.

"Possibly by train. Doctor Baldwin had a railroad security agent out here to check things out."

"The man with one arm?"

"Yes."

Nurse Andrea looked about at her patients, who were wandering around the tent. If living here had caused such a stir, how would they ever survive a train ride to Oklahoma?

"Are you taking them all?" Andrea asked.

"Yes," she said.

"The security ward as well?"

"As I said. Which brings me to why I'm here. We're trying to determine how many of the staff would be prepared to make the move."

"My home is here, Doctor Helms. I would have to leave everything behind."

Helms pulled out a black appointment book that she kept in her pocket and looked in it.

"One way or the other, Baldwin Asylum will be closing. If it's moved, then you will have to move as well if you wish to continue employment.

"Think about it, but not too long. There are a great many decisions to be made. Now, if you'll excuse me, I have a session."

After Doctor Helms left, Andrea sat down on a cot and rubbed at her face. She'd lived in Barstow her whole life, had inherited her parents' house. Everything she had was here.

With the first peal of the fire bell, Andrea's stomach knotted. And then it came again. She stood, paralyzed by the sound.

"Oh, God," she said aloud. "This can't be happening."

Gathering her wits, she ran from the tent to look about for fire or smoke. The bell rose in a crescendo from across the yard, and Andrea's heart pounded in her chest.

Inmates spilled from the buildings and from out of the tent. Some sat in the grass, rocking back and forth, while others clung to one another. Doctor Helms and Doctor Baldwin ran toward them from across the compound.

Andrea headed for the fire bell. As she drew near, she covered her mouth with her hand.

"Esther," she said. "Oh my god."

Esther pulled the rope with wide swings of her body.

"Ring it," she called out to Andrea. "Ring it like this."

That night, Andrea sat at her kitchen table and sipped a glass of wine. She rubbed the fatigue from her arms and looked about the kitchen. The saltcellar on the stove had been her mother's, and the footstool used to reach the top shelf. Her father's toolbox still sat in the garage, and her old bicycle from the sixth grade. She'd never lived anywhere but Barstow.

How could they ask her to leave her home? And no person should ever live through another day like she'd just experienced.

As the sun lowered, she turned on the radio and closed her eyes. She wondered how her patients were doing. They were so easily stampeded, so fearful. She would have stayed with them, but the staff had insisted she come home and get some rest.

If she were to go to Oklahoma, she'd be leaving behind her whole life. But the truth be known, her work and her patients *were* her life now. Without them, nothing remained but this house.

She knew that she had to go, to make certain that they arrived safely. Once there, if things didn't work out, she could always return and find another line of work.

Turning on the light, she dialed Doctor Helms's number.

"Baldwin Asylum. Doctor Helms speaking."

"Doctor Helms, this is Nurse Delven."

"Yes," she said.

"I've decided to go."

Helms paused on the other end of the line.

"Put it in writing, Andrea, and give it to Doctor Baldwin in the morning."

6

SETH AND HOOK walked down the tracks toward the supply shed. The morning sun struck their shadows across the rails.

"Don't seem right walking down line with a yard dog," Seth said.

Hook paused to light a cigarette, offering one to Seth. "How do you think it makes me feel?" he said, striking the match on the track.

"Did you talk to Division?" Seth asked.

"You don't really talk to Eddie Preston," Hook said.

"What did he say?" Seth asked. "Or is it a national secret?"

Hook looked out from under his brows. "I can still run you in, you know?"

"Is hanging with a yard dog illegal? Probably ought to be," Seth said.

"Eddie's getting political heat, if you got to know, from the California governor, or the Barstow mayor, or the mayor's cousin. Who the hell knows? They're running scared that those inmates out to

Baldwin's going to cost them a vote. Crazy folks got less rights than criminals like yourself."

"But we got yard dogs to contend with," Seth said. "And you bastards carry firearms."

At the supply shed, Hook popped the pickup hood, took out the oil dipstick, and dripped a little oil onto the joint of his prosthesis.

"Maybe it's time you took it in for an oil change," Seth said.

"Damn thing freezes up once in a while. Other than that, she's just like new."

Dropping the hood, Hook said, "Division needs to come up with a special train. They can't put inmates on the Chief. All those celebrities out of Los Angeles might not like the competition. And then there's soldiers and equipment. There's no trains left for moving mental patients halfway across the country. It's going to be hell making up a special on this short notice.

"To make matters worse, Baldwin figures the employees out there aren't going to pack up and move for a job no one wants in the first place. I figure he's right."

"What are they going to do?"

"Another fire like that last one, and they aren't going to have to do anything except hire another dozer to push over their problems."

"That's an army answer," Seth said. "No answer at all."

"Look, I'm just a yard dog. I got half the country bumming my trains, like you for instance, and Division's got me out here dealing with an insane asylum. As far as I'm concerned, Baldwin could turn the whole bunch loose. I figure no one would ever know the difference."

Seth got inside the pickup and waited for Hook to get in. Starting the engine, Seth said, "Which comes first, being a jerk or being a yard dog?"

Hook looked over at him and grinned. "Get me out to Baldwin before I change my mind and run you in."

In the Baldwin parking lot, Seth waited for Hook to get out.

"Wait here for me," Hook said.

"All the same to you, I think I'll go on back."

Hook smiled. "Be here about three and don't let anything happen to this truck. The disciplinary board's after my ass as it is."

"I was thinking to strip her down and sell her for junk," Seth said, pulling out.

After checking in with security, Hook made his way to Baldwin's office, where he found the receptionist with her head in the files.

"Oh," she said, pulling down her skirt. "May I help you?"

"Hook Runyon, Santa Fe Railroad," he said. "Doctor Baldwin, please."

"One moment, Mr. Runyon. I'll see if he's available."

When she came out, she left Baldwin's door open and directed Hook in.

"The doctor has an appointment in thirty minutes," she said, as he passed by her.

Baldwin rose to greet him. His hair had not been combed, and his clothes were rumpled.

"Mr. Runyon," he said, drawing his fingers through his hair. "Have a seat. Forgive my appearance. Things have been a little hectic around here."

"Thanks," Hook said.

"Excuse me for one moment, please," he said, stepping out.

Hook took in the doctor's office: a few volumes on his book shelf, medical books by the looks of them, and diplomas hung on the wall behind the desk. A small bronze of Einstein sat on the table under the window. Hook took another look, decided it wasn't Einstein but Sigmund Freud instead.

"Sorry to keep you waiting," Baldwin said. "I've sent for Nurse Andrea Delven to show you around the institution. Perhaps it will give you a better idea of what we are dealing with here."

"Doctor Baldwin, before we get into this thing too far, you and I should talk about some practical matters."

"For example?"

"This move you're proposing is a high-risk venture at best. I have serious doubts we can come up with a special train in time for your needs. There's a shortage of equipment.

"And then there's the matter of security. This is a particular problem since firearms can't be used. As for men, I doubt seriously if we could come up with enough. Even if we did, they would be untrained in dealing with mental patients."

He looked up at Baldwin, who hadn't moved. "Frankly, my best advice is for you to reconsider this whole plan."

Baldwin took his glasses off and rubbed at his face. "I appreciate your advice, Mr. Runyon. I suspect that you consider me to be a little naïve, but let me assure you that's not the case. I've a medical degree from the University of Pennsylvania, and my experience in these matters is considerable.

"As a young doctor, I spent three years in Fergus Falls, Minnesota, a state institution, where I worked with some very challenging patients. From there, I worked as a psychiatrist with the Texas Department of Corrections. I've seen the worst this world has to offer. But I believe in what I am doing, and I believe I make a difference.

"In short, I have no intentions of giving up here. If you can't help me, I'll find another way."

Hook laid his prosthesis across his lap. Dust had gathered on the hinge where he had dripped the oil. The damn thing looked like the tie rods on a junked car. Taking out his handkerchief, he wiped it away.

"Doctor Baldwin," he said, "have you considered the possibility that the fire here might have been arson?"

Baldwin's brows lifted. "No matches or flammable materials of any kind are permitted on the wards. The wiring in these old buildings is quite inadequate. It's pretty clear the fire started in the wall of the orderly's room. Unfortunately, it effectively cut the inmates off from escape."

"There was no other egress?" Hook asked.

"Even though we are not a prison, we have to maintain tight security. Too many exits lead to problems."

"Then shouldn't an orderly be on duty at all times, Doctor Baldwin?"

"Frankie Yager *was* on duty, but he also made rounds downstairs, where the less troublesome inmates were housed. This never took more than a few minutes."

"One orderly for two floors?" Hook asked.

"Help is very difficult to come by out here, Mr. Runyon, and then with the war. In any case, most people are frightened by mental illness."

Hook rose and walked to the window. From there he could see the burned-out building and the fresh grave up on the hill. He could see the young nurse working her way toward the office.

Baldwin had nailed it. There *was* something frightening about the mentally ill. With criminals he always knew where he stood. They were the enemy. They wished him harm. He watched his back, and he trusted no one. But here, the rules weren't clear. These people were not the enemy, though they could be just as dangerous.

He turned. "Alright, Doctor Baldwin," he said. "I'll do what I can, but there are no guarantees."

"Thank you, Mr. Runyon. In my business, I'm accustomed to no guarantees.

"Oh, here's Nurse Delven now."

She smiled at Hook as she came through the door. She struck him as prettier than what he remembered from the funeral, petite, and with a spray of freckles across her nose. Her mouth turned up at its tip, and behind her round glasses were eyes the color of gunmetal.

"Nurse Delven," Doctor Baldwin said. "This is Hook Runyon, special agent with the Santa Fe."

She held out her bandaged hand and then withdrew it.

"Sorry," she said. "I forget."

Hook held up his prosthesis. "I've carried this chunk of iron around for years, and I still forget sometimes."

"We call her Nurse Andrea around here," Doctor Baldwin said. "She volunteered first among the few to help us out with the move."

"Just Andrea," she said. "Will you be involved in the transfer, Mr. Runyon?"

"It looks that way," he said.

Baldwin came around his desk and put his hand on Hook's shoulder.

"Mr. Runyon would like a tour of the place, Andrea. I'll get someone to cover for you if you'll show him around."

"The security ward, too?" she asked.

"I'll arrange for Doctor Helms to be there," he said.

"Alright," she said. "If you'll follow me, Mr. Runyon, I'll introduce you to Baldwin Insane Asylum."

7

SETH DROVE BACK to town at an easy pace and rolled his window down to let in the morning breeze. He'd forgotten how good it felt to be driving, to go somewhere without waiting for a freighter to break on the horizon. He lit a cigarette and turned toward the jungle. Maybe some of the boys would be up and about, and he could show off the company truck.

Just then he spotted Roy from the jungle coming down the street. He could tell Roy's walk anywhere. He swung his arms high and dug the heels of his boots in with a thump. Drill sergeants had taught him that. Roy said he'd forgotten how to walk any other way, like he'd been reborn and had learned to walk all over again.

Roy hailed from Kentucky and hadn't been anywhere else his whole life until the army took him, though he claimed to have ridden all the way to Louisville once on his sister's bicycle. When pressed, and when under the influence of busthead liquor, Roy would admit that he didn't actually go *into* Louisville but could *see* Louisville from atop a nearby hill. He said the world's tallest building resided right there on the banks of the Ohio River, which put Ethan, who had lived in New York City, into a frenzy.

Seth pulled over, shut the engine off, and waved at Roy to come over.

"Hey, Seth," Roy said, pushing the hair from his eyes. "Where'd you get the truck?"

"It's a railroad company truck," Seth said. "They provide this vehicle as a benefit of my employment."

Roy dug out an empty pack of cigarettes, crumpled it up, and threw it into the back of the truck.

"You got a smoke, Seth?"

Seth rolled his eyes and handed him a cigarette. "Where you going?" he asked.

"Headed for the still. Got a prime batch just finishing up. Maybe you could give me a lift?"

"I'm on company business, Roy."

"Doing what?"

"Mostly I escort the railroad yard dog to the Baldwin Insane Asylum. Then at night I take him back to the depot."

"They let him go home at night?" Roy asked.

"He's just working out there, Roy."

"I thought you said he was a yard dog?"

"He is."

Roy's brows, which were like thick bushes, converged over his nose.

"They have trains in the insane asylum?"

"No, they don't have trains. He's lining up security and such. Goddang it, Roy, the point is I can't be using the company truck for taking you to your still."

Roy lit his cigarette and hooked his arm over the side mirror of the truck.

"We're running a tad low on shine down at the jungle," he said.

"Soon enough we'll all be drinking Barstow river water. Why don't we just make a quick run, Seth?"

Seth rocked the steering wheel and looked up at Roy. "I can't be using the company truck for carrying people to moonshine stills. Stills are illegal, as you well know. Anyway, this is a full-time railroad job. It isn't like unloading trucks over to the grocery or mowing old man Johnson's yard."

"Maybe some of us boys could hire on with the railroad, too, Seth."

"I don't think so, Roy. It's professional business, though it wouldn't hurt to ask, I suppose."

"I thought you said you dropped the yard dog off in the morning and picked him up at night?"

"I did say that. I can say it again if you didn't hear it the first time."

Roy took a drag off his cigarette. He studied the red coal on the end.

"So what do you do *between* morning and night?" he asked.

Seth flipped down the visor. In the dust on the back someone had drawn a picture of Kilroy with his nose over the fence.

"I don't know yet. Maybe when it gets hot, I'll stop in at Barstow Drug for a root beer or drive out to the wigwag crossing and take a nap under the truck. Maybe I'll visit the mayor or go to the chief of police and tell him about all the asshole cops he's got on the force. How do I know what I'm going to do?"

"Jeez, Seth, you don't have to get so riled up. My still is just out there by the salvage yard. I don't mind walking in the heat."

"Your still is by the salvage yard?"

"I built it close for supply parts. Them radiators can be damn heavy, especially when you don't have no company truck to haul things around in."

"Alright, goddang it. Your mother should have pinched your goddang head off when you were born. The whole world would be better off. I damn sure would be."

Roy came around the truck and got in. "If a man's got to be in Barstow living under a bridge," he said, "he ought be there with a friend like Seth Durand, a man who's never uppity, even when he's driving a company truck."

Seth cranked up the engine, checked the side mirror, and pulled off down Main toward the salvage yard.

Pretty soon Roy said, "It's been a good long while since I had a root beer."

Seth glanced over at Roy. "We're going to the still, Roy. That's what you said."

"That's right, the still is where we're going." He took out his pocketknife and worked at a nail. "Takes a lot of effort to keep a still up. It's art, you know, like painting or figurines."

"Just don't think I'm going to do this every time you want to go to your still."

"I'm not one to be asking favors," Roy said, turning his shoe up to pry out the pear cactus thorns in the bottom. "Far be it from me to interfere with your plans. You want a root beer, just go ahead and get one. It won't bother me a bit."

Seth sighed. "You got money for a root beer, Roy?"

"Hell, Seth, did I ask for one? Anyway, you're the man with a steady job and a private truck to drive around. I'm just a goddang hillbilly, thanking the Almighty my mother didn't pinch off my head while I lay in the cradle."

Seth whipped a U-turn and pulled in at Barstow Drug. They went in, and he ordered two mugs of root beer. Roy drank his down and then watched Seth drink his. Finally, Seth ordered him a second round so he wouldn't stare anymore. After that, they drove past the salvage yard and, from there, down a dirt road to Roy's still, which he'd tucked back in an arroyo.

"What do you do when it rains?" Seth asked, looking over the steering wheel.

"It don't rain in Barstow."

Seth got out and examined the still, which Roy had fashioned from a Buick radiator.

"Then how did this arroyo get here?" he asked.

"It's always been here, Seth. Any fool knows that."

Roy drew a sampling of the run and handed it to Seth.

Seth looked into the cup before shooting it down. Tears welled in his eyes.

"Good God," he said.

Roy filled the cup again and took a swig himself, swishing the liquid around and around in his mouth. A red blush crept down his neck and disappeared beneath his collar.

"Just right," he said. "There's a case of canning jars over there. I'll do a draw."

When finished, Roy said, "Damn, there's one jar too many. It won't fit into the box."

Seth walked around the jar and then looked over at Roy.

"Guess we could dump it," he said.

"I know men been shot for dumping busthead," Roy said.

"We could put it back in the still," Seth said.

"Taint's up. Just as well dump it."

"We could carry it in the front of the truck," Seth said.

"I knew a man once who broke a quart of shine in his truck," Roy said. "It was a sad thing."

"What happened?"

"Ignition set it off. Burned him alive. When they opened the door, he just crumbled away into a pile of ashes."

"Well, I don't want something like that on *my* conscience," Seth said.

"Be hard to live with alright," Roy said, picking up the quart and holding it against the light. "Guess the only thing to do is drink it."

"I suppose that's the right thing," Seth said.

Roy unscrewed the lid and took a pull before handing it over to Seth.

"Shine in and yeller out," Roy said. "Like dawn and dusk on the Mojave."

When they had drained the last drop, they sat the empty quart on top of the still and loaded the box of quarts into the back of the truck.

Seth got in on the passenger side and waited for Roy to get in.

"It's your goddang company truck, Seth."

"Oh, yeah," Seth said, getting out and going back around to the driver's side.

Roy fumbled for a cigarette. Not finding one, he said, "Got a smoke?"

Seth took one for himself and tossed the package to Roy.

Seth looked at his watch. "That yard dog is a little short on the fuse," he said. "I ought get on."

"I had a rail dick throw me off a doubleheader at thirty miles an hour," Roy said. "The son of a bitch didn't even look back."

Seth said, "I broke into a caboose over at Needles looking for something to eat. Came nose to nose with the meanest dog I ever saw, and a crazy man chased me halfway to Barstow in his underwear."

"I knew a preacher once what kissed rattlesnakes," Roy said. "He claimed it upped the plate donations and made the girls damp."

"The thing is, I've reason to believe it was the same railroad bull I'm working for now, Roy. I think he knew who I was when he offered me this job."

"Well, there's no figuring yard dogs or preachers neither one," Roy said.

"Oh, hell," Seth said, looking around. "I've lost the damn truck keys."

"They're in your hand," Roy said.

"Oh, yeah," Seth said.

"Listen," Roy said. "I'm running short on corn for the still. I spotted a couple of boxcars on a siding out by the army base and popped the seal, just for a look, you know. Hundred-pound sacks of Iowa corn were stacked clean to the roof. Course, without a truck there wasn't much could be done but leave them there."

"Those boxcars are for the army-base mess, Roy."

Roy squashed out his cigarette and shrugged. "It's not like we haven't done our duty for the army, Seth, fighting Germans, sacrificing for our country, and them leaving us to starve under a bridge. A couple-three of those sacks off the top, and we'd be set for a good long while.

"We could drive down the right of way, come in from the back, and no one would ever know."

"This a company truck, Roy. I can't be stealing corn in a company truck."

Roy rolled down his window and hooked his elbow out. "I suppose a man with a full-time job can afford store-bought liquor. Course, the rest of us just have to do without, though it's about all we got left in the world."

Seth swung the key back and forth on his finger. "How long do you figure it would take?"

"An hour. No more."

Seth looked at his watch again. "Just so it's understood that I'm doing this for the boys."

By cutting onto the right of way at the wigwag, they could drive behind the sided cars, thus blocking the view from the base, which lay beyond the security fence. They eased out of the truck and climbed into the back.

"She's still open," Roy said, pushing the door of the boxcar back.

"I'll give you a leg up," Seth said, locking his fingers together. Roy boosted up and scaled the sacks like a mountain climber. Within moments, five sacks were stacked in the truck.

Once back in, Seth dropped her into reverse and brought her

about. They were nearly to the crossing when a military jeep appeared in Seth's rearview mirror.

"We've been tagged," Seth said. "They must have spotted the broken seal and figured some fool would be back."

Seth pushed the pedal to the floor. The truck engine roared, and black smoke drifted skyward. When he looked again, the jeep had dropped behind a hill.

Just then the turnoff to the still presented itself. Seth slammed on the brakes and spun the wheel hard as he could. The truck slid sideways, down into the ditch, and up onto the road again. Shoving her into second, he goosed her hard, and they careened behind the salvage-yard fence before coming to a stop.

They waited, listening to the jeep as it went on down the road. Seth dropped his head against the steering wheel.

"I got a notion to break your leg and leave you to die in this junkyard, Roy."

"How was I to know they'd be waiting, Seth? The goddang army don't ever mind their supplies. If it's stole, they just get more."

Seth checked his watch. "Let's get this corn unloaded. I got to get back for that yard dog."

After unloading the sacks, they covered them with an old car hood that Roy had dragged in. They smoked a cigarette and waited to make certain that the soldiers hadn't circled back. After that, Seth pulled out on the road and checked his rearview mirror.

"Looks like we've lost them," he said.

"Glad those boys aren't fighting Germans," Roy said. "We'd be drinking beer and dancing the polka."

"I can't be taking this shine to the jungle in broad daylight, Roy."

"I got an oil drum buried on the riverbank just past the stockyards," Roy said. "I keep my extra stash there, and it ain't that far from the jungle. Turn up there," he said.

Seth turned down a rough path that led to the river. Roy held his hand against the roof of the truck to keep from hitting his head, and when they came to the top of a slope, Seth pulled up.

"Too goddang steep," he said. "We'll have to carry it the rest of the way."

Turning the truck about, Seth backed it up to the lip of the slope and set the hand brake.

It took half an hour and a load switch before they reached the bottom. Seth checked his watch again.

"So where is this barrel, Roy?"

Roy turned and said something. Seth knew this because he could see his lips moving. But he never understood what it was Roy said. A screeching noise rode down into the valley and drowned him out. It sounded like a giant winged bird or the hot brakes of a runaway train charging down grade.

At that moment Seth and Roy looked up to see the company truck plunging toward the river in a cloud of dust.

8

HOOK FELL IN beside Andrea as they walked across the compound. She guided him onto the sidewalk. She smelled of Juicy Fruit.

"Here we are," she said. "As you can see, they've put the women in the tent."

The inmates' faces were pale from lack of sun, and they wore plain cotton dresses with no belts or accessories. Rocking chairs, on which some of the women rocked, lined the perimeter of the tent.

From the building across the way, Frankie Laine's music *The Mule Train* rose in the morning quiet.

"That's Frankie Yager, the orderly," she said. "He's been playing that record player for days.

"As you can see," she said, "these inmates are mostly nonviolent, though they forget that from time to time. Many of them suffer from depressive disorders. We also have a number of dementia patients and anxiety disorders as well.

"The one rocking there with the doll is Lucy. She has Habit

Disorder. Once she begins a movement, she can't stop. We have to keep a close watch that she doesn't harm herself."

"What's the doll about?" he asked.

"Her baby was taken by the state when she was admitted here. As you can see, it's a pain that she has never gotten over. Mental sickness does not necessarily diminish the need to be human or to be cared about by others.

"Take Ruth over there. She is our local exhibitionist. She has managed to entertain the entire institution since the fire, but, aside from that quirk, she can be a loyal and loving friend."

Sitting on the bunk near the entrance was a young girl. Her hands were folded in her lap, and she held her head down.

"What about her?" he asked. "She's so young."

"That's Elizabeth," she said. "She was to be married, you know. And then one day she didn't come home from work. They found her three days later. She had gotten lost on the way and had nearly died from hypothermia. Shortly after that, she was diagnosed with a brain tumor and brought here to Baldwin. I'm afraid her chances are slim."

"But shouldn't she be with her family?" he asked.

"Actually, no one ever came to see her again, not family, not even her fiancé. She did receive a card and a fruitcake for Christmas. But it was too late by then."

"They abandoned her?"

"Mental confusion can be both a frightening and shameful thing for a family," she said.

"You have a difficult job here," he said. "It would be like keeping up with a room full of children."

"Nothing is ever quite finished. You just move from one problem to the next." She put her hand on her waist. "They depend on me, and I'm attached to them as well.

"Now, do you have any questions?"

"The obvious, I guess. How do you keep the men and the women apart?"

Andrea smiled. "No one has managed that since Adam and Eve, have they?

"Okay," she said. "Though greatly diminished since the fire, the boys' ward has taken up residence in what used to be our facility. Let's go see."

Frankie sat behind the desk with his feet up. He was reading a magazine and had his music turned up to a painful volume. A crumpled potato-chip sack lay next to the trash bin.

Some of the boys were gathered about into groups. Others sat alone in the corners of the room or on their bunks. A few were behind locked doors, looking out from a single small window. Many of the boys were tattooed or bore scars on their arms.

Andrea motioned for Frankie to turn the record player down, which he did.

"Frankie, this is Mr. Hook Runyon, a special agent with the Santa Fe. He will be in charge of security during the transfer."

Frankie laid a limp hand in Hook's. His eyes were close set, turning slightly to the center, and he smelled of tobacco.

"Will you be going along?" Hook asked.

Frankie shrugged. "There ain't many can handle these boys but me," he said.

Andrea said, "A lot of these inmates exhibit antisocial behavior. Many of them have been abused or have been abusive themselves in one way or another: suicide attempts, self-inflicted wounds, uncontrolled anger."

"It's rules they understand," Frankie said, "and consequences."

Andrea glanced over at Hook. "Others have borderline intellectual functioning," she said. "Schizoid disorders are prevalent as well. Add all this into the normal developmental upheavals of male adolescence, and you can see the problem."

Hook said, "I see you're a Frankie Laine fan?"

"I was named after him," he said. "I got Dizzy, too, and Artie Shaw."

"You were pretty lucky your records didn't burn up in the fire. You seem to be very attached to them."

Frankie pursed his lips and rolled his shoulders. "Left my player downstairs. I move it around for the boys. When they do good, they get to listen."

"Nice meeting you," Hook said.

Once outside, Hook tapped his pocket. "Mind if I smoke?" he asked.

"Not at all," she said. "It's not permitted on the wards, especially nowadays. Sometimes Frankie lets his boys smoke in the back."

Hook lit a cigarette and rubbed at the tension that had gathered in his neck. "So, now what?" he asked.

Andrea checked her watch. "That leaves the security ward," she said. "We should go before Doctor Helms starts her appointments."

The security ward building, located at the back side of the compound, had been built of brick, and bars had been installed over the windows. A guard awaited them at the front entrance.

"This is Agent Runyon," Andrea said to the guard. "He's a railroad detective for the Santa Fe. We are to meet with Doctor Helms."

"Do you carry a weapon?" the guard asked.

"Yes," Hook said.

"Check it here, please. Weapons aren't permitted beyond this point."

Hook slipped his P.38 out of the shoulder holster and handed it to the guard.

Unlocking the door, the guard said, "I believe you'll find Doctor Helms in the therapy room, Andrea."

Doctor Helms, dressed in a gray suit, gathered up her keys to the ward and motioned for them to follow. Hook suspected that beneath that suit somewhere lurked a sensual and willowy body.

"These inmates are wards of the court," Helms said, unlocking the door. "In large part they have committed crimes for which others would have received the death penalty. Because they were deemed insane at the time of their crimes, they were sent here to be treated."

Sounds issued from the ward, not the sounds of criminals behind locked doors, not the cursing and vulgar language Hook had known in prisons, but the random and hopeless sounds of madness.

Helms adjusted her skirt and folded her arms over her breasts.

"Doctor Baldwin has asked that I escort you through," she said. "There's a red panic button at the end of the ward. If something untoward should happen, hit it and help will be sent in due time."

"Without weapons, how do you control these men?" Hook asked.

Doctor Helms pointed to a locked cabinet. A number of bottles sat on a table next to it.

"We rely heavily on medications," she said, "though restraints are sometimes necessary."

"And what are those sitting out unlocked?" he asked.

"Placebos," she said, picking up one of the green bottles. "They come in different sizes and colors, but they are simple sugar pills."

"Sugar pills? And what would those be for?" Hook asked.

"They serve as controls in our research programs. In addition, we have many hypochondriacs under our care. Placebos can be effective in treating imaginary ailments without doing harm to the inmate.

"And then, of course, there is malingering, those who pretend mental illness to escape justice. Such inmates will often respond positively to placebo treatment, thinking they are fooling us into believing that the medication is effective. Distinguishing criminal intent from mental illness can be difficult. Some believe that no differences exist."

"And are any of these men ever released from the institution?" he asked.

Helms lifted her chin. "Rarely," she said. "But it's been known to happen."

Though the floors had just been scrubbed, the area still smelled of urine and sweat. The rooms were stripped of all accoutrements except bunks and bedding. Cotton pads hung from the walls, and bars replaced the door windows.

Doctor Helms stopped at the first room. A man with a pocked face and lifeless eyes peered over her shoulder at Hook.

"Robert Smith," she said. "Robert is a sexual sadist who tied up his neighbor's daughter and butchered her with his penknife. They searched for her for weeks before the stench behind his garage wall alerted them to her location. No one knows how many more might be out there somewhere."

As they moved away, Hook said, "He's so docile."

Andrea nodded her head. "He's on medication."

"And the jury found him innocent?" he asked.

Doctor Helms paused. "The jury found him insane. According to the court, his acts were evil, but Mr. Smith is not.

"This man *here* is narcissistic," she said.

Hook looked in at the man sitting on his bunk, his legs crossed. Black molten eyes looked back for a moment and then turned away.

"He cares for nothing in this world but himself, not his mother, not his wife, not his own children. He is incapable of feeling your pain or anyone else's. All of the men here in some way suffer from narcissism. It's the basis of most crime."

As they moved from cell to cell, Doctor Helms described each, men so delusional that they barely slept, men who picked sores on their arms, who paced the rooms like wild animals, who cried and laughed for no apparent reason.

She paused at the last room. "In here we have Bertrand Van Diefendorf, a pyromaniac," she said.

"Fire?" Hook asked.

"Exactly," Doctor Helms said. "Mr. Van Diefendorf got up one night, went downstairs, and set the curtains on fire in his living room. By the time the fire department arrived, his entire family had perished. They found Mr. Van Diefendorf in the bushes masturbating.

"True pyromania is quite rare in the world of mental illness, though fire setting is not. The motivations for setting a fire can be quite varied."

Hook looked in at the man sitting on the bunk, fairly young, perhaps in his early forties, with wheat-blond hair and red rabbit eyes. Blue veins corded beneath skin as translucent as skimmed milk. He stared into another world, and his hands trembled ever so slightly in his lap.

"What are the motives in fire setting?" Hook asked.

"Most people set fires to cover a theft or insurance fraud or to destroy evidence, that sort of thing. If they set fires for no apparent reason, they are diagnosed as pyromaniacs."

Andrea looked into the room. "What is the underlying cause?"

Doctor Helms drew her arms over her chest. "The obvious answer is the lack of impulse control. But there's a high correlation with ungratified sexual desire. We believe the fire itself causes sexual arousal. Perhaps it's the manifestation of some primal urge. After all, men have been sitting around fires for some time now. In other words, Van Diefendorf here *enjoys* watching people burn.

"Well, then," she said. "Are there any questions, Mr. Runyon?"

"Just one," he said. "How am I supposed to get these men all the way to Oklahoma on a train?"

Helms turned up her hands. "You've asked the one question I can't answer, Mr. Runyon. That's why you're here."

9

HOOK PICKED UP his weapon on the way out of the security ward, relishing its weight there in the shoulder harness once again.

Andrea looked up at the sun. "Anything else you'd care to see?" she asked.

"I'd like a chance to visit with you about some things," he said. "Could it be arranged?"

"You've missed your lunch," she said. "Perhaps you'd care to share mine?"

"I couldn't take your lunch."

"I bring extra anyway," she said. "The ladies are always begging for this and that. Doctor Baldwin has my post covered, and there are tables under the trees. It's up to you, of course."

"Alright," he said.

On the way back to the women's tent, Andrea said, "The security ward can be a bit of a shock."

Hook paused long enough to light a cigarette. "You're right about that, and I've run into some pretty tough characters."

"Doctor Baldwin and Doctor Helms spend a great deal of time with their therapy. I don't know how they maintain their optimism."

"Having them together in one herd like that," he said, "it's like making a large monster out of smaller ones."

Andrea stopped and studied him for a moment. The sunlight danced in the gray of her eyes and lit the singed tips of her hair.

"I hadn't thought about it that way," she said. "Any single act they've committed is horrifying. Put them together, and it's incomprehensible.

"Here we are," she said. "I'll be back in a second."

Andrea returned with her sack lunch and a couple of drinks. "Up there," she said, pointing to a concrete picnic table that sat beneath the trees.

Hook watched her as she set out the lunch, placing the napkins just so.

"I hope you like cheese sandwiches because that's as good as it gets.

"So," she said, sitting down. "What is it you want to talk about?"

"I've got to be certain about some things before I take this on. Moving a trainload of folks across country is always a problem. Moving a load of folks like you have here could be downright dangerous. You can see that?"

"I can," she said. "But sometimes you don't have much choice, I guess."

He took a bite of his sandwich and looked back at the freshly dug grave.

"I've been wondering about that fire," he said.

"Awful," she said, shuddering. "I'll never forget those horrifying screams."

"Did you see anything that day?"

Andrea slid over the dill pickle she'd cut into quarters.

"What do you mean?"

"Anything out of the usual? Anybody about that shouldn't have been there?"

Andrea shook her head. "Frankie Yager, Doctor Baldwin, and Doctor Helms were there. I had Esther ringing the bell. Before long, people were running everywhere."

"Where were you when you first saw the fire?"

"In the women's building. I just happened to look out the window. First, I saw this flicker, and the next thing I know smoke is pouring out of the windows of the boys' ward."

"It came on pretty fast?" he asked.

"These old buildings are like kindling," she said.

"What did you do then?"

She dropped her chin in her hand as she thought. "I ran to help," she said. "No more than that. By the time I got to the top of the stairs, the fire raged out of control. I wasn't much help in the end, I'm afraid."

"And what about Frankie?"

She shrugged. "I don't know. I guess he was downstairs. When I opened the door to the boys' ward, a blast of hot air and flames shot out." Andrea looked away for a moment and then said, "I could see those boys. I could see them moving in the flames."

"I'm sorry to put you through this again, Andrea, but I've got to know if someone started that fire or not. Would any of the boys have done it themselves?"

Andrea opened her drink and thought about the question. "It's possible, I suppose. But the others would have intervened, wouldn't they?"

"Did you consider going for help?"

"The fire . . . I didn't think I had enough time. I put Esther to ringing the bell in hopes that others would come. I've wondered if I did the right thing, of course. I mean, all those lives."

"You decided to help the boys instead? That was your judgment?"

"Yes," she said. "That was my judgment."

"But Frankie decided to go find someone, to go for help instead?"

Andrea wrapped the last of her sandwich.

"Frankie's decisions are sometimes questionable. In spite of his physical presence, he's very childlike. In a way I'm not surprised that he sought out other adults. I've wondered if he could have saved those boys had he done otherwise. It's easy to second-guess, though."

Hook folded his napkin. "Doctor Helms said that the buildings were insured. Do you know anything about that?"

"No," she said.

"Do you know if the asylum had any money problems?" he asked.

"I know what you're thinking, but we had to turn patients away. The Baldwin Asylum enjoys, enjoyed, a good reputation."

"Well," he said. "My ride should be here by now. Thank you for lunch. I hope you get some weekend."

"Doctor Baldwin has found some relief for me, thank goodness. I plan to sleep for a week."

Hook was still waiting in the parking lot for Seth when Andrea left for home.

As she approached, she said, "Is everything alright?"

"My ride didn't show," he said.

"Where do you need to go?"

"I'm staying in the crew rooms at Casa del Desierto. It's not far. I'll just walk."

"It's on my way."

"I've already taken up half your day and eaten your lunch. I need the exercise anyway."

"Don't be ridiculous," she said. "My car is just here."

Andrea pulled into the depot and waited for Hook to get out. He stuck his head back in.

"Listen," he said. "I'm a book collector and thought I might get in some browsing while I'm here. Any recommendations?"

She looked over the tops of her glasses. "A book collector? Really?"

"Yeah, I know," he said. "But it's my thing."

"There's a couple places that have books," she said. "I doubt there would be anything a collector would want."

Hook turned when someone called his name. "Oh, that's my driver," he said. "Anyway, thanks for the lift."

Seth, who had been sitting on the bench just outside the depot, stood when Hook came toward him.

"Where the hell were you?" Hook asked. "I said three o'clock."

Seth looked at his feet. "I had a little trouble, Hook."

"Trouble? What kind of trouble?"

Seth shoved his hands into his pockets. "With the truck," he said.

"It wouldn't start?" Hook asked. "Damn thing hasn't been tuned up since it came off the factory line."

"Not that," Seth said. "It's in the river."

Hook rubbed at his face and looked down the line of track.

"Say again."

"It's in the river, Hook."

"What the hell you talking about?"

"Hell, Hook, I had time to kill, so I decided to go fishing up river by the stockyards. Food's a little hard to come by for poor vets like myself. So I backed the truck in, see, pulled the hand brake, and went on down to snag a catfish. First thing I know that truck came racing down the bank and right into the river."

"Jesus Christ, Seth, the company truck went into the river?"

"Not the engine, Hook. The engine's dry as dry."

"Jesus," Hook said. "Do you know what Division's going to do to me? It's just what that prick Eddie's been waiting for."

"I'm sorry, Hook. I didn't know that hand brake didn't work."

"Why didn't you get it out of the river?"

"They want ten bucks for a tow, Hook."

"That would be *your* ten bucks, wouldn't it, Seth?"

"Hell, Hook, I'm sleeping under a goddang bridge."

"I ought to take it out of your hide."

"I'm just a poor vet, Hook, waking up with night sweats from the war. It would be un-American."

By the time Hook got back, the last of the sun had sunk below the horizon. He pulled in at the bridge to let Seth out, who hadn't said a word all the way. The fire flickered from the jungle beneath the bridge.

"I'm real sorry, Hook," Seth said. "Soon as I get ten bucks, I'll pay you back."

"I won't be holding my breath on that one," Hook said.

"Me and the boys been talking," he said. "We got a proposition. You think you could come over tomorrow?"

"What you going to do, Seth, hit me over the head and throw me in the river along with my truck?"

"Naw," he said. "Roy's cooking his ham and beans. There's no better this side of Mexico."

"Well," Hook said, "it's against my better judgment, but I reckon I couldn't be in more trouble than I am."

Seth grinned. "Thanks, Hook. See you tomorrow, and I'm real sorry about the truck."

Hook waited until the supply clerk went down to the loading dock before ducking in to leave the truck keys on his desk.

Back at the depot sleeping rooms, he took off his clothes, which smelled like river mud, and threw them onto the floor of the shower to soak. After showering, he shaved and splashed on a heavy dose of aftershave.

He went to bed but couldn't sleep. After seeing the security ward, he was more convinced than ever that moving them as a group was a misguided strategy. Add in the missing links of a fatal fire, and it all came down to a dangerous assignment indeed.

'10

HOOK HEADED FOR the jungle under the bridge after deciding to leave the company truck at supply. It had been pretty much a mess when he left it, and he didn't feel like explaining to the supply clerk.

The Mojave sun blazed low on the horizon, but the heat still lingered. He wiped the sweat from his eyes. He would have preferred a little book scouting, but there would be time enough for that tomorrow.

As he approached the bridge, he smelled the fatback and beans wafting up from the jungle, a smell he'd encountered often enough on the line.

He slid down the bank and ducked under the bridge. A pot of beans simmered over a small fire, and clothes dried over one of the bridge beams. Bedrolls lay about here and there, old blankets mostly, tied up with ropes and pieces of wire.

"Seth," he said.

Seth rose from the patch of weeds just beyond, and then two or three others cropped up behind him.

"That you, Hook?" Seth asked.

"No, it's the president come for dinner," he said.

Seth clambered up the embankment. "Glad you could make it, Hook. Sorry about the greeting. The cops been keeping pretty close watch lately. I guess they figure we might be a threat to America."

"Well, they're probably right about that," Hook said.

"Come on up, boys," Seth said, waving the others in.

The men who climbed the bank looked more like bums than war vets. Their clothes were worn thin, and their eyes were dark and hollow.

"This is Hook Runyon, a friend of mine," Seth said. "We met in the yards, you might say."

"This here is Santos," Seth said, pointing to the Mexican fellow. "Santos is from El Paso or Juárez. We haven't figured that out for sure. Either way, he's a hell of a soldier. He wiped out a whole squad of Germans. Only problem was, one of them turned out to be his first lieutenant. They weren't sure if they should give him a medal or kick him out. They kicked him out."

Santos dropped his eyes, which were black as night. His hair was cropped military style. He stood as tall as Hook and was a fourth again as large, but he moved in a smooth catlike way.

"Santos," Hook said, shaking his hand.

Seth nodded toward the skinny one standing off from the others.

"That's Roy," he said. "Out of Kentucky, though he won't say exactly where. He cooked for the army, good, too, which requires some doing in the army. The Krauts shot one of his nuts off when he was dumping garbage one day. He says he was tired of the damn thing banging against his knees anyway."

"You make Kentucky shine, Roy?" Hook asked.

"It ain't lawful," Roy said.

"And that's Ethan over there," Seth said. "He's from New York City, but his people died off while he was away to war. We're about as close to relatives as he's got. He was gut shot making a hill. He made the hill alright but with half his intestine strung out behind. He's been a bit on the frail side ever since. He can't do much about that, I guess, or his looks either one. Ethan says living under a bridge is just like living in the Bronx, except quieter. He don't look like much wet, but there's a half-dozen dead enemy wished they hadn't met up with him."

Roy moved in closer. "Where'd you lose your arm, Hook?" he asked. "Land mine?"

Hook shook his head. "Car wreck. It wasn't much count but for sticking in my pocket, anyway."

Seth said, "Sit down, Hook. Roy's got the beans on and cornbread cooking in the iron skillet there. Santos came up with an onion from the grocery, and Ethan pulled greens in the backwash."

"Thanks," Hook said. "Smells right at home."

Ethan folded his legs under him. "You get a medical out of the army, Hook?"

Hook held up his prosthesis. "Lost it before the war. Never got in."

"Army prefers limbs intact when you enlist," Ethan said. "They're less particular about how you muster out."

"I hear you been working yard dog?" Roy said.

Hook glanced up at Seth. "I'm not here in an official capacity today."

"Bulls can be a dangerous lot," Roy said.

"I'm not on duty. Anyway, you boys would never hop my trains, would you?"

"Oh, hell no," Roy said. "But once I rode the Chief from Tucumcari. Drank martinis with Clark Gable the whole way. Beat him in three games of no-limit hold 'em poker. Poor ole Santos drank tea with Katy Hepburn the entire run."

"That a fact?" Hook said.

Santos grinned and added wood to the fire.

Pretty soon Roy gave the beans a stir and then poked a grass stem into the cornbread, which had turned golden brown. He served up the beans in tins that had been stored on top of the bridge beam. He cut the cornbread into pie-shaped slices and handed them around.

"I didn't get the flowers picked for the table," Roy said.

"Here I had my heart set on a nice bouquet," Hook said, digging in.

Afterward, they all sat back and had cigars that Santos had bought when the grocery clerk wasn't looking.

"I believe those are the best beans I ever ate," Hook said, "except maybe those I had at Bogie's house one time."

Roy shrugged. "Seems to me Bogie always shorted the fatback."

Hook dusted the ash off his cigar and gave it some thought.

"Your point's well-taken, Roy. I believe your beans *are* the best ever."

"Sure would like a taste of shine, if it wasn't against the law, I mean," Roy said.

Hook studied the end of his cigar. "Being somewhat of an expert on legal matters, it's my understanding that shine can be cooked up so long as it's in small batches and so long as the taxes are paid up."

"That a fact?" Roy said.

"So I've been advised," Hook said.

"Just happens I got a mighty small batch, and it's my intention to be paying taxes up before year's end. Would you care for a taste?"

"Long as it's a small batch," Hook said. "And long as the taxes are scheduled, I don't see what it could hurt."

Roy fetched a mason jar from behind the bridge pier, unscrewed the lid, and handed it to Hook. Hook took a sip and handed it back.

"That's fine busthead, Roy," he said. "You aren't related to a fellow by the name of Runt Wallace, are you?"

"Not so's I remember," he said.

"He's a man talented such as yourself," Hook said, "though his bean-cooking skills are somewhat lacking."

Seth took a swig of shine and handed it to Ethan. "It's a rare man can cook beans and shine with equal skill," he said.

Ethan took a long drink and shuddered. "Better hope the Waldorf doesn't get this recipe, Roy. We'll be paying forty dollars a quart."

Roy grinned. "You bastards know how to butter a man up, don't you?"

Hook took another drink and held the quart up to the firelight.

"What proof is that, Roy? I think my life's slipping away."

"Can't say," he said. "But you might not want to hold it too close to the fire."

Hook took another sip and passed it over to Seth.

"So," Hook said, "what is it you boys wanted to talk to me about?"

Seth picked up a stick and poked at the fire, which sent a spray of embers into the air.

"Well," he said, "you know how you're looking to hire security to move those inmates out of the Baldwin Insane Asylum?"

Hook took the jar and tipped it up. "I recall that," he said, wiping his mouth. "Too bad you boys don't have another small batch stored away somewhere, isn't it?"

Roy stood and dusted off his pants, reaching up under a bridge support.

"By golly," he said, handing the jar to Hook. "I believe there's one left."

Hook unscrewed the lid and gave it the smell test. "And you'll be paying up taxes on this one, too?"

"Oh, yes sir," Roy said. "Right along with my church tithe."

Hook took a long pull and passed it around. "Now," he said, tugging at his nose, which had now disappeared altogether, "about this proposition. You're telling me you want to hire on as security to help transport mental patients from California to Oklahoma?"

"It's not exactly a matter of want to," Seth said.

Hook looked at the men, the firelight flickering in their eyes.

"You boys don't have much training in such matters, do you?"

"Hell, Hook," Seth said, handing him the quart back. "We've been fighting Germans for years. We ought be able to move a few folks across country."

Hook took another drink, and the bridge shifted a little to the left.

"Maybe we should have talked about this before Roy found that second small batch of shine," he said.

"Every one of us been in combat, Hook. Dead center of it, too."

"But you had weapons," he said. "Besides, how would I tell security from the inmates?"

"Pick out the crazy ones," Roy said. "They would be security."

Hook started to take another drink, when Santos stood. "Listen," he said.

All fell quiet, their ears trained into the darkness. When it came again, Ethan bolted to his feet. "Cops," he said.

A flashlight beam shot from out of the darkness, and they all scrambled for the weed patch beyond the bridge. Hook jumped to his feet, only to discover that he had no feet, and he pitched headlong down the embankment. He struggled to get up, but by then a cop had his knee on his neck and was snapping on a handcuff.

"You'll get thirty days for this you son of a bitch," the cop said, cuffing Hook to a bridge support. The cop motioned for the others to follow. "The bastards are headed for the weeds, boys," he said. "Circle round. I'll be back for *you*," he said to Hook.

Hook could hear the cops as they circled out through the weeds, their breathing labored. Eddie Preston prayed for just such a calamity. There'd be thirty days in the slammer with the disciplinary board just waiting in the wings.

Voices rose up, and flashlights shined this way and that as the cops searched out the area. Hook tugged at the cuff, at that moment realizing that it had not cut into his wrist. He pulled again.

"I'll be damn," he said.

Within moments he climbed his way up the embankment, his prosthesis swinging from the bridge support like some macabre lynching.

Hook ducked into the depot and headed down the hall just as the operator stepped out of the bathroom.

"Hello, Hook," he said.

Hook lowered his head and grunted.

"Hey," the operator said. "Where the hell is your arm?"

Hook stopped. "I don't ask where your goddang arm is, do I?"

The operator wrinkled his brow. "But I ain't never lost one, Hook."

Hook turned for his room. "Just mind your own goddang business in the future," he said, "or you might."

Hook showered for the second time in one day and climbed into his bunk. If he ever found Seth again, he planned to kill him and place his body on the tracks. How had he managed to get mixed up with a bunch of castoffs in the first place?

Outside his window, a switch engine took the slack out of a line of cars and then growled off for the yards. Hook's head thumped from Roy's mighty small batch, and he had a patch of hide missing from his cheek.

At first he thought a thunderstorm had gathered up in the distance, but when the thump came again, he sat up on the edge of his bunk. He could see a silhouette against the yard lights outside his window. He reached for his sidearm and slid open the window.

"Hook?" Seth said. "It's me."

"I ain't shot a burglar all week," Hook said. "What the hell you want?"

"I got your arm," he said.

"What?"

"We conked that son of a bitch on the head and took his cuff keys. For a minute me and the boys thought they'd hung you off the bridge."

"Well, give it to me," Hook said, "or had you figured on charging me for it?"

Seth handed the arm through the window. "Roy dropped it in the river, but it ain't hurt.

"Listen, Hook, about that proposition?"

"You got about two seconds to get out of my window," Hook said, "before I empty this gun."

"Right," Seth said. "Good night, Hook."

11

WHEN THE TELEPHONE rang, Andrea rolled over and searched for the receiver.

"Hello," she said, sleep in her voice.

"Andrea, this is Hook."

"Who?"

"Hook Runyon, you know, with the railroad."

"Oh, yes," she said. "Is something wrong?"

"No, no, nothing wrong. I was just wondering about those bookstores you mentioned."

"I could get the addresses and call you back."

"That would be alright, but then I was hoping to talk to you actually. I've some concerns about that fire and thought you might have some ideas."

"Well," she said.

"And I don't have a ride, this being the weekend and all. I thought maybe we could sort of do it all at the same time."

"I did have plans to get some things done here," she said.

"Oh, sure. I understand. Another time."

"Well," she said, pausing, "I suppose I could show you where they are."

"That would be great. I'll be waiting out front of the depot. I'm the guy with one arm."

Andrea sat on the edge of the bed. She had misgivings about meeting Hook, not that she disliked him, but he *was* a yard dog. With Barstow being a railroad town, she'd grown up aware of the transient nature of railroaders and of yard dogs in particular.

On top of that, her breakup had been a difficult one, and she wasn't at all certain that she was emotionally prepared to deal with a man on any level. Still, he'd given her no reason to believe that he was interested in anything but getting his job done in the safest way possible. She guessed she owed her patients that much.

Hook finished his coffee and headed out of the depot. When he walked by the ticket office, the operator turned to his ledger without speaking.

The day shined bright and clear, and the pigeons gathered atop the depot, chortling and gurgling like teapots. Hook lit a cigarette and checked out the new scratches on his battered prosthesis.

When Andrea drove up, he doused his cigarette and slid in next to her. She wore a white ball cap that lit up her freckles and her slate-colored eyes.

"Morning," he said. "Hope I haven't ruined your weekend."

"Glad to be of help," she said. "What exactly are you looking for?"

"Books," he said. "So any place I can find them cheap and plentiful."

"There's a thrift."

"Works for me," he said.

Andrea checked her mirror before pulling out. "What happened to the face?"

Hook touched his cheek. He'd forgotten that the cop had parked a knee on his head.

"Jackrabbit kicked me," he said.

Andrea looked over at him. "A mighty big one by the looks of it."

"You never know what you're going to shake loose in a rail yard," he said.

When they passed the bridge, Hook rolled his window down. He wondered where Seth and the others had spent the night. He figured the cops hadn't left much of the jungle.

"Have you heard any more about getting a train for the asylum?" Andrea asked.

"I didn't call Division again," he said. "Thought I'd let it simmer for a bit. Too much information too fast shunts Eddie onto a siding, and he forgets where he's headed."

"There," she said, pointing to an old Quonset. "It's a pretty shabby place. You sure you wouldn't prefer a bookstore?"

"It's the hunt more than the finding," he said. "I like poking around, digging up treasure where no one else sees it. Problem is, it gets in your blood, and pretty soon you can't see out your windows for the books."

A cowbell attached to the door with a rope rang when they entered. An old guy with eyes the color of milk nodded and turned back to his reading. The Quonset smelled of dust, old clothes, and grease. Hook checked out the usual array of mismatched dishes, pots and pans, and toasters with frayed cords. Racks of accessories were near the window: belts, leather purses, scarves, and costume jewelry. Used furniture had been stacked in the back, kitchen chairs with the seats missing, crippled tables, and old sewing machines.

"It's all so disorganized," Andrea said.

Hook pushed aside the kitchen chairs and looked under the table.

"Keep focused on what you're looking for or you go home with a ton of junk. See those boxes under there? Treasure," he said. "But like all treasure there's a certain amount of overburden to dig through."

Andrea got down on all fours and pulled the boxes out, the white of her back peeking from under her shirt.

"Good Lord," she said, dusting her hands. "There's hundreds of them. We'll be all day."

"I'm going to talk to the clerk," he said. "Be right back."

When he returned, he said, "Okay. Got what I need."

"You found the book you wanted?" she asked.

"I bought them all."

"What?"

"This sort of thing takes time."

"I should be getting back."

"Oh, sure," he said. "Let me buy you lunch first. I owe you that much."

They stopped by the Mojave Hamburger stand before driving to the park. After they'd eaten, Hook put the boxes on the picnic table.

"A quick look," he said. "It won't take long, I promise."

"We're already here, I suppose," she said. "It's old books you're looking for, right?"

"It's rare books," he said. "Sometimes they're old and sometimes not. Condition is everything, and dust jackets are essential. We want first editions, signed if possible. Beware of book-club editions. They're not worth a damn. You can tell by their weight, or lack of it, I should say."

"But how do you know what titles to collect?"

Hook thumbed through a book, checking the title page and the series of numbers at the bottom. "Practice," he said. "Even then, it's easy to make a mistake. Look for an author's first book. It tends to be the smallest print run. Beware of bestsellers. Everybody in the country will have a copy just like yours."

Andrea picked up a book and examined it. "But what do you do with them once you've collected them?" she asked.

Hook looked over at her. "Own them," he said. "One day you die, and somebody else owns them. That's how it works."

Andrea studied him. "That's a little weird."

"It's a lot weird," he said.

An hour later, Hook leaned back and lit a cigarette. "That about does it," he said.

Andrea looked at the books Hook had set aside. "Out of all those, you have only two?"

"Not just *any* two," he said. "This one is Steinbeck's *Cup of Gold*, his first. Not many of those published. It will be valuable someday. And this one is Lawrence's *Lady Chatterley's Lover*. Not much now but a groundbreaker. Someday it will be important."

Andrea gathered her knees into her arms. "You've quite an interest in all this?"

"An obsession, and I'm not the best company when I'm in the midst of a hunt."

Hook started putting the books back into the boxes. "So tell me about yourself."

Andrea shrugged. "My life's pretty simple," she said.

"No life is simple. How did you wind up at Baldwin?"

"Went to nursing school first, of course. Took my internship with the nuns. I've always been a pretty good student. Things were going well until I discovered something about myself."

"What would that be?"

"I couldn't deal with blood. This is not a good thing for a nurse."

"Or for yard dogs," he said.

"But I'm pretty good with what I'm doing, at least I like to think I am."

"I'll bet you are," he said.

"So how did you get to be a yard dog?" she asked.

Hook held up his prosthesis. "My life began and ended with this," he said. "Car wreck, and then I sort of went out to get even with the world."

"And did you?"

"I hit the skids and learned a lot about survival. Then, with the war came a shortage of men. Hiring a one-arm yard dog doesn't seem so unreasonable when there's no one else. I've been at it awhile now. Me and the railroad have had our ups and downs over the years."

"Married?"

"Never been asked," he said. "You?"

"I've been asked," she said. "And then he changed his mind."

"Sorry," he said. "I didn't mean to pry.

"The law turned out to be something I could do, and I had spent a lot of time riding the rods by then. I have a pretty good eye for detail and tend to think like a criminal, all necessary in a job like mine."

"Where do you live?"

"Caboose," he said.

Andrea plunked her chin in her hands. "You're kidding me?"

"It's like living at the tail end of a bullwhip," he said.

"Do you have relatives?" she asked.

"Not that I admit to. Other than Mixer, that is."

"Mixer?"

"My dog. He fights everything that comes along, and it doesn't matter a damn how big or mean it is. Don't know how he's managed to stay alive. Section foreman's taking care of him back in Needles."

"And now you're charged with moving an entire insane asylum," she said.

"It just might be the end of a fine career," he said.

"Why do you say that?"

"Other than there's about a thousand things that could go wrong, I've some real concerns about that fire out there."

"I wake up in the night thinking about that horrible accident," she said.

"If it was an accident," he said.

"You don't think so, do you?"

"I don't know. That's just the point, but I can't have an arsonist running around loose on my train. I can't take that chance."

"They said it was the electrical wiring."

Hook picked up the boxes of books and took them to the car. When he came back, he said, "What do you think?"

"I guess it could have been."

"But how do they know? There was nothing left of that building but ashes. Did the fire department investigate or the local police?"

Andrea gathered up the papers and sacks from lunch and put them in the trash can.

"Both came," she said.

"And?"

"They looked around, talked to Doctor Baldwin."

"If the fire had been anywhere but in an insane asylum, do you think things would have been handled differently?" he asked.

Andrea fell silent for a moment. "I've gotten used to people's indifference when it comes to the mentally ill. As far as other people are concerned, those inmates out there are already dead. They didn't spend that much time investigating, I guess."

Hook sat down on the table and lit a cigarette. A squirrel peeked around a limb before vaulting to the top of the tree.

"If I can't be certain it was accidental, I can't be certain it wasn't set," he said.

"But why would anyone do such a thing?" Andrea asked. "There would have to be a reason."

"That's usually the case," he said. "Unless what Doctor Helms says is correct, that pyromaniacs don't need a reason."

"Like Van Diefendorf?"

Hook shook his head. "Anyone who would burn his house with his family in it might enjoy setting fire to his fellow inmates."

"But that's the security ward," Andrea said. "The place is locked down twenty-four hours a day."

Hook snuffed out his cigarette. "Maybe security has been breached. Men who are locked up can be unusually clever in finding ways to get what they want. Perhaps there is someone on the outside who's involved."

Andrea thought for a moment. "There's the guard, I suppose, but he's worked there for many years now. The staff has access. Other than that, no one can even get in there."

"How are they fed?"

"Food is brought in from the cafeteria. Everything is searched going in and coming out."

"The safety of those boys lay with Frankie. How do you figure he let such a thing happen?"

"He had two floors to cover. It's not easy to keep track of so many, believe me."

"Does he have friends, a girlfriend maybe?" he asked.

"Not that I know of. Frankie has his music, and he goes out to a movie occasionally, but I've never seen him with a girl."

"How does he get along with Doctor Baldwin?"

"He doesn't interact with people much one way or the other."

"And so what about you, Andrea? What made you decide to make this trip?"

"Am I a suspect as well?"

"No," he said. "You came after the fire had started, and you tried to put it out. There are burns on your hands to prove it."

Andrea turned her hands over. "I'm going so that I can look out for my patients. If not for them, I wouldn't be going. Everything I have is here.

"Look, I don't mean to tell you your business, but have you considered the possibility that this was just a tragic accident?"

"I've been a yard dog a long time now. Being suspicious has kept me alive." He looked over at her. "I admit that sometimes I see the world through a broken glass."

"Well," she said, standing, "I really must be getting home. What do we do with all these books you don't want?"

"Take them back to the thrift," he said.

"But you've already paid for them."

"Lots of people depend on these for their reading material," he said. "I've found what I wanted."

Back at the depot, Hook got out of the car. "Thanks for showing me around," he said, "and for answering my questions. I'll be seeing you soon."

Andrea watched him walk toward the depot. He was nearly at the door when she called after him.

"It's the sedation mostly," she said.

Hook turned. "What do you mean?"

"I've seen those men in the security ward stare at a bowl of soup until it was stone cold. No one under that much sedation could plan a crime, even if he weren't locked up."

12

Hook sat in the phone booth for several minutes before he called Eddie at Division.

When Eddie came on, he said, "Preston here."

"Eddie, about this asylum deal."

"Runyon, I just got a call from the Barstow supply clerk."

"The supply clerk?"

"He says you brought the company truck back in a goddang mess."

"I don't know what you're talking about, Eddie."

"He's says it was full of mud. You don't have enough Brownies yet?"

"Mud? This is Barstow, the Mojave for Christ's sake. Besides, you can't believe anything that a supply clerk tells you."

"What does that mean?"

"I think he's been stealing supplies."

"You got any evidence of that?"

"It's a feeling."

"You got too much riding on this board hearing to be playing games, Runyon."

"Listen, I think I've located some men for security."

Eddie paused. "How many?"

"Four. It isn't enough, but this is not the best job in the world either."

"Who?"

"Soldiers," he said. "Vets. Heroes. These bastards are disciplined heroes."

"Where did you find them?"

"They come highly recommended. I'll get the paperwork in so you can get them on the clock."

"What does Baldwin have to say about it?"

"I'm headed out there this morning. He'll be damn glad to get these boys. How many times you get the chance to hire true American heroes?"

"This better be on the level, Runyon."

Hook took a deep breath. Talking to Eddie was like going under for the third time.

"Did you locate a passenger train?" Hook asked. "Baldwin's got inmates scattered everywhere out there, and some of them are pretty scary characters."

"We have a war going on, remember?" he said.

"Yeah, I heard that."

"The section foreman out of Needles called," Eddie said. "He says someone's popped the spikes on a length of track."

"It's a maintenance problem, Eddie. The whole damn line is in need of repair. What the hell am I supposed to do about it?"

"Get back there and take a look. We can't take a chance on some nut sending a train airborne."

"Jesus, I'm kind of busy out here."

"And call if you find something."

"Yeah, you're first on my list, Eddie."

Hook walked down to the supply shack to get the truck and found the clerk in the back counting out lightbulbs. He looked up when Hook came in and then went back to his counting.

"Like to sign out the truck," Hook said.

The clerk pushed the box back. "What the hell you been doing to my truck? The damn thing smelled like swamp mud."

"No time to chat," Hook said.

"I'm signing out no truck until I get an explanation."

"Well, I am kind of rushed this morning, seeing as how I've got to get my report on supply finished up and sent in to Division."

"What report?"

"My investigation."

"On supply?"

"After that, I got to get out to the Baldwin Asylum. Seems like I never get caught up."

"What supply report?"

"That sort of thing is confidential, but I will say this. The company disapproves of shoddy inventory. You know what I mean?"

The clerk stood. "Now look, Runyon, I run a tight shop here. Nothing goes out but what's signed for."

"I understand you wouldn't do anything like that yourself, but you know how these other bastards are, carrying things home in their lunch pails.

"I caught a man stealing signal wire out of the Needles supply shack. Had the damn stuff rolled up under his shirt. What the hell could he have been thinking? He got a year in the slammer on that one."

The clerk dug in his pocket for the truck key and handed it to Hook.

"I run a tight shop here, Runyon."

"Yes, sir, so I've heard. I doubt I'll find a thing in a shop such as this."

Hook had no sooner opened the door to the company truck

when a police car pulled in. The cop that got out stretched the kinks out of his legs. Gray tinged his hair, and a bandage had been taped behind his ear.

"I want to talk to you," he said.

Hook closed the door. "Start talking."

"What's your name?" he asked.

"Hook Runyon, railroad agent. What's yours?"

"We raided a jungle last night," he said.

"Were they on railroad property?"

"Under a city bridge."

"Out of my jurisdiction," Hook said. "You see one on railroad property, give me a call."

"Thing is, I caught one of them and cuffed him to the bridge support. When I got back the son of a bitch had escaped, gone, but his arm was hanging from the bridge. Someone cracked me behind the ear, and when I woke up, damn if that arm hadn't disappeared."

"What does all this have to do with me?"

"So far, you're the only one-arm son of a bitch I've seen."

Hook lit a cigarette and looked at the cop through a cloud of smoke.

"With all these army boys about, my guess is that there's more than one man in Barstow with an arm missing."

"The son of a bitch better not let me catch him," he said. "Any man cracks me on the head's going to get his ass kicked."

"Mind moving your patrol car?" Hook said. "We got rules about blocking the right of way."

Hook pulled up at the bridge and got out, checking to make certain he hadn't been followed. The cops had done a fair job of wrecking the jungle. What they couldn't break up, they had thrown into the river.

"You boys can come out," Hook said.

One by one they emerged from the weed patch.

"Hello, Hook," Seth said, cocking his hat. "Some night."

"You can figure those cops will come back," Hook said. "And they're a little pissed, especially the one with his head cracked."

"I hit my head all the time on these bridge supports," Seth said. "It can sure make you mad."

Roy buried his hands in his pockets. "You come for more shine, Hook? I got a small batch down there in the weeds."

"Last time I drank your popskull someone tore off my arm," Hook said, "and I didn't even know it."

"I lost a nut the same way," Roy said. "Woke up and the damn thing was gone."

Hook worked his way into the shade. "I'm here about that proposition."

Seth joined him. "Baldwin?"

"It's against my better judgment, but I need men. The railroad's agreed to put you on the payroll from now until we unload in Oklahoma. After that, you boys would be on your own."

"Hear that?" Seth said.

"I figure you can get a little experience while we are waiting for a train. Working with those inmates requires know-how, and there's no weapons allowed."

"Kind of like going to the front in your underwear, ain't it?" Seth said.

"Least you'll be riding on the *inside* of the train for a change," Ethan said.

Santos rolled his shoulders and looked around. "No weapons? Maybe, I don't know."

Hook shook his head. "That's the way it's got to be. These inmates aren't criminals, Santos, and they aren't Germans neither."

"Do we get a company truck?" Roy asked.

"No truck, and I expect you boys to be professional."

"Oh, sure," Roy said. "We know how to do that."

"Okay. We're going to load up and go talk to Doctor Baldwin. All you boys have to do is nod your heads once in awhile."

"You got the truck?" Seth asked. "How did you manage that?"

"I reminded the clerk of my investigation powers."

"He's stealing?" Ethan asked.

Hook shrugged. "I never knew one who wasn't."

Before going into Baldwin, Hook walked the men past the mass grave. Roy held his hat in his hand. Ethan's jaw rippled when he asked how many had died.

"Thirty," Hook said, "more or less. I just wanted you men to see how it is out here. This place is under a lot of pressure. Now let's go see Baldwin. Try to act like you haven't been living under a bridge."

Doctor Baldwin and Doctor Helms stood when Hook and the men came in. Hook made introductions all around.

"Veterans?" Baldwin asked.

"True American heroes every one," Hook said.

Doctor Helms folded her arms over her chest.

"Have any of you men worked with mental patients before?" she asked.

"We been in the army, ma'am," Seth said. "It don't get any crazier than that."

"I'm afraid this won't do," she said.

Doctor Baldwin pushed his glasses down to the end of his nose and looked over the tops, his huge eyes shrinking.

"Normally, I would agree, Doctor Helms, but we've had a major tragedy here. Sometimes you have to make do with what you have. These men have served their country and have suffered great hardships. They've demonstrated their ability to adjust to difficult situations. Perhaps we should give this a chance?"

Helms walked down the line of men, stopping in front of Hook. She wore a thin gold chain about her neck.

"Have you explained the security ward to these men?" she asked.

Doctor Baldwin said, "What Doctor Helms means is that the security ward is made up of criminally insane inmates. That's where you will be needed the most during the transfer."

Helms sat back down and crossed her legs, and a garter snap at the top of her nylons peeked out.

"You should understand what you're getting into," Helms said. "These inmates have committed horrific crimes. They did so without provocation and without the slightest remorse. Given an opportunity, they would do so again."

"Sounds like my old drill sergeant," Roy said.

Hook shot Roy a look. "I been thinking a short training period would be in order," Hook said. "Division's having trouble locating a passenger train. In the meantime, these men could be instructed on how to handle these inmates."

"I'm not sure the security ward is the place for training," Doctor Helms said. "One mistake and someone could lose his life."

"Well now," Doctor Baldwin said. "We've trained others, haven't we?"

Helms uncrossed her legs and adjusted her skirt.

"But they worked in the institution for years before transferring to the security ward," she said. "It's a very dangerous place."

Doctor Baldwin picked up his pen and commenced doodling on his desk pad.

"Your point is well taken, Doctor, but the fact is very few of our employees have agreed to the move. We don't have a lot of choice.

"We could start these men in the boys' and the women's wards. When the time comes, we'll move them to the security ward. With your supervision, I'm certain things will work out."

Doctor Helms stood. "I'll do as you say, of course, Doctor Baldwin. But I think it's inadvisable. We cannot afford another calamity like we just had. Baldwin Asylum would not survive."

Baldwin said, "Place two of your men with Nurse Andrea, Mr. Runyon, and two with Frankie Yager in the boys' ward."

"Right away," Hook said.

"And, Mr. Runyon, would you have any idea when a train might be located?"

"I'm sorry, Doctor Baldwin, but I can't be sure. Division is trying to put something together. Equipment is difficult to come by. With a little luck, something will break soon."

"I do hope so," he said. "I received a call from Oklahoma last evening. Word has gotten out about our move. The community there is less than happy about our opening an asylum in their town. The longer this goes on, the worse things are likely to become."

Hook left Seth and Ethan at the boys' ward. Frankie Yager rolled his eyes and turned back to his magazine.

Santos stood behind Hook as he explained the situation to Andrea.

"They've never worked with patients before?" she asked.

"They're good boys, Andrea, a little rough here and there."

Andrea looked at Santos, who peeked over Hook's shoulder.

"What's the matter with him?" she asked.

"Santos is shy around women, I think," Hook said. "Roy here will keep an eye on him. Won't you, Roy?"

Roy didn't answer inasmuch as he was watching Ruth, who sat on the cot with her legs apart.

Andrea lifted her brows. "Are you sure about all this, Hook? This *is* an insane asylum."

"No," he said. "I haven't been sure about anything since I left Needles. I just get up every morning and do what's in front of me. Once in awhile it works out. I needed men, and these are the ones I found."

Santos said, "Without fear, I once killed a German soldier in a mud hole, but this place . . ."

Andrea took Santos's arm. "It will be alright. You just go about your business, and pretty soon you'll forget all about it. Lots of people are afraid at first."

"Roy," Hook said, "when you're done there, Andrea is going to show you around."

"Sorry, Miss," he said. "What do we call them?"

"By their names," Andrea said.

Hook said, "I have a little business to take care of, Andrea. Needles is having rail trouble, so I might be out of pocket for a few days.

"Roy, you boys stay out of trouble while I'm gone."

"Yes sir," Roy said. "Everything's under control here."

13

ANDREA ARRIVED AT work early. Santos and Roy were waiting outside the gate for her. Both had gotten haircuts and wore new shirts with the hanger creases still in them.

"Morning Nurse Andrea," Roy said. "Seth and Ethan went on to the boys' ward."

"Morning," Andrea said. "Are you men ready?"

Santos ducked his head and Roy said, "It's like going over the top and not knowing if there's a bullet waiting."

"Well, there's no bullet. Most of this is just common sense."

They trailed behind Andrea like little boys at their mother's dress tail. She paused outside the tent.

"These women are here because they're deeply troubled," she said. "Their judgment, for one reason or another, is impaired, so you are responsible, not only for them but for yourselves. Do you understand what I'm saying?"

"What happens if they attack?" Roy asked.

"That's not likely, Roy. But if it happens, you have to protect yourself, of course, but do so in the least physical way possible. Words are the weapon of choice here."

"Santos only has about two words," Roy said. "And they're both in Mexican."

"Santos will do just fine," she said and led them inside.

"Now, Esther over there suffers from dementia. She's quite harmless but confused. Don't expect her to follow directions."

"Seth don't follow directions, either," Roy said. "But he's just contrary."

"Ruth is in the general category of paraphilias, specifically exhibitionism."

"Someone ought tell her to keep her dress down," Roy said.

"That's just the point, Roy. She gets intense sexual urges to exhibit herself. Her behavior can be quite disturbing. It's best to not reinforce it. Do you understand?"

"I'll do my best," Roy said, "though it's right disturbing, as you say."

"The same is true with Bertha, who is sitting over there by the tent flap. She has what we refer to as Histrionic Disorder. She often misreads her relationships with others as being more intimate than they are in reality. It's an odd form of narcissism, in a way."

"Those are sure big words," Roy said. "I don't think Santos understands them."

"Well, don't worry about the words. Just tread carefully in these situations."

"Santos freezes up around women," Roy said. "But he's damn handy in a fight."

"Anna, the old lady over there by the tent pole, has never recovered from her husband's death. She believes she caused it and can't forgive herself.

"Elizabeth, the young girl on the cot, has a malignant brain tumor. Her condition is deteriorating, and her depression has deepened as well."

"Why won't she look at you?" Roy asked.

"She has trouble focusing now, and she sometimes thinks she's back home again with her people."

"Doesn't she have anyone left?" Roy asked.

"None to see her through," she said.

Roy looked at the girl, who had turned her back to them. "I seen boys on the front just the same," he said, "waiting for word. It's a pity when it don't come. Ain't much left after that, I guess."

"Okay, we'll meet the others later," Andrea said. "Questions?"

"What do you want us to do first?" Roy asked.

"You should just get acquainted. The inmates need to get comfortable with you. Mostly what we need is help in managing the daily chores. It has become particularly difficult under these conditions. We have to take them to the cafeteria each day to eat, and the nights are getting colder. Bathing has also become complicated.

"Anyway, for now, just circulate. Talk to them if they want or just sit quietly."

"Okay," Roy said. "Come on, Santos. Be sure and don't talk too much."

Andrea turned to go get the medications ready and then paused.

"About Hook?" she said.

"He caught the east-bound for Needles early this morning," Roy said.

"I was just curious about the train."

"Oh, yes ma'am," Roy said. "I can see where you would be."

Frankie's record player cranked up over in the boys' ward while Roy and Santos made the rounds. Bertha soon took to Santos's reticence as a sure sign of his infatuation with her and started following him about the tent.

Roy and Santos escorted a small group to the restrooms while Andrea finished her meds. She bandaged Esther's hand, which had been pinched in the tent rope, and looked up to see Doctor Baldwin approaching from across the compound.

"Nurse Andrea," he said, adjusting his glasses on his nose. "May I speak with you for a moment?"

Andrea picked up her tape and gauze. "What is it, Doctor Baldwin?"

"I've decided to call a staff meeting in my office. Do you think you could attend?"

Andrea looked about the tent. "Well, we were just getting ready to take the inmates to lunch."

"Perhaps you could get someone else to do it."

"There's Roy and Santos, but they've never done it before."

"Thank you, Nurse Andrea. I wouldn't ask if it weren't important."

Andrea lined up the women, making certain that Ruth had all her clothes on and that Esther had gotten in line. Bertha took her place next to Santos, gazing up at him.

"Now," Andrea said, "their meds have been administered. All you have to do is walk them to the cafeteria. When they've finished eating, bring them back here. I'll be along as soon as I can. Do you think you can do that?"

"Why, sure," Roy said. "How hard can that be?"

Doctor Baldwin looked up from his papers when Andrea walked in. Doctor Helms stood at the window.

"I'm glad you could make it, Nurse Andrea," he said. "Please take a seat."

Doctor Baldwin filed his papers before beginning. "There, now," he said. "The reason I've called the meeting, the reasons, I should say, are because some pressing matters have arisen."

Doctor Helms took her chair and fished a pen and paper out of her purse.

"Doctor Baldwin," she said, "I've left the security ward in the hands of the guard."

"I will get right to the point. I've received word that the insurance company has delayed payment. They've decided to conduct an investigation of the fire."

"Do they suspect foul play?" Andrea asked.

"It's just precautionary, to make certain that arson didn't play a role in all of this. I don't anticipate a problem except that it does delay payment. That means I'll have to tap the general fund to pay for the transfer."

"This could be a problem," Helms said.

"We should be alright, but it does put a strain on the budget. On top of that, I've had three more locals quit. We are running dangerously low on help. I've called you here to get your advice."

"Advice?" Andrea said.

"My biggest concern is how to transfer the security ward. Manpower is limited at best, and to move them such a distance and without sufficient help is risky. I can't afford an incident."

Andrea looked over at Helms and then back at Doctor Baldwin. "I have a suggestion," she said. "It's only a suggestion, of course."

"Please," Doctor Baldwin said. "That's why I asked you to come."

"Well, given the situation, why couldn't they be sedated? Most of them are on meds now. It would be a matter of increasing the dosage for a temporary period of time. Restraints could be used as a backup when necessary."

"This presents an ethical problem," Helms said. "Drugging inmates for our convenience is a questionable procedure."

"But how ethical is it to risk these men escaping?" Baldwin said.

"Frankly, in my opinion the security ward should not be moved as a group. It puts both the public and the inmates in danger."

"Time is critical here," Baldwin said. "The community where the fort is located has become increasingly agitated about having the asylum located there. They've organized a committee and have made their objections known to me."

Helms checked her watch. "Doctor Baldwin, there is another alternative that you haven't mentioned."

"Oh?"

"You've intimated that the Baldwin Asylum faces financial problems. Are you sure it's prudent to move all these people to some abandoned fort and without proper funding? If this institution is facing insolvency, then perhaps that issue should be addressed first."

"I didn't say it was insolvent. Barring complications, I see no reason why we can't reestablish the asylum."

"But that's exactly the problem," she said. "If there's one thing I've learned about an insane asylum, it's that there's never a shortage of complications."

As Andrea walked back to the tent, she thought about what Helms had said. If the situation had been dire enough to call a staff meeting, Baldwin could be in more of a financial bind than he was admitting.

When she rounded the corner, she stopped, covering her mouth with her hand. "Oh my God," she said.

Her patients were coming up the hill from the cafeteria with Roy at the lead and Santos bringing up the rear. In between, the women marched in single file, their hands locked behind their heads prisoner style.

As Roy approached the tent, he said, "Arms down."

The inmates dropped their arms and remained at attention.

"At ease," Roy said. "There you go, Nurse Andrea. Fed up and ready for their naps."

Andrea clamped her hands on her waist. "What *are* you doing?"

"We had a little trouble getting them to line up," Roy said. "But not for long. One time me and Santos marched a whole squadron of German soldiers fourteen miles the very same way. Didn't have a bit of trouble, did we, Santos?"

"These are patients, Roy, not prisoners of war," Andrea said.

"Yes, ma'am," he said. "That's what I told Santos when he wanted to make Bertha do push-ups 'cause she wouldn't leave him be. I says, 'Santos, Bertha there is a hysterectomy, and you can't be making her do push-ups.'"

"By the way," he said. "Just so you know, Ruth dropped her britches in the cafeteria, and the cook spilled a pan of biscuits. We ate them anyway. You learn not to be persnickety in the army."

"Perhaps this is enough training for one day," Andrea said. "I'll see you men in the morning."

Andrea watched as Roy and Santos made their way to the gate. She looked back at the security ward and wiped the palms of her hands on her skirt. She hoped she had made the right decision to go along with this move. It would be all too easy to wind up a thousand miles from home with no job and no future.

14

Pap Gonzales waited on the Needles platform for Hook to disembark from the east-bound Chief.

"Well look who's back from the insane asylum," he said. "Glad to see you got your britches on. Hope you feel better 'cause you sure as hell don't look it."

"I figured you'd be retired or dead by now," Hook said. "You ain't dead, are you?"

"Just as well be," Pap said, "living in this hole."

Hook hefted his bag over his shoulder. "So what's so important to drag me across the desert, or are you just lonesome to see me?"

"I have track torn up. Looks to me like someone's been tampering."

"You section hands are always looking for a reason to blame someone else."

"Truth is, I wanted you to come get this goddang dog. He's more trouble than a railroad official."

Mixer leaped out of the motorcar when he saw Hook. His ears were shredded, and one eye had swollen shut.

"Jesus, Pap," he said. "You been beating my dog?"

"No, I ain't been beating your dog, though I can't say I hadn't thought about it."

Hook loaded his bag on the motorcar and lifted Mixer into the back. He waited for Pap to spin the engine up.

"What's he been up to?" he asked, as they clattered off down the track.

Pap goosed the engine, and the wind flapped Mixer's ears like a bird taking flight.

"He chased a badger into a culvert," he said. "Big as a goddang mountain lion. That idiot dog of yours went in after him." Pap adjusted his hat. "I never heard such a racket. Pretty soon, here comes Mixer out the other end looking just like he does now."

"What happened to the badger?" Hook asked.

"I don't know, and I damn sure didn't go into that culvert to find out."

Hook grinned, lit a cigarette, and leaned back to enjoy the wind and desert.

Within the hour, Pap idled down the car and brought her to a stop just short of a crossing. A lonely dirt road stretched out into the desert, and buzzards circled high in the blue.

Hook walked up the tracks and then back down. He stopped at the motorcar. Mixer marked all four wheels before climbing aboard to lie down.

"Well?" Pap said.

Hook propped his foot up and leaned in on his knee.

"It's just poor maintenance, Pap. If you boys would spend more time working and less time shooting craps under the bridge, we wouldn't have these problems."

Pap rolled his eyes. "If you'd turn this stuff in once in awhile, maybe we could get a little more help around here. Can't you see someone has taken the spikes out?"

"They worked loose, Pap. Those ties are rotten."

Pap walked up a ways and then came back. "Then where's the spikes, Hook? Someone has pulled them."

"Just picked them up, probably selling them for scrap. The only place they're missing is where the ties are rotted. Get your boys out here and replace those ties, and I think you'll find your problems will be over."

Pap climbed back on the motorcar. "I see where that dog of yours gets his mean streak," he said. "Where to?"

"Yard office. I need to call Eddie."

Back at the yard office, Hook climbed out with Mixer right behind him.

"I'll walk back to the caboose when I'm finished here, Pap. You have any more trouble, let me know."

"Just be wasting my time, wouldn't I?" he said. "Least I won't have that dog following me around all day."

"See you later, Pap."

The yard office clerk looked up from his desk when Hook walked in.

"Well," he said, "if it ain't Hook Runyon. When did they let you out? What I mean is *why* did they let you out?"

"They figured it was time someone straightened things out around here," he said.

The clerk grinned. "There's a sack full of mail for you over there. I was just getting ready to toss it out when you walked in."

"Thanks," Hook said, picking up the phone.

Eddie answered on the third ring. "Division," he said.

"Eddie, this is Hook. I just got back from that crossing Pap was squawking about."

"What did you find?" Eddie asked.

"The ties haven't been replaced in about a hundred years. Somebody has been picking up the spikes, probably kids or something."

"Tell Pap to get them replaced then. We get a derailment out there somebody's going to swing."

"Pap's got his hands full. How about sending him a little extra help out here once in awhile?"

"Right," Eddie said. "Did you get those men lined up for Baldwin?"

"Oh, sure. It's working out fine. Those guys are top-notch."

"Listen," Eddie said. "I get this call from Barstow, see. Their supply clerk's gone, and they can't find him anywhere. They checked the supply inventory. Turns out the son of a bitch has been stealing."

"Yeah," Hook said. "He probably concocted that truck deal to sidetrack my investigation. I'll keep an eye out for him.

"Have you put together a train yet, Eddie? These people can't hold out forever."

"I found something," he said. "It will be coming in a couple days."

"What is it?"

"Well, it ain't the Chief, but it ought get the job done."

"Put in an order to pick up my caboose."

"Do you know that caboose weighs forty thousand pounds?"

"Part of my deal, Eddie."

"I'll put in the order, but I'm siding the train *outside* Barstow. I don't want mentals hanging out at Casa del Desierto."

"I always said you were a sensitive guy, Eddie." Hook paused as he deliberated on the next question. "About that disciplinary board thing?"

"No decision," Eddie said. "The Flagstaff foreman can't make up his mind if you were drunk or just crazy. I figure both. My advice is to stay on the straight and narrow. The railroad might let you get by with murder, but they'll hang your ass for drinking."

"Thanks for the support, Eddie. Maybe someday I can return the favor."

Hook hung up and looked over at the clerk. "What the hell you grinning at?"

"Well, it ain't pretty," he said. "Don't forget your mail or that dang dog out there, either. Somebody ought shoot the poor thing and put out him out of his misery."

Hook picked up his mail. "Better be glad they don't shoot *people* for ugly," he said.

Hook headed down the track for his caboose. Mixer followed at a distance, keeping his eye out for anything deranged enough to intrude on Santa Fe property.

The caboose smelled of stale air and metal, and a cobweb stretched across the room. He opened both doors to let the heat escape and set his new books out on the table. With a little luck he'd have enough time to do some reading this evening. Mixer curled up in the corner and went to sleep.

The sun settled onto the horizon, an orange ball quivering with heat, and locusts serenaded the coming of night with a symphony of thousands.

Hook dumped the sack of mail out on the table and sorted through it. There was nothing of importance or in need of attention. His ties to the past had long since faded.

After that, he lay in his bunk and read until the lantern light fluttered and went out. He tried to sleep, but it wouldn't come. Lots of problems awaited him back in Barstow. So why did he find himself so anxious to return?

Maybe it had to do with his need for change, an affliction he'd struggled with throughout his life. Or maybe it had to do with a nurse with gunmetal eyes and a fierce loyalty for those in her care.

15

SETH MADE THE rounds in the boys' ward while Ethan carried out the morning trash. The inmates barely acknowledged his presence, shying away or glowering silently from their rooms.

Frankie Yager sat behind his desk working on his fingernails. Periodically he would rise from his chair and walk the length of the ward while slapping his leg with his magazine. Now and then he would pause and peer into the rooms like a ferret.

When the record player came on full volume, Ethan rose up with his jaw set. Seth grabbed his arm.

"Take it easy, Ethan."

"Somebody needs to shoot that bastard behind the ear," Ethan said, pulling away.

Frankie smirked from his desk and turned to his magazine.

"I couldn't agree more," Seth said, "but our jobs depend on us getting along. I'm sick and tired of living under a bridge."

Seth's night sweats and bad dreams had worsened with the rigors of jungle living, and now that the nights were getting colder, he hardly slept at all. The constant harassment by the law kept him on edge, and the stress of the new job nibbled away at his nerves. Sometimes his hands shook so badly that he had to bury them in his pockets.

But he didn't want to disappoint Hook, a man who did what he said he'd do, a man tough but fair. Seth liked the way Hook went about his life, the way he let others do the same.

Later that morning, men from the insurance company came to see Frankie. They talked in hushed tones out on the porch. When Frankie came back in, he threw his magazine into the trash can.

"I want this pigsty cleaned up," he shouted. "I want it cleaned now."

At noon, Frankie said, "Take them to lunch. I got errands."

"We've never done that before," Seth said.

"Well, it's high time," Frankie said. "And don't lose them when that cow from the women's ward drops her pants."

Seth and Ethan walked the boys to lunch without incident. Seth saw Roy and Santos from across the cafeteria. A big-bosomed woman sat close to Santos and gazed up at him.

They ate meatloaf, mashed potatoes, and gravy. Compared with Roy's cooking, it tasted pretty good, though in all fairness cooking out of a pot under a bridge had its disadvantages.

After lunch, Seth watched the boys while Ethan sneaked a smoke in the bathroom, and then Seth took his turn, fieldstripping the butt before flushing it down the toilet.

That afternoon about two o'clock, Ethan disappeared from the ward. When he returned, his face had turned the color of paste, and a bead of sweat glistened on his forehead.

"I feel like hell," he said.

Within the hour, one of the boys complained of a stomachache, and then another boy fell sick. Ethan sat at the table, his head down on his hands. Seth stood and grabbed his own stomach, which had twisted like a wet rope inside him. His head spun, and a cold chill swept through him.

Soon, the entire ward moaned and groaned, and the stink of sickness filled the room.

"Go get Doctor Baldwin," Seth told Frankie.

"I ain't bothering Doctor Baldwin," Frankie said.

Seth rose, locking his eyes on Frankie. "I said get him."

Doctor Baldwin arrived a short time later. He walked through the ward shaking his head and then went to check on the women.

When he returned, he said, "We've got people going down everywhere. I'm calling the health department."

The people from the health department came with their clipboards, checking the cafeteria coolers, the bathrooms, talking to the cooks.

Doctor Baldwin returned to the boys' ward and stood in the doorway, his face ashen and tired.

"Food poisoning," he said. "There's little to do but wait it out. Keep hydrated and rest as you can."

"What caused it?" Seth asked.

"They can't be certain. Everything appears to be in order."

"What about the others?" Seth asked.

"The women's ward got hit pretty hard. Luckily, Nurse Andrea brought her own lunch, and, as you know, the security ward doesn't eat in the cafeteria. Their food is prepared earlier in the day.

"Needless to say, the health department frowns on this sort of thing. They would have shut us down, but they didn't know what to do with all these people. They've agreed to send in extra help for a few days, so you men can go on home until you've recovered. Come back as quickly as you can."

His legs still shaky, Seth helped Ethan under the bridge, where he found Roy and Santos already there.

Roy took hold of Ethan to help him down. "You look like a chicken with the pip," he said.

"Yeah, but I'm just sick," Ethan said. "What you have is permanent."

They leaned Ethan against the bridge support. His hands lay open at his sides, and there were dark circles under his eyes.

"He's hit pretty hard," Seth said. "He can't keep anything down."

"I once saw him eat half a sandwich out of a dead German's hand," Roy said.

Ethan shook his head and coughed. "That's before I lost half my guts on a hillside. Besides, he wasn't dead yet."

"I'll boil up some water," Roy said. "Get the skeeters out. I think Ethan's all dried up."

So Roy built the fire and boiled the water. He stirred in a little baking soda, but Ethan spewed it back. Seth put his hand on his forehead.

"He's running a fever," he said. "Maybe we should take him somewhere."

"But where?" Roy asked.

"I don't know," Seth said, "the army base maybe."

"They might still be looking for their Iowa corn," Roy said.

Ethan rolled his head back and forth. "No army base," he said. "I've had enough of army hospitals. Get me a blanket. I'll sleep it off."

And so they wrapped Ethan in a blanket and folded another to put under his head.

As darkness enveloped the jungle, the fire sputtered and went out. Seth checked on Ethan, who slept deeply, his breathing slow and steady. Each took to his own bed then and drew into his own thoughts. Stars showered into the blackness of the cold desert night as the men slept once again under the bridge.

The sun had yet to rise, only a dim glow on the eastern horizon, when Seth rose from beneath his blanket to check on Ethan. He pulled aside Ethan's covers and laid his hand on his cheek. He sat back on his haunches. Ethan's fever raged, and his skin had turned dry as paper.

"Ethan," Seth said. "How are you doing?"

Ethan worked at a smile, which faded with weakness. "Not so well," he said. "My insides are burned away."

"I'll fix you something."

"No, Seth," he said.

"Let me get you to a hospital."

"Wake the others," he said.

Shivering in the morning cold, they gathered about Ethan. All there had watched comrades die before, the disinterest that came into the eyes, the looking away.

Ethan rallied. "Are you here?" he asked.

"We're here," Seth said.

"Bury me in the jungle," he said. "Don't tell anyone. It will only bring trouble. I've no one else. And don't be making crosses over my grave, Santos."

Santos pulled at his chin and looked off into the morning sun.

"When you come here, put a stone on my grave. It's the way of my people."

He fell silent, his breathing stopping for the longest moment, and then he said, "You boys will be alright?"

"We'll be alright," Roy said.

His breathing slowed to a rasp. "Did my life matter?" he asked.

"There ain't a one of us would be here without you," Roy said.

Ethan turned his face away. "I've not been such a good friend," he said.

They buried him next to the main pier, wrapping him in his blanket. Roy found Ethan's dog tags. He put them in an empty shine jar and placed it in the grave. They covered dirt over him with their hands, and each laid a stone to mark his place.

After that, they built a morning fire and cooked eggs and fatback. They recounted the time Ethan hid in his wall locker to avoid KP duty, how the latch had locked, and how no one had found him for several hours. They laughed about how they had to drag him to his bunk because both his legs had gone to sleep. They laughed and laughed until tears came to their eyes.

16

PAP AND HOOK waited on the Needles platform for the asylum train to arrive. When the black smoke rose up on the horizon, Hook looked over at Pap.

"It's a goddang ole kettle," he said.

Pap shook his head. "They haven't used those for anything except switching and work trains since the steam engine was invented."

The old engine churned down the alley like a worn-out workhorse. Clouds of steam and smoke boiled up around her as she chugged in. Hook could smell the grease and smoke. Water dripped from out of her boilers, and she sighed like an old woman settling into her rocking chair.

Hook kicked gravel down the track. "I could walk to Oklahoma faster than that galloper will get us there."

Pap looked down the line of cars. "Hell, those are section-hand outfit cars. They must be forty years old."

The brakes screeched, and the cars rumbled and clanged off down the line.

"Eddie Preston must have rescued that hog out of the salvage line," Hook said. "The day I retire, I'm going to kill him and bury his body under the turntable."

The engineer climbed down from the cab. He peeled the wrapper from a new cigar and stuck it in his cheek.

"Frenchy?" Hook said.

Frenchy peered at Hook from underneath his hat. "Well, I'll be a son of a bitch, if it ain't Hook Runyon. I figured someone left you on the rods for dead by now."

"There's been a couple tried," Hook said. "They dig you and this coffeepot out of the same junk pile?"

Frenchy fished a match out of his pocket and lit his cigar. The flame dipped up and down as he worked it to life.

"You might say," he said, blowing out his match. "They ain't got much use for either one of us anymore."

"You get orders to pick up a caboose?" Hook asked.

"We've got a bobtail scheduled to bring her into the yards. You still living in that bouncer?"

"If you call it living," Hook said. "You know Pap?"

"More or less. How you doing, Pap?"

"Good seeing you again, Frenchy. Weren't you in Amarillo for a while?"

"About a year. I been bumped so many times, I forgot where my wife lives," he said.

"I best be on my way," Pap said. "Good luck."

"Thanks for taking care of Mixer," Hook said. "If you want to visit him, just let me know."

Pap waved his hand over his head as he walked away. "Oh, sure, sure," he said. "Maybe I'll have him over for Christmas in about twenty years."

"I'm not exactly clear on who we are picking up in Barstow," Frenchy said.

"I guess Eddie forgot to give you the details."

"Eddie lies about everything but forgets nothing," Frenchy said. "So I figure it's something no one else wants to do."

"They had a big fire out to the Baldwin Insane Asylum. They're moving the inmates to Fort Supply in Oklahoma."

Frenchy took his cigar out of his mouth and stared at Hook. "Mental patients?"

"Looks that way."

Frenchy took off his hat and rearranged a few wisps of hair on his bald head.

"That son of a bitch," he said.

"Thing is, about twenty of them are classified as criminally insane."

Frenchy looked off down the tracks and then put his hat back on.

"The insane train," he said. "That's us. Well, I hauled a load of railroad officials to Chicago one time. Couldn't be any worse than that."

"At least these boys are in straitjackets," Hook said.

Hook sat in the cupola of the caboose and watched Needles disappear into the dusk. Mixer had fallen asleep before they were out of the yards, and now the steam engine crawled across the desert like a caterpillar on a stick.

Soon darkness descended. He listened to the click of iron against iron and smelled the smoke churning down the line. Hook climbed from the cupola and stretched out on the bench. They should be in Barstow by morning if they didn't break down, which could easily happen.

A lot of uncertainty lay ahead, but he'd be glad to get the assignment underway. Most of all, he would be glad to see Nurse Andrea once again.

Hook picked up the company truck from the operator in Barstow, who, with the disappearance of the supply clerk, had taken over the sign-out sheet.

He drove directly to Baldwin Asylum and found Andrea washing down the chairs and tables with disinfectant. She looked up and smiled when he ducked under the tent flap.

Pushing aside her hair with the back of her hand, she said, "You're here."

"And with the train," he said. "She's sided outside of town. I'm afraid she's not much to look at."

"Well, anything will be better than this," she said.

Hook looked around. "Where's Seth and the others?"

"They aren't back yet," she said. "We had a little bad luck."

"Oh, no. What did they do?"

"Food poisoning," she said.

"What?"

"It's been a long week for all of us."

"Is everyone alright?" he asked.

Andrea slipped off her rubber gloves. "Esther's still not up, but she's doing better. Luckily, I brought my lunch that day, as I usually do. I don't know how we would have managed otherwise. Thank goodness no one in the security ward came down."

"And the boys' ward?"

"Several down," she said. "Doctor Baldwin sent your men home to recuperate. I'm looking for them back anytime now."

"And Frankie?" he asked.

"He left the compound that day to run errands."

Hook walked to the end of the tent and looked over at the boys' ward.

"Has anyone checked as to why the food spoiled?"

"The health department came," she said. "They found nothing out of order."

"Did they check the temperatures on the freezers, things like that?"

"They said there were no problems with the equipment."

"I'm going over to the cafeteria," he said.

Hook found the head cook, a Mexican fellow with flour up to his elbows, kneading a pile of dough as big as a five-gallon can.

"I'm with railroad security," Hook said. "Maybe you could answer a few questions?"

The cook dusted the flour from his hands and the front of his shirt.

"The health department say okay," he said.

"That's what I understand," Hook said. "What do you think happened?"

The cook shrugged.

"What about the coolers?" Hook asked.

"No problem."

"You saw nothing out of the usual?"

He picked up his rolling pin and commenced working out the ball of dough.

"I check coolers like always," he said.

"I see. Well, thank you for your time."

Hook turned to leave, when the cook said, "Maybe the oven lights."

Hook stopped. "The lights?"

The cook nodded. "Number five breaker."

"Do the ovens have their own circuit?" Hook asked.

"Sí," he said.

"Maybe you could show me the breaker box?" Hook said.

"In back," he said, laying down his rolling pin.

Hook followed the cook into the utility room. It smelled of Lysol, and a single bulb cast its yellow glow into the darkness.

"Number five there," the cook said.

"And what is that one just next to it?" Hook asked.

"Number six," he said, lifting his brows.

"I mean, what does number six go to?"

"Coolers," he said.

"But number six hadn't been thrown when you came to work?"

"Number six okay. Coolers okay. Nothing wrong with my kitchen."

"No, I don't think you did anything wrong," Hook said. "Thanks for your help."

Doctor Baldwin hung up the phone when Hook walked in.

"Mr. Runyon," he said, "I've just gotten a call from Eddie Preston. I understand our train has arrived?"

"When Eddie said it wouldn't be the Chief, he wasn't kidding," Hook said.

"Well, we've had a bit of bad luck around here."

"So I hear."

"Unfortunately, it has delayed our preparations for the transfer."

Hook crossed his legs and spotted a hole in his sock the size of a quarter where Mixer had chewed. He put his leg down.

"Doctor Baldwin, do you have any reason to believe that someone would do you or this institution harm?"

"No. Why do you ask?"

"You've had lots of bad luck lately."

Doctor Baldwin rose out of his chair, turning his back to Hook.

"This is an insane asylum, Mr. Runyon. There are lots of troubled people here and many with checkered pasts. I suppose there's the potential for that sort of thing. But I've always run a compassionate program, and I know of no one who wishes me harm."

"I'm not a big believer in coincidences, and you've had a pretty fair run of them," Hook said.

"Are you suggesting a connection between the fire and the food poisoning?"

Hook stood. "Just a thought. When do you think you'll be ready for the transfer?"

"The beginning of the week, with a little luck."

"And what about the security ward?"

"We've decided to administer extra sedatives, chloral hydrate specifically. The side effects are minor, gastric irritation, nightmares, flatulence, but it should work, providing that the journey does not take too long."

"I see. I don't mean to press, but the company frowns on its equipment sitting idle. The sooner we get this on the road, the better."

"I'll do my best, Mr. Runyon. Do you happen to know when your men will be back?"

"I'm headed there now," Hook said. "I'll let you know."

Hook parked the company truck on the side of the road and picked his way down to the bridge. Pigeons winged upward into the blue as he ducked under. He waited for his eyes to adjust to the shade. A breeze swept in, and ashes swirled up from the cold fire. The men had to be around somewhere, given they'd not gotten their first pay yet.

"Hello," he called out, but no one answered.

Perhaps they were at the pool hall or down at the courthouse where they went sometimes to wash up in the bathroom.

The sound behind him had a quiet danger, and he whirled about. A man towered over him. Hook reached for his sidearm.

"Go on," the man said. "I need a reason to blow off your goddamn head."

Hook lowered his hand. He knew the voice, had heard it somewhere before. When the man stepped forward, he could see his badge.

"You," Hook said.

The cop smirked and rubbed at his whiskers with fingers the size of sausages. His barrel chest heaved up and down.

"Criminals always return to the scene," he said.

"Had *I* cracked your head, you'd still be in the dirt with your brains leaking," Hook said.

"You talk pretty tough for a one-arm son of a bitch," he said.

"I'll take off my weapon and badge," Hook said. "Maybe you'd like to do the same?"

The cop smiled. "Between you and me?"

"That's how it will be," Hook said, taking off his badge and sidearm.

The cop lowered his head and growled, charging across the opening like a Mexican bull. Hook sidestepped, catching the cop's foot with his own. The cop slid down the embankment headfirst and into the campfire. When he got up, there were ashes on his face and in his hair.

Hook circled, keeping to the high ground. Once again, the cop rushed him, his yelp quivering and pitched. Hook delivered a blow from the shoulder, catching him hard in the nose. His head jolted back, and blood sprang from his nostrils, streaming into the corners of his mouth. His legs wobbled, and his eyes filled with water. Cursing, he shook the fog from his head.

Again, he rushed, maneuvering Hook into a bear hug. He stank of booze and tobacco, and his hair dripped with sweat. Hook struggled for breath and for enough strength to break away. When the cop's ear presented itself, Hook chomped down. The cop screamed and grabbed his ear, which now dangled in a bloody flap.

Hook broke away and seized him behind his neck, driving him headlong into the bridge pier. The cop staggered and dropped to his knees. Drool spilled from his lips, and his eyes rolled white as he pitched forward into the dirt.

As Hook slid his sidearm back into its holster, Seth rose from out of the weeds. Santos and Roy stood up behind him.

"I been waiting a long time to see that," Seth said, grinning.

Hook dusted the dirt from his pants. "Thanks for the help, boys."

"Man oh man," Roy said. "That cop has got a powerful headache on the way."

Santos walked around the cop and smiled. "You want him in the river?" he asked.

"I think he's had enough," Hook said. "You boys didn't see any of that, right?"

"I'd sure like not to see that again sometime," Roy said.

"Where's Ethan?" Hook asked.

The men looked at one another. "Ethan went home," Seth said.

"Back to New York?"

"His momma fell sick," Roy said.

"I didn't think Ethan had family."

"Maybe he just got tired of living under a bridge," Roy said. "I sure as hell am."

Hook walked over to the main pier where the three stones were laid out in a row.

"I understand you boys have been under the weather?"

Seth shook his head. "Sober, too."

Hook knelt and studied the newly turned soil and the stones.

"I reckon Ethan won't be coming back this way anytime soon?"

"He said he was real sorry that he had to leave," Seth said. "But he didn't want to bother no one with his troubles."

"Well, a man's got to do what's in his mind," Hook said, taking out his billfold. "Here's a little advance. You boys can pay me back out of your first check. I want you to get a room, clean up, and come back to work on Monday. We got a train in, and things are on the move. Baldwin's in need of help."

"What about the cop?" Seth asked.

"I'll take care of this. You boys get on out of here."

Hook waited for them to gather up their belongings and climb the embankment before he rolled the cop over on his back. The knot on his forehead was the size of a walnut, and dark rings had already gathered under both of his eyes. But he breathed with a steady stroke, and his lids flickered.

Hook gathered up the cop's sidearm and badge and tossed them on his chest before climbing up the embankment. The patrol car had been pulled onto the side of the road. He opened the door and hit the switch on the two-way.

"Central, central," he said. "This is Bye-Bye Bluebird. You got a man down under the Fourth Street Bridge. Better get out there with an aspirin."

As he drove back to the caboose, he thought about Ethan and about how a man could slip out of this world without so much as a ripple.

17

ANDREA FOUND ESTHER under her cot rubbing black pepper into her nose.

"Oh, Lord, Esther," she said. "You mustn't steal the pepper shakers. Do you understand me?"

Esther sneezed, and her eyes filled with water. Andrea took the shaker and cleaned Esther's nose with her handkerchief.

"Why do you do that?" she asked.

"Feels good," Esther said, pulling at her nose.

Lucy, whose head still bore the marks from the tent pole, tapped Andrea on the arm.

"Esther's leaving," she said, holding her doll over her shoulder.

"Oh, dear," Andrea said. "Esther, come back here."

Esther wandered back toward the tent with her bottom lip stuck out. She had one shoe on, the other in her hand, and her dress turned wrong side out.

"I'm going home," Esther said. "It's my turn."

"No, Esther," Andrea said, handing her a washcloth. "You have to clean the tables for me."

Esther grinned and proceeded to scrub the tabletop. "I'm in charge," she said.

"Yes, you are," Andrea said, pushing the hair back from her eyes. "When you're done with that one, clean the next one, too."

"Nurse Andrea," Lucy said. "Ruth has her tit out."

"Ruth," Andrea said. "Button your blouse up before you cause a riot."

Ruth shrugged and buttoned her shirt.

Even though Doctor Baldwin had sent Andrea a couple of ladies from the kitchen to help out, they were inexperienced and could do little more than watch. But at least most everyone had recovered from the food poisoning, and Frankie had not cranked up his record player.

An hour behind schedule, Andrea had the meds ready. As she worked her way through the list, she realized that Bertha was missing.

"Keep a lookout," she told the kitchen help. "I've got to find Bertha."

Andrea searched the parking lot and then the picnic area but found nothing. Though Bertha could be difficult, she had never left on her own before. Andrea walked up to where the mass grave had been dug and then down the hill to where the bushes thickened along the fence.

"Bertha," she called.

When Bertha stepped out of the bushes, Andrea jumped.

"Bertha?" she said. "Good heavens, you scared me. What are you doing out here?"

Bertha's face and neck were flushed, and the buttons on her dress were mismatched with their buttonholes. Leaves clung in her hair.

"Picking grapes," she said.

"What?"

"Grapes."

"Bertha, there are no grapes out here."

Bertha brushed the leaves out of her hair.

"Come along," Andrea said. "You mustn't wander off like that. You wouldn't want to be confined to a cell, now would you?"

Andrea took her by the arm as they walked back toward the tent. Just as they were crossing the parking lot, she spotted Frankie Yager going into the boys' ward. He looked over at them as he closed the door behind him.

"Bertha, you weren't out there with someone, were you?" Bertha shook her head. "You would tell me, wouldn't you? You know it's against the rules?"

"I know," she said.

Andrea knocked on Doctor Helms's door and waited.

"Yes."

"May I speak with you for a moment, Doctor Helms?"

Helms looked up from her desk. "Is it urgent? I'm rather busy."

"It's just that Bertha ran away this morning."

Doctor Helms looked over the tops of her glasses, her eyes as black as tar.

"And did you get her back?"

"Yes," Andrea said.

"Then what is it you need?"

"The thing is, I think she'd been with someone in the bushes by the fence."

"Oh? I see, but then these things happen in an institution, Andrea. You must have seen it before."

"Yes, I suppose I have."

"Well, then, take away her privileges for a while. It's about all we can do."

"In most cases I would agree that it's not so important, Doctor Helms. But I think this requires attention."

Doctor Helms took off her glasses and unfolded her legs from beneath her desk.

"Could you be more specific?"

"I believe she'd been with Frankie Yager," she said.

"You saw them together?"

"I saw him coming back just as we did."

Doctor Helms came around the desk. "These are serious allegations. You'd have to be quite certain."

"I didn't literally see them together, if that's what you mean."

Helms walked to her bookcase, pulled a book out partway, and then pushed it back in.

"I'll keep an eye on things. If your allegations prove to be true, I'll see that disciplinary procedures are put into place. Until then, please keep this to yourself."

"Alright," she said. "But I want no harm to come to my patients."

"I understand, Andrea. And thank you for reporting this to me first."

Andrea stood outside of the door for several moments. Back at the tent, she gathered up her things.

"I'm going home now," she said to the ladies from the kitchen.

"And leave us alone?"

Andrea checked her watch. "I've been here ten hours without relief. That's long enough. If you need help, I'm sure that Frankie Yager would be happy to oblige."

As Andrea got in her car, she glanced back at the boys' ward. Frankie was sitting on the porch smoking a cigarette, watching her.

The real estate agent had placed a for-sale sign in the front yard of Andrea's house, a red and white banner as big as a tabletop. Andrea sat in her car for some time looking at it. The old house wasn't much, but it was all she had, all her parents had managed after a lifetime of hard work. Selling it now smacked of betrayal, even though she knew in her heart they would have understood.

Once inside, she took a shower and then poured a large glass of wine. Her legs ached, and she'd barely had time enough to eat. Why she had agreed to go off on this crazy trip, she couldn't fathom. It was not like they appreciated her.

And then that business with Frankie Yager, having taken advantage of her patients. She hadn't seen him, but she knew what was going on. She took another drink before opening the curtains. The sunset, Barstow's saving grace, blazed on the horizon. Her stomach tightened. Why had she volunteered to go? Maybe the reasons were more personal and less about her patients than she'd allowed herself to think.

One had much to be cautious about when it came to Hook Runyon. A man didn't become a railroad bull without a proclivity for the hard side of life. And she knew little about him, though she sensed the toughness, the aggression lying just beneath the surface, the way his eyes followed every movement like a stalking cat.

Andrea watched as the sun oozed below the desert rim. She finished her drink and rose to turn on the light. The phone rang out of the darkness.

"Hello," she said.

"Andrea?"

"Yes. This is she."

"Hook here. I thought you might like to do the flea markets with me?"

"I've really a lot to do before the trip."

"Around ten? I have the company truck."

"Well, then," she said. "I suppose. I am feeling the need for a break."

"Great," he said. "I'll pick you up."

Andrea lay in bed and listened to the far-off whistle of a train as it raced through the desert. So why then was she drawn to this man? Perhaps it was *because* of his intensity and unpredictability, his raw intelligence and rough edges hacked out like an axe carving. Perhaps the very things she found wanting were what set him aside and made her anxious for tomorrow.

18

ANDREA STEPPED FROM the front porch when Hook drove in. She slid in beside him and hiked her foot on the dash to tie her shoe. Her hair lay in wet curls.

"Hi," she said, looking over her shoulder. "I'm moving slowly. The hours at Baldwin are killing me."

"Hi back," he said. "So where is a good flea market?"

"Take a left on Main. It's out by the fairgrounds. I haven't been in a long time."

Hook shot a U-turn and rolled down his window. The town still slept, and the morning air smelled of the desert. He pulled in at Jan's Restaurant and bought them coffee.

"Good," she said, blowing the steam from her cup. "So what are we looking for today?"

"Shakespeare's first folio," he said.

Andrea rolled her eyes. "In Barstow?"

"Well, barring that, I'd settle for some bargains."

The vendors were still setting up when they drove in. Andrea followed Hook's pace as they made their way to the stalls.

"I admit it feels good to get away," she said.

"Let's start over there," he said, "and make the loop."

They poked through costume jewelry, racks of musty clothes, kitchen utensils, and stacks of old hubcaps. Andrea sifted through a collection of thimbles, a table heaped with Carnival glass, and a basket of agate marbles.

At noon they ate hot dogs topped with mustard and homemade chow-chow, washing it down with Dr Peppers fished out of a horse tank filled with crushed ice.

At each opportunity, Hook picked through the books, checking the title pages and the dust jackets with care. When he could carry no more, he looked over the stack in his arms.

"What say we go?"

"It's either that or bring in the truck," she said.

So as the sun lowered in the west, they drove down Main with Hook's loot safely ensconced in the back.

"How about a Mojave burger?" he asked.

Andrea lifted her brows. "I guess it's too late to save my figure at this point anyway."

Hook wheeled in at the Mojave Hamburger.

"It would take more than a burger," he said.

Andrea blushed. "Yeah?"

"I'm the law," he said, "and cannot tell a lie."

"I'm not good at flattery," she said. "It comes from being a caretaker my whole life."

"Say," he said. "Let's order to go. I'll show you my caboose."

"Now there's an invitation," she said. "But I think not."

"You can meet Mixer, my dog," he said.

Andrea glanced up at him. "It's safe, this invitation?"

"You can fault me for lots of things, but forcing myself on a woman isn't one of them. Too much pride, I suspect."

"I guess it would be alright," she said. "But only for a little while."

When they pulled onto the right-of-way, Andrea looked down the line of outfit cars. The old steamer sat as cold and silent as a dinosaur. For some time she didn't speak.

"We're taking the inmates in that?" she asked.

Hook nodded. "It's all they could come up with. She's old but functional. That girl has hauled many a load across the desert in her time."

"And that's your caboose?"

"Come on," he said. "I'll show you my collection."

Mixer met them at the door with something in his mouth.

"Oh, dear," Andrea said. "I believe he's eating one of your socks."

Hook sat down his books. "Goddang it, Mixer."

Mixer dropped the sock, looked at it, and then looked up at Andrea.

Andrea got down on her knee. "It's alright, Mixer," she said. "You want Hook's sock, you can just have it."

Mixer wagged his tail and snuggled into Andrea's lap.

"That dog requires a strong hand," Hook said. "Undermining my discipline is not good."

"Perhaps if you picked up your socks," Andrea said.

"Oh, now I see how it is."

Andrea stood, taking in the surroundings. Books were stacked everywhere, some still spilled on the floor from the trip across the Mojave.

"Oh, my," she said. "Do you really need all these books?"

Hook looked about the caboose. "Essential," he said.

They ate their hamburgers, sharing with Mixer. Andrea sat cross-legged on the floor and watched as Hook examined each of the new acquisitions.

"Ah," Hook said, holding up a book. "This is the one that makes it all worthwhile, Sinclair Lewis's *Ann Vickers*. I've been looking everywhere for it. It's in fine condition, too."

Afterward, they sat on the steps of the caboose while Hook smoked a cigarette. Mixer worked his way down the outfit cars, marking each as he went, and then came back to curl up at Andrea's feet. The sun eased down, and the sky erupted in a blaze of color.

"Andrea," Hook said, "I've been thinking."

"I know," she said.

"About that fire."

"You are still not convinced of an accident, are you?"

"Well, I can't be certain, of course, but arsonists have their ways."

"What do you mean?"

"Knowing they're about to burn something up gives them an advantage. They're not inclined to burn what they value, not when they can save it ahead of time."

Andrea rubbed her hands together against the cooling evening. "I don't understand."

"Take Frankie Yager, for example. That record player and those records are pretty important to him."

Andrea looked over at Hook. "Yes. He drives everyone to distraction with them."

"And they weren't in the fire?"

"No, they weren't."

"And he failed to eat lunch at the cafeteria the day everyone came down with food poisoning."

"So did I."

"But you never eat at the cafeteria."

"I like having a minute to myself. I bring my own lunch every day."

"And no one in the security ward came down sick?"

"No. I don't think so."

"Doctor Helms, the inmates, the security guard?"

"Not that I am aware of. Often their food is prepared ahead of time so that it can be taken to the ward."

"And then there's that business with the breaker," he said.

"The breaker?"

"Suppose I wanted to spoil the food without anyone knowing it. I could switch off the cooler breaker early the night before so the temperature would rise and spoil the food. Turn it back on later, and no one would ever know."

Andrea hooked her chin in her hands and looked over at him. "Do you think someone threw the cooler breaker?"

Hook put his cigarette under his heel, squashing it out.

"The breaker to the ovens had been thrown. It just so happens it's positioned right next to the cooler breaker. Given the dim light of the utility room, well, you can see what I mean."

"You think the oven breaker was thrown by accident and not reset?"

"It's another coincidence in a long line of coincidences."

Andrea shivered. "Something happened the other day I haven't told you about," she said.

"Oh?"

"Bertha came up missing from the tent, and I found her in the bushes over by the compound fence. I think she had been with someone."

"It's my understanding that sort of thing happens," Hook said.

"I saw Frankie coming back to the ward shortly after that. I think she had been with him."

"Did you report it?"

"Doctor Helms wants more proof before she initiates anything."

"Frankie does get around," he said. "There's just one problem with this whole business."

"What?"

"Why set a fire that kills a bunch of people and then poison the entire compound? A man would have to have a lot of hatred to do something like that. What would he have to gain here?"

"He's a pretty simple man," she said. "He responds to his immediate needs and little else. Frankie is a reactor, not a planner. Who knows what might set him off?"

Andrea leaned her head against Hook's shoulder. When he turned, she put her hand behind his neck and brushed her lips against his.

"Andrea," he said.

"Oh, dear," she said. "I didn't intend for that to happen. I'm sorry."

"It's just that there's things about me."

"You're married?"

"No, and there's probably good reason for that."

"But there's someone else?"

"I'm not much of a catch for a woman. Some say I'm too quick to drop the hat. Others say my drinking gets in my way. Right now my job's on the line for a thing in Flagstaff. If it goes against me, I've no place else to work."

"That's what others say. What do you say?"

"Me? In my line, if you wait too long to drop the hat, someone else drops it for you. As for the drinking, it's true, I guess, though it rarely is more than a bit of fun. As for the arm, it's damn hard to button my shirt or tie my shoes. Beyond that, I just keep on living like everyone else. I get done what needs to be done one way or another."

"Maybe you aren't the only one who isn't perfect," she said. "I've been known to pout for days on end, and once I stole my dad's whiskey out of his liquor cabinet and wrecked his car. I've got two arms, but I can be dog lazy when I take a notion. Sorry about that Mixer."

Mixer lifted his head and then went back to sleep.

"You sound like a real risk to me," Hook said.

"The fact is, I've just gone through a bad relationship. This could be a rebound thing, and I don't want that for either of us."

"Come on," he said. "I better get you home."

———

Hook pulled up in front of Andrea's house. She ruffed Mixer's head and got out.

"Thanks. I had a good day," she said. "I'll see you tomorrow."

"The men will need to spend a little time in the security ward before we leave, Andrea."

"Things have settled down in the women's ward. Move them if you need. We should be alright."

"And I think we're going to be a man short."

"Oh?"

"Ethan," he said. "He's taken off, some sort of trouble at home."

"Do you think he'll be back?"

"No," he said. "I don't think so."

"Look," she said, "about what happened. I don't know how all this is going to work out. But we've been honest with each other. No one can say we weren't warned."

19

SETH HAD BARELY slept with all the snoring and clamor of the Barstow Workers' Hotel. That, on top of an especially disturbing nightmare, had made it a short night indeed. He preferred sleeping under a bridge to staying in a flophouse. At least the air was fresh, and the nights were quiet.

He stood in front of the long line of sinks, deciding on the one nearest the door. The previous man's whiskers still lined the sink, and a sliver of soap liquefied on the backsplash.

He took a long look in the mirror, which had a crack radiating from one corner to the other. The scar on his face had faded with the desert sun, and the droop of his eye had lessened as his weight had returned. But a sandwich board could not have been more effective than the scar in reminding folks of the war, something most preferred to forget.

After shaving, he rousted Santos and Roy from their bunks.

"Goddang it, Seth," Roy said. "Such a dream don't come along all that often."

"Hook will be waiting," Seth said. "And he ain't so patient."

On the way to the Harvey House, they stopped at the back door of the Barstow Café and Grill, which could be good for a cup of coffee, sometimes a biscuit with butter if the Mexican cook was on duty.

"You think that cop died?" Roy asked, munching on his biscuit. "That bridge support rang like a Chinese gong."

"Cops got heads thick as boiler patches," Seth said.

"You figure we're going to the security ward?"

"Soon enough," Seth said, finishing off his coffee. "They didn't hire us to march a bunch of women back and forth to lunch. Anyway, things are getting out of hand between Bertha and Santos here."

"She like it hot," Santos said.

"That's why she's in the nutty," Roy said. "Anyone fall for you has to be bonkers."

Santos dropped the remainder of his biscuit into his mouth and grinned.

Hook waited as Santos and Roy climbed out of the back of the pickup. He flipped his cigarette butt out the window and turned to Seth.

"I've got to get locks put on one of those outfit cars for the security ward today, Seth. We can't take any chances with those boys. Now, I called Baldwin this morning, and he wants you to go ahead and report to Doctor Helms."

"We're going to the security ward then?" Seth asked.

"Looks that way."

"I fought Germans bare-handed, Hook," Seth said, "but I got to tell you, the security ward scares the bejeezus out of me."

"You just keep your wits about you, Seth. You'll be alright. Doctor Helms will be there to give you an orientation and such. Don't let Roy be poking fun at those inmates. They haven't the sense of humor I do. Any questions?"

Seth looked over at the gate. "I been hoping to get paid before I got killed."

"Well, it isn't payday, and the railroad doesn't pay until it's payday."

"Exactly what *is* criminally insane, Hook?"

Hook pulled at his chin. "It isn't altogether clear to me. They're either criminals or they're insane, but they can't be both at once."

"They got to be one or the other?" Seth asked.

"That's right. A criminal commits a crime because he wants to. An insane criminal commits the same crime, but he doesn't want to. That way he isn't a criminal, he's just insane."

"He can do it as long as he doesn't want to? It ain't against the law that way?" Seth asked.

"That's right."

"Hell, Hook, that's crazy."

"Exactly. That's why there are doctors and then there's us. So just don't try to figure it out. Do what you're told."

Seth opened the door. "Okay, Hook, if you say so."

Helms, looking like a blue heron, waited at the door of the security ward as Seth, Roy, and Santos climbed the steps.

"There's no smoking," she said, pointing to Seth's cigarette, "and no matches allowed in the ward."

Seth snuffed out his cigarette and gave her his matches. Roy searched his pockets and came up with nothing.

"Follow me," she said.

Sounds issued from the bowels of the ward when the men stepped in. The smells reminded Seth of the flophouse they just left, the pungency of urine, sour clothes, and sweat. But the sounds were nothing he'd ever heard, an eerie concoction, like a mourner's wail and a jackal's howl all mixed together in sadness.

"These cells are locked at all times," Doctor Helms said. "Your duties here are simple. You'll help administer the medications I've prepared, and you'll bring the meals from the cafeteria. Do not talk to the inmates more than giving instructions, and do not go into a cell under any circumstances. If there's an emergency, call me immediately, and I'll arrange for restraints. Is that clear?"

They all nodded their heads.

"Good. Now, this man in room six is Robert Smith. He's a sexual sadist and extremely dangerous. Believe me when I tell you that he would have no compunction about slitting your throat and watching you choke on your own blood."

Seth looked into the cell. Smith sat on the edge of his bunk staring at the wall. He was small, not much bigger than a boy, really, and his face, pockmarked from acne, displayed no emotion. Suddenly, he turned toward Seth and blinked his eyes with the slow deliberateness of a serpent. His tongue slid from his mouth until it reached nearly to his chin. Seth's bowels churned, and he turned away.

"Van Diefendorf over here is a pyromaniac," Helms said, "among other things. He is not to be trusted under any circumstances. *Any* circumstances. Understood?"

They all nodded and looked in at Van Diefendorf.

"All of these inmates suffer from a range of psychotic disorders, most so severe that traditional therapy is ineffectual. Whatever dysfunctions you see in the general population exist here as well, except to the extreme, including insomnia, sexual deviance, eating disorders, identity disorders, and substance abuse of every ilk. Self-mutilation is common.

"This man in room five sawed open his wrist with a can lid. In room eight is a seventy-year-old grandfather who picked his nose until he destroyed his septum. We tried everything to stop him but to no avail."

She stopped and turned to the men. "Do not think for a minute that these men see the world as you do. Do not think they are stupid because they are insane. Many planned their crimes with the most exacting detail and executed it in ways so despicable they cannot be described in mixed company. Some eluded their captors for years through carefully planned deceptions. To assume them to be dull-witted could be the biggest mistake of your life.

"Now, here in this room is a man you do not have to worry about. He will do you no harm, not now, not ever again. He murdered his teenage daughter for kissing the neighbor boy. In order to avoid punishment, he left his car running in his garage. Unfortunately, he bungled the job. The end result is what you see before you; that was over twenty years ago. The state pays for his care."

Seth peeked into the window. The man leaned against the wall. His hair had worn from the back of his head, and the smell of feces seeped from under the door. His hands lay open at his sides, and drool spilled from his lips, soaking the front of his shirt. His eyes reflected outward like mirrors, absorbing nothing from the outside world.

Roy looked over Seth's shoulder. "I once dated a girl from Pikesville looked just like that," he said. "Except she wore heels and shaved every Saturday night, need it or not."

Helms turned and looked at Roy. "Jokes are inappropriate. I suggest you dispense with them."

Roy glanced at Seth and then at Santos, who was busy studying his feet. "Sorry," he said.

Helms then took them to the end of the hall. "This is a panic button," she said. "It's called that for obvious reasons. If you should become engaged in a situation, push this button immediately. An alarm will be sounded throughout the compound." She paused, looking at each of them. "It is the only access to help. Be mindful of where it is in relation to where you are at all times."

That morning Seth swept the main hall while Doctor Helms prepared medications for each of the inmates, placing their pills in paper cups, writing the room number on each with a pencil. Roy and Santos went for bathroom and cleaning supplies, sneaking a smoke on the way back.

At noon, Doctor Helms called Seth into the medications room.

"I've therapy sessions scheduled, Mr. Durand. You are to give these medications to the inmates. The room numbers are on the cups. Slide them through the opening and watch to make certain they are taken. Sometimes they hide the pills under their tongues. If there is a problem, simply wait until I return."

"You're leaving us here?" Seth asked.

"I'll be back around three. The other men are to go to the cafeteria and bring back the food carts. Count the eating utensils going in and coming out."

"But this is our first day, Doctor Helms."

"Under normal circumstances, I would not leave the ward under the supervision of new employees, but these are hardly normal circumstances. In any case, the inmates need to become familiar with you and your men since you will be working with them during the transfer. In the final analysis, all you have to do is maintain security. Are you clear on that?"

"Keep them locked up," he said.

"Yes," she said. "Exactly."

After Roy and Santos left for the cafeteria, Seth stacked the cups of pills on the tray. At each room, he handed the medications through the slot and waited for them to be taken. Most took their medications without comment before turning back to their demons.

Van Diefendorf in room nine swallowed his in a single gulp, crumpled up the paper cup, and threw it at the window. Seth jumped back, nearly spilling the tray.

Voices rumbled down the corridor. Seth turned to see the inmates watching him through their windows. Their eyes were still and insidious. His ears went hot.

When he came to room six he called out Robert Smith's name. Smith didn't move, staring at the wall.

"Medications," Seth said. "Doctor Helms's orders."

Smith rose from his bunk to stand at the window, looking at Seth with cougar eyes, the eyes of a predator that kills instinctually and without guilt. Seth's pulse ticked up as he searched through the cups for room six.

When he pushed the medicine through the slot, Smith reached out and touched Seth's hand. Seth jerked it back, the coldness of Smith's touch lingering on his fingers.

Smith tipped the cup up and swallowed the pills. Then, smiling, turned the cup around to where Seth could see that it had the number 9 written on it rather than the number 6.

"Oh, shit!" Seth said.

Smith slid the cup back through the slot, went to his cot, and sat down. Seth's heart thumped in his chest. What had he done, two inmates with the wrong medications? Maybe he had killed them both. But then maybe it would be alright. It was just one dose after all, and crazy *was* crazy. Maybe no one would know.

He finished the last three rooms and returned the tray to the med room. He went back to Smith's window, and his heart stalled at what he saw. Smith lay unconscious in the corner of his room, his head slumped over.

"Oh, God," Seth said, looking about. "I've killed him. I have killed him sure."

But the ward had fallen silent behind him. No one said that it would be alright, that he'd just had an accident, just a simple mistake and that no one could blame him.

His hands trembling, he fumbled for the room key, opening the door. Bending over Smith, he put his fingers on his neck to check for a pulse. He'd seen plenty of death in the war. He knew the stillness, the cooling of the skin, the smell of leaking bowels.

But in that single moment, the moment Smith's pulse tripped on Seth's fingertips, he realized his mistake, the biggest mistake of his life.

Smith came up, driving his fist hard into Seth's throat. Seth screamed, but nothing came out as his esophagus convulsed under the blow. He struggled to breathe, to stand, to make it to the panic button, now a million miles away.

If only he could get to the door, escape the madness intent on taking his life. But Smith hit him again, a driving blow that sent Seth reeling. Black spots swam in his eyes, and a high-pitched ringing wormed through his head like a corkscrew.

Through his fog, he could see the top of Smith's head, the thinning spot on the back where beads of sweat were gathered, and he could feel Smith's hands and his hot breath. Fire ripped up his groin and settled into the pit of his stomach like molten lava.

Roy caught Smith under the chin with his knee, snapping his head back against the wall. Smith slid onto the floor, his eyes rolling white. Santos pulled Seth from the room by his arms, and within moments the door to room six slammed shut.

Roy retrieved water from the medications room and dabbed it on Seth's face. Seth sat up and looked about, his eyes still filled with terror.

"It's alright now," Roy said.

Seth rubbed his face and looked over at the locked door.

"The son of a bitch tricked me," he said.

"Maybe we shouldn't tell Helms about this," Roy said. "She ain't much for joking around. We'll all lose our jobs."

Seth steadied himself on trembling arms.

"Roy, I got to tell you, I'm not so sure about taking this job anymore. It's a hell of a long trip we got ahead."

"I'm mighty tired of sleeping under bridges, Seth, and there's a chance we could hire on with Baldwin after we get there."

Seth looked over at room six. Robert Smith stood at the window with blood in the corners of his mouth. He smiled.

"But what about him?" Seth said.

Santos helped Seth stand, steadying him by the arm.

"You don't need him," Santos said, grinning. "I share Bertha."

20

BALDWIN SAT BEHIND his desk, his great, sad eyes even sadder on this day.

"It feels a hundred years since I graduated from the University of Pennsylvania," he said. "I had such dreams." He turned in his chair to face Hook. "My father worked as a physician for nearly forty years. He had all these expectations for me, none of which included psychiatry."

Hook said, "Sons fall short, no matter."

Doctor Helms folded her long legs one over the other.

"There's a great deal yet to do," she said.

"Yes," Baldwin said. "There's much to be done. I've arranged for cuffs and chains for the security ward. After the inmates are medicated, the process should move along rapidly. Once they're in the train, perhaps we can take off the restraints."

"I think that's a bad idea," Hook said. "I'd recommend they stay cuffed to their seats. Perhaps we could get by with just the leg restraints."

"I would agree," Doctor Helms said. "These men are capable of great harm."

"Well," Baldwin said, folding his hands over his stomach. "It strikes me as a bit inhumane. The trip will be strenuous."

"It shouldn't take that long if all goes as planned," Hook said.

Baldwin walked to the window. "Security is your job, Mr. Runyon, so I leave the decision to you for now. But I want it understood that these people are not criminals. They are mental patients and are to be treated as such."

"I understand," Hook said. "But they *are* dangerous and cunning. I can't take any chances with the safety of the others. Perhaps after we are on our way, we can reconsider."

"Well, then," Helms said. "We best get this started?"

"There is one other thing I'd like to discuss," Hook said.

"And what would that be?" Baldwin asked.

"Frankie Yager."

"What about Frankie?" Baldwin said.

"Do you know anything of his background?" Hook asked.

"Baldwin personnel are thoroughly vetted before they're employed," Helms said. "Frankie Yager came highly recommended."

"What's your point?" Baldwin said.

Hook stood and rubbed his shoulder. The weight of the prosthesis hung like a sack of rocks.

"As you know there have been a number of unhappy incidences here at Baldwin. They have all involved Frankie Yager in one fashion or another."

"Could you be more specific?" Helms asked.

"Frankie just happened to be absent when a fire burned his ward to the ground," he said. "And then he somehow managed to escape food poisoning."

"Go on, Mr. Runyon," Baldwin said.

"I found the oven breaker thrown, which just happened to be located next to the cooler breakers."

"I don't understand," Baldwin said.

"I believe that someone may have tripped it accidently when they threw the cooler breaker."

"That's quite a stretch, isn't it?" Baldwin said.

"I also believe him to be abusive."

"Frankie has been effective at keeping his ward under control," Doctor Helms said. "Believe me, not everyone can handle those inmates. The fact is we have less trouble with his ward than any other."

Hook said, "I'm not certain of this, but there's some indication he might be sexually involved with one of the female patients."

"Oh?" Baldwin said.

"You mean Bertha?" Helms said. "Nurse Andrea mentioned this to me. What you must realize is that this sort of allegation can easily get blown out of proportion in an institution such as this. You see, Bertha is in here for pestering her neighbor until the poor man lost his family over it."

Hook walked to Baldwin's bookshelves. He had a nice 1913 *Interpretation of Dreams* by Freud.

"All I know is that in the real world coincidences are rare. At this point Frankie Yager has had more than his lifetime share."

Doctor Baldwin paced behind his desk, his hands clasped at his back.

"Doctor Helms is right," he said. "This *is* an insane asylum. One has to be careful with allegations made by patients."

"I think Frankie deserves the benefit of the doubt here," Helms said.

"Perhaps you should consider removing him from the boys' ward as a precaution," Hook said. "Keep him away from the women until we have a chance to check things out. We can't afford trouble on this trip."

"Nor can we afford to run help off," Helms said. "Frankie is experienced and capable."

Baldwin shrugged. "We could assign him to the security ward section of the train, I suppose," he said. "Until we know if these allegations have any merit."

Helms glanced at Hook. "Would that work for you, Mr. Runyon?"

"For the time being," Hook said.

"Then so be it," Helms said.

"Fine, then," Baldwin said. "We'll assign Frankie to the security ward for the duration. Now, I must be on my way."

"Will you not be assisting in administering the chloral hydrate to the inmates?" Helms asked Baldwin.

"Perhaps you could handle it, Doctor Helms. I've arranged to meet with the Howard Real Estate Agency in town. It's my hope to sell the property here soon."

"The train is ready for departure the moment we're loaded," Hook said. "Any delay invites trouble."

"I'll meet you at the train," Baldwin said.

"I've requested sandwiches be prepared at the Harvey House," Hook said. "Apparently meals were not arranged for today."

"My fault. I'm afraid it slipped my mind," Doctor Baldwin said. "I've been preoccupied. I'll see the food is delivered."

After leaving his sidearm at the office, Hook and Doctor Helms walked over to the security ward. Roy met them at the door.

"I thought maybe you and Seth ran off to Germany where it's safe," Roy said.

"I can't say it didn't cross my mind," Hook said.

"I been here by myself," Roy said. "It's right uncomfortable."

"Where's the security guard?" Helms asked.

"He just up and left. Said most likely he wouldn't get his pay anyway."

"You've been here alone?" Hook asked.

"No, I been here with the biggest collection of misfits this side of Texas."

"I might put you up for a medal, Roy. It's damn fine duty you pulled."

"To tell you the truth, I'm a little nerved up myself, Hook. The inmates are all in a stir, figuring something's amiss what with the comings and goings."

"I have the chloral hydrate in pill form," Helms said. "It's mild enough to induce calmness, not so strong as to put them to sleep, at least not right away."

"I could use a little chlorine myself," Roy said.

Helms looked over her glasses. "We'll start at the far end with Van Diefendorf. He's usually compliant in these matters."

Hook and Roy waited as Helms prepared the doses. She placed cups of water on a tray and handed it to Roy.

When they approached Van Diefendorf's cell, he moved to the back.

"We'd like for you to take your medication now," Doctor Helms said.

Van Diefendorf turned his back to them and edged into the corner.

"It's alright," Doctor Helms said. "Just something to calm you."

Van Diefendorf hung his head.

"Maybe he'd drink some shine," Roy said.

"We want him calm, not comatose," Hook said.

Helms unlocked the door. "I'm going in," she said.

"Are you certain?" Hook asked.

"Roy, bring the water."

"Me?"

"He won't hurt you here," she said. "It's not his style."

Roy followed Helms into the cell and looked back over his shoulder at Hook.

"I think I like living under a bridge," he said.

She took Van Diefendorf by the arm. "You must take your medications."

Suddenly Van Diefendorf lurched toward Roy, knocking him off balance. Roy tipped the tray, sloshing the cups of water. Hook started to move in, but Helms held up her hand.

"It's alright," she said, taking a cup off the tray. "Here, Mr. Van Diefendorf, I know how much you dislike the straitjacket."

Van Diefendorf hesitated, took the cup, and washed down his pill.

"Good," Helms said. "Now to the others."

They worked their way down the cell block. Most of the inmates took their medications without protest, peering over the tops of their cups with blank eyes. It took longer with the inmate who had failed in his suicide. He repeatedly spewed the pill back until it had dissolved on his chin and had to be replaced.

Finally, Helms said, "Robert Smith's the only one left now."

"I ain't going in there," Roy said.

"Maybe he will take it on his own," Helms said. "Sometimes he's cooperative. Other times not."

Hook looked in. Robert Smith sat on the end of his bunk, his hands clasped between his knees. He looked up with cold eyes.

"He doesn't look cooperative to me," Hook said.

"Robert," Helms said. "We need you to take your medications now."

Robert didn't move, except for his leg, which bobbed up and down at a rapid pace.

"Robert," she said again. "You know you have to take your medications."

Suddenly, Robert stood and walked straight to the window, his face only inches from the bars. Helms stepped back.

"Okay, then. Good," she said, regaining her composure. "Here's your pill."

Robert held out his hand, steady, but small like a child's hand.

Helms gave him the pill and slipped the cup of water through the bars. Smith dropped the pill into his mouth and drank down the water, a drop clinging to his lip.

Helms glanced over at Hook. "There," she said. "Not so hard."

Hook turned to Roy. "Do you smell something?"

Roy sniffed. "Smoke," he said.

"Oh, no," Helms said. "It's coming from Van Diefendorf's room."

Smoke boiled from his window and under his door. Helms worked at the lock. All the while Van Diefendorf coughed and sputtered from somewhere inside the cloud of smoke. When Helms swung open the door, Hook took a deep breath and went in.

Van Diefendorf lay naked on the floor, his bedding smoldering in the corner of his room. Hook stamped out the flames and dragged him out by his arm. Van Diefendorf flopped onto his back, his eyes at half-mast, a box of matches clutched in his hand.

The ward burst into pandemonium behind them. "Fire boy, fire boy, fire boy," someone chanted.

Helms pried the matches from Van Diefendorf's grip. "Where did he get these?" she asked.

"They look a bit like mine," Roy said. "Though all matches are more or less similar."

"Didn't I tell you no matches in the wards?" Helms asked.

"I forgot," Roy said.

She narrowed her eyes. "Next time you follow instructions, do you understand? You'll get us all killed."

"Yes, ma'am," Roy said, hanging his head.

Van Diefendorf lay on his back in a stupor, soot under his eyes and around his mouth.

"Get him dressed," she said.

By the time Hook and Roy managed to get Van Diefendorf secured, a quiet had fallen over the ward. Hook checked the cells one by one. To the last man, they were either asleep or staring off into space. Robert Smith, too, lay curled on his cot, his eyes closed, his knees drawn into the fetal position.

"I'll be damn," Hook said. "I could use a little of that stuff out on the line."

"Let's get them cuffed and on their way before they're all asleep," Helms said.

They cuffed the inmates, leading them into the hallway, where they slumped against the wall in silence. Helms opened the door to Robert Smith's cell.

"You did see him take his pill?" Hook asked.

"Yes," she said.

"He drank it down," Roy said.

"Let me check his eyes," she said.

Helms leaned over to open his eyes when Smith sat straight up, shoving the door closed behind her. A scream issued from Helms's throat, a cry so pitiful that it caused the hair on Hook's neck to prickle.

When Hook next looked, Smith had cuffed Helms to the bedpost. Opening his hand, he showed Hook the pill and the room key. A slow smile spread across his face as he began unbuttoning Helms's blouse.

"Nooo!" Helms cried, jerking against the cuffs. "Help me. Help me."

Hook tried the door but to no avail. Smith stepped in close to Helms, slipping his hand into her blouse.

Roy looked at Hook.

"There's no key," Hook said.

"My office," Helms cried out. "Top drawer. Hurry, for God's sake. Hurry."

Roy stood still, mesmerized at what played out before him. "Go get it, Roy," Hook said.

"Maybe you better go, Hook."

"Roy, goddang it."

"Right," he said.

By the time Roy got back, Helms was pleading with Smith, which had only served to spur him into a frenzy.

"Here's the key," Roy said.

Smith turned just as Hook shoved him hard into the corner. Picking up the pill, Hook stuck it down Smith's throat.

Helms adjusted her blouse and pushed her way past Roy, who was standing frozen in the doorway.

At her office, she turned. "Don't either one of you say a word about this," she said, slamming the door shut behind her.

21

Hook retrieved his sidearm and waited at the front door of the security ward as Helms and Roy brought out the inmates. They exited in single file, Helms at the lead, Roy bringing up the rear. The inmates shuffled out, their chains rattling like a Georgia chain gang.

"The bus is ready," Hook said to Helms.

"These men won't stay medicated forever," she said. "If it should wear off, we'll have chaos on our hands."

"I'll meet you there," he said.

"You aren't coming on the bus?"

"I'll follow in the pickup," Hook said. "I need to leave it at the depot and check in with Division. The security-ward passenger car has locks on both doors, and the windows are inoperable. As soon as you're settled, we'll be moving out."

Hook fell in behind Roy as they climbed the hill to the bus, the shuffle of the inmates' chains the only sound coming from the Baldwin Insane Asylum.

"I'll be putting Frankie in security," he said

"Oh, sure," Roy said. "Now that they're all blitzed on Clorox."

"That would be chloral hydrate," Hook said.

Roy shrugged. "That's what I said. Don't you ever listen, Hook?"

As they passed the mass grave, Hook fell back and lit a cigarette. A crop of dandelions had taken root, nearly covering the grave. With no marker and no one to care, those buried would soon enough pass into oblivion.

He turned for a last look back at the Baldwin Insane Asylum. Pigeons gathered on the roof of the security ward, and the smell of the desert hung in the air. He squashed out his cigarette and hurried on to catch up with the bus just pulling out of the parking lot.

Hook dropped the truck off at supply before calling Eddie.

"We are loading the last ward now, Eddie," he said. "But I got my doubts that old bullgine you sent will make it out of the city limits."

"The company needs that work train, Runyon. The railroad ain't happy about putting rip-track up in no hotel."

"There could be trouble on the other end of this deal, Eddie, if we ever get there."

"What does that mean?"

"Apparently the town in Oklahoma isn't all that happy about bringing in a trainload of mental patients as permanent citizens."

"That ain't our worry. It's your job to get them there. Period."

Hook lit a cigarette and studied the spider that hung by a silver thread from the light fixture.

"I don't know if I can make it to Topeka for that hearing, Eddie."

He could hear Eddie wheezing on the other end. His two-pack-a-day habit would be his end.

"You don't show, they'll pull your card, Runyon. Neither the railroad nor the union tolerates boozers."

"I wasn't drinking, Eddie. I just didn't get the goddang truck off the track."

"I ain't the one you got to convince, Runyon."

"I'm having trouble hearing, Eddie."

"And tell Frenchy to lay up when his trick's over. I don't want no shift violations."

As Hook walked the track toward the train, smoke rose from the engine stack. Frenchy had her stoked and ready to go by the looks of it. Took some doing to keep an old rust bucket like her up to throttle.

Heat ribbons quivered up from the tracks, and the smell of creosote settled in at the back of Hook's throat. On a summer day in Barstow, the rails could burn the skin right off your hands.

He stopped at the caboose and let Mixer out, who in turn hopped up and down, his tongue lolling out like a wet mop.

"Here, Mixer," he said, patting his head. "You better get a run in. It's a long ride to Needles."

Mixer took off down the tracks, his ears flopping as he wound in and out of the cars. Hook stopped in to check on Andrea. She leaned against the doorway and pushed the hair back from her face.

"We're loaded," he said. "Everything okay here?"

Andrea looked over her shoulder. "They're not happy, but at least they're fed," she said.

"How's Seth doing?"

"Esther locked him in the bathroom," she said. "We had to pry the door open to get him out. He looked like he'd been hung by his thumbs."

"I'll see you later?"

"Okay," she said, smiling.

He found Frankie in the end seat of the boys' car with his feet up. Santos sat at the opposite end. Most of the boys, having risen early, slept in their seats.

"You've been reassigned to the men," Hook said. "We need the extra help in there."

"Baldwin assigns my duty," Frankie said, pulling in his chin.

"Not on this train, he doesn't."

Frankie shot a glance at Santos. "That Mexican can't handle this ward," he said.

"I'll check in on him from time to time," Hook said. "Meanwhile, you can come with me."

Frankie scoffed and picked up his gear. They worked their way through the cars, the heat, the smell of grease and iron in the air. Doctor Helms peeked through the door before unlocking it.

"Frankie will be joining you," Hook said.

"Alright," she said, stepping aside. Frankie pushed his way past without a word.

"Are you prepared to leave?" Hook asked.

"There are a few complaining of headaches from the meds, but the side effects are no more than a mild hangover."

"Wouldn't know about that," he said.

"Doctor Baldwin stopped by," she said. "He wants the restraints removed."

Hook looked in at the men, who sat like zombies in their seats.

"And what do you think?" he asked.

"Frankly, I think it's misguided. These men are dangerous."

"I'll talk to him," he said.

"You know this whole operation could come flying apart. It would be quite impossible to get it back together."

"That has occurred to me," he said.

"In the meantime, will you remind Doctor Baldwin that more meds must be administered in two hours?"

"The engineer will blow the whistle before we pull out," he said. "You have trouble, send someone."

Helms nodded and closed the door. Hook waited until he heard it latch before leaving.

When Hook stepped from the car, Mixer leaped from behind the wheel carriage and stuck his butt in the air.

"Come on," Hook said. "No time to play. Let's go find Frenchy."

Frenchy rolled his cigar into his jaw and pushed back his hat.

"It's about goddang time," he said. "You know Ron Jarrett, my fireman? This is the cinder dick, Hook Runyon."

"Ron," Hook said, shaking the fireman's hand.

"Where the hell you been, Hook?" Frenchy asked. "We burned up half our fuel just keeping the air up."

"She's set, Frenchy. I'll take a last walk through and give you the signal from the caboose."

"Well," he said, lighting his cigar, "crossing the Mojave is best done at night anyway, providing this ole calliope holds together."

"Eddie says he doesn't want you to exceed your twelve-hour shift limit, Frenchy."

Frenchy checked his gauges. "Maybe I'll retire after this run, Hook. Me and this ole bucket have about seen our day, so you can probably figure out what Eddie can go do to hisself far as I'm concerned.

"We'll lay up in Needles for a little rest. Far as Eddie knows I just now came on shift anyway, and Ron here can't tell time without the sun up. That's why they made him a fireman."

Hook leaned out on the ladder and looked down the line. "You have any idea how long this trip will take, Frenchy?"

"Not long on the Chief," he said. "But we ain't on the Chief. And then there's that spur."

"What spur?"

"Hell, Hook, how long you worked for the railroad? The main line don't run to Fort Supply. I worked it once a few years back. The only thing going there is an ole doodlebug line used for delivering mail and hauling wheat. That track looks like a snake's back, and the grade's a son of a bitch through them canyons. I don't know if this hog can make it without a pusher."

"I got a train full of trouble back there, Frenchy. The sooner we can get there the better."

"Yes, sir. I'd be there now had I not been waiting on you."

Frenchy fired up his cigar and snuffed out the match with his fingers.

"Word is you might be having a little difficulty with the disciplinary board, Hook?"

Hook dropped off the ladder. "You know the railroad, Frenchy. They aren't happy unless they got you by the balls."

"If you need someone to speak up, Hook, just let me know."

"Thanks, Frenchy. I'll remember that."

Hook found Doctor Baldwin in the supply car sitting behind a makeshift desk of spike kegs and bridge planking. His tie hung over his chair, and a wisp of hair had fallen across his eye.

"May I come in?" Hook asked at the door.

"Oh, Mr. Runyon. Yes, come in and have a seat. I've been trying to get the institution records in some sort of order. I'm afraid they're hopelessly scrambled."

"I've just talked to the engineer. We're ready anytime now."

"Yes, yes," he said.

"Is there something wrong, Doctor Baldwin?"

"Wrong? No, no, nothing wrong. Well, maybe. It's just that I've had a little bad news."

"Oh?"

"Nothing that can't be resolved."

"Can I help?"

Baldwin picked up the stack of records and dropped them into a wooden crate next to the desk.

"Just between us," he said, "the insurance company has declined to pay on the fire."

"I'm sorry," Hook said.

"There's a lawsuit pending, which means the property can't be sold until things are settled. It's a run of bad luck."

"Sorry to hear it," Hook said.

"Yes," he said. "Then I can't be entirely certain of the condition of the facility when we get there. It has sat empty for some time now. Who knows how much will be required to bring it up to par. The government can be quite strict about these things."

"Well, maybe it will work out," Hook said. "By the way, Doctor Helms asked that I remind you of the medications schedule."

"Oh, yes."

"And I wanted to discuss the restraints for the security ward. Doctor Helms is concerned about safety. Frankly, so am I."

Baldwin stood, paced the length of the car, and sat back down.

"Doctor Helms does not fully accept a rehabilitative prognosis for the security-ward inmates. Nonetheless, the balance between protecting ourselves and providing treatment is a delicate one.

"Frankly, having seen their situation in the car, I'm more convinced than ever that cuffing them for such a long trip is unacceptable."

Hook said, "Perhaps a compromise, Doctor Baldwin. Keep them restrained until we are on our way. After that, release them one at a time for exercise, bathroom breaks, that sort of thing. This arrangement would help to keep things under control while at the same time providing some relief from their confinement."

"Yes," he said. "Perhaps that would work. There is one other thing, Mr. Runyon."

"What would that be?"

"I must ask that you relinquish your weapon. The courts have declared these inmates as patients, not criminals."

"This is not the insane asylum, Doctor Baldwin, but my train. Its safety is my responsibility. The weapon stays."

Baldwin drummed his fingers on his desk and studied Hook. "Very well, then, if you insist. But for the record, I don't approve."

"Noted," he said.

As Hook walked the line back to the caboose, Mixer scoured the territory with his nose for past transgressions. The sun had dropped low in the sky, and the day had cooled.

Once inside the caboose, Hook lit the lantern and took a last look around before stepping out on the platform to signal.

A patrol car had pulled into the right-of-way behind the caboose, its lights on, and a man carrying a flashlight walked toward him. As he got closer Hook recognized him as the cop from the jungle. Mixer growled, and his hackles rose on his neck.

"Hold up," the cop yelled, shining his light in Hook's eyes. "I got a complaint filed against you."

"And what would that be?" Hook asked.

"Indecent exposure."

"Say what?"

"Some woman with her rear out a bus window, one of those beanies from the asylum."

"Would like to visit," Hook said. "But I'm in kind of a hurry."

"This time I keep the badge on, you bastard," the cop said, moving toward him.

Maybe it was the flashlight or the sudden movement that sent Mixer off the end of the platform. Whatever the cause, no man or animal stopped Mixer or escaped his wrath once he'd committed. The cursing and thrashing that followed confirmed that no exception had been made for the Barstow law.

Hook leaned out on the grab iron and swung the lantern. Frenchy's whistle rose, and the train bumped up slack, grumbling and moaning down line. Hook called out for Mixer, who came running at full choke down the track. Reaching out, Hook scooped him up.

Sitting on the platform, Mixer in his arms, Hook watched the cop's red lights spin in the blackness behind them as the insane train chugged off into the desert night.

22

AFTER PUSHING THE books from his bunk, Hook slipped off his prosthesis and his shoes. He lay down, and Mixer curled into a ball at the foot of the bed. The clack of the wheels beat its rhythm as the train crawled through the night. Weariness swept over Hook, and he slept.

The moon cast through the window of the cupola and awakened him sometime in the night. The caboose waddled and pitched, a movement as familiar as his own heartbeat, and then turned hollow as they passed onto elevated track. Ancient, dry lake beds pocked the desert like moonscape.

He sat up, lit a cigarette, and drew the blanket over his shoulders. He wondered about Andrea, how she was managing with a car full of disturbed women, but then Andrea managed well no matter the situation. She had about her a strength and calmness unusual in one so young. But in his experience, character trumped age every time. And she had Seth, who made a good hand in spite of his bitching.

The train bumped and ebbed and bumped again as it leaned into a curve. Even in its enormity, a train moved with grace, except in the slightest turn, which caused it to moan and groan like an old woman.

Tossing off his blanket, Hook climbed the ladder into the cupola. The moon hung like a lantern in the sky, and the passenger cars, with darkened windows, drove through the night. The headlight beam of Frenchy's engine shot into the desert, and smoke drifted over the moon like black lace.

When he spotted the ruby smudge of light under the car, his pulse ticked up.

"Hotbox, Mixer," he said, climbing down. "Showing color, too. I hope to hell Frenchy's awake."

Hook slipped on his prosthesis and lit the signal lantern. He stepped out onto the platform, the wind, smelling of smoke and steam, cold against him. He waited until the engine banked full into the turn before swinging the lantern in a slow-stop signal. After a full minute, he repeated the signal. Frenchy's whistle rose in the night, and the brakes screeched as he brought her down.

"Stay here," Hook said to Mixer. "We're on a trestle. You fall through a hole and that would be that."

Holding his lantern out, Hook edged his way down the track, taking care to negotiate the ties. He couldn't be certain as to the depth of the grade below, and he damn sure didn't want to find out. He could see Frenchy's light coming toward him.

"What's going on?" Frenchy asked, his cigar a red spot in the darkness.

"I spotted a blazer back there on the curve," Hook said.

"Let's take a walk," Frenchy said. "See if we can smell her out."

Just then Andrea and Seth stepped from the car, and then Roy from the security car.

"Be careful," Hook said. "We're sitting on a trestle."

Baldwin dropped a window on the supply car and stuck his head out.

"What's going on?" he asked.

"Think we have a hotbox. Just need to check it out," Hook said.

"Let's get a move on," Frenchy said. "We need to get this trestle cleared."

As they worked their way along, Frenchy examined the journals one by one. When they came to the back wheel carriage of the boys' car, Hook stooped over.

"I smell her," he said.

Frenchy lay his hand against the journal and jerked it away.

"Goddang it," he said. "Scorching hot." Taking out his pliers he lifted the packing lid. "Hell, there ain't no packing left. She's dry as the Mojave. It's a wonder we didn't burn her to the ground."

"Can we move?" Hook asked.

"Depends if there's any brass left in her. Don't want that axle dropping down." Frenchy relit his cigar, pinching out his match. "We'll oil her up. See if we can't limp on in. Sons of bitches should have packed those journals in the yards," he said.

"Eddie had his way, we'd be riding in cattle cars," Hook said.

Hook waited with Andrea and Seth on the steps of the women's car while Frenchy and the bakehead packed up the journal.

Within the hour, Frenchy came back. "Okay," he said. "We're going to give her a go. You keep an eye out, Hook. She flares up, I'll head for a siding until we can get some help out here."

"Seth," Hook said, "you and Andrea better go back in."

"I ain't shut my eyes in three days," Seth said.

Hook rode in the cupola, watching for any sign of fire while Frenchy nursed her down the track at walking speed. By the time the sun rose over Needles, they were pulling into the El Garces depot.

Hook helped Santos and Roy unload the boys for breakfast while the car was shuttled off for repairs. Baldwin made arrangements for food to be delivered to the security ward. Hook went to help Andrea and Seth take the women in to eat.

Andrea and Seth met him at the door.

"We have a problem," Andrea said, her face pale.

"What is it?" he asked.

"We just took head count," Seth said.

"What's going on?"

"It's Elizabeth," Andrea said.

"Elizabeth?"

Andrea shook her head, her eyes welling. "The young girl with the brain tumor. She's gone, Hook."

"Gone? Are you sure?"

"We've looked everywhere," Seth said.

"This is my fault," Andrea said.

"Now, take it easy," Hook said. "When's the last time you saw her?"

"After we pulled out of Barstow. She had fallen asleep like everyone else."

"That's the last time you checked on her?"

"Everyone had gone to sleep," she said. "It didn't seem necessary."

"Seth, what about you?"

"I didn't hear a thing," he said.

"She has to be on the train then," Hook said. "Have you gone through the cars?"

"Every last one," Seth said. "She's not on this train."

"Elizabeth suffered depression, and her tumor had worsened lately," Andrea said.

"You think she might have hurt herself?"

"We never left the car," Seth said. "How could she have?"

Andrea glanced up at Hook. "Not until . . ."

"Not until that trestle," he said.

"I'll never forgive myself if something has happened to her," Andrea said.

Hook walked to the end of the car and then back. "Tell Baldwin. And then call the sheriff."

"What are you going to do?" Andrea asked.

"I'm going back to that trestle."

"I'll go with you," Seth said.

"No, Andrea needs you here," he said.

Hook found Pap Gonzales at the yard office preparing for the day's work.

"Well," Pap said, pushing up his hat, exposing a tan line that cut his forehead into two exact hemispheres. "If it ain't the law come calling."

"Hello, Pap. I need a favor."

"I ain't taking care of no goddang dog, Hook."

"That's not it, Pap. I have a trainload of mental patients waiting at the depot."

"What else is new?"

"We had to shut down to oil up a blazer last night. When we rolled in this morning, one of our patients had disappeared. I think she might still be out there."

"Goddang it, Hook, I got a crew waiting."

"Run me out there in the popcar. I have to make certain she wasn't left behind."

"Goddang it," he said, sticking his hat back on. "We'll have to get a clearance card, 'less you want to risk riding back to Barstow on the front of a cowcatcher."

"Thanks, Pap. I wouldn't ask if it weren't an emergency."

"It's always an emergency unless it comes to my switches."

The day had turned hot by the time they'd fueled the motorcar and cleared the line west. Pap cranked the engine and throttled up.

"How far out, Hook?" he asked.

"I can't be certain."

"You ain't figuring on hunting out the entire line, are you?"

"I don't think we crossed another trestle after the hotbox," he said.

"That last trestle ain't so far out," Pap said.

"We crippled in pretty slow," Hook said. "It's a wonder she didn't melt out the axle at that."

Pap took out a cigarette and covered the match with his hands against the wind.

"Rumor is you're in trouble over that truck deal in Flagstaff, Hook."

"You know it doesn't take a lot to get Eddie worked up," Hook said.

"You can't leave your truck on the tracks, Hook. You'd think a goddang bull would know better."

"I appreciate the advice, Pap. Next time I'll get a valet before I chase down a bum."

Pap studied a lone hawk sitting atop a Joshua tree. "You figure that girl has come to some harm?" he asked.

"She has a brain tumor, Pap. Things hadn't been going her way for quite a while. Andrea said she was dropped off at the door, and no one has been back to see her since."

"I got a daughter," he said. "I'll be a grandpa come September."

"Yeah? I figured someone old as you had been a grandpa for twenty, thirty years by now."

"It's a goddang long way back to Needles," he said. "Especially walking."

"You ought take good care of me, Pap. I put you in my will."

"You did?"

"Left you all my books and my dog."

"And here I thought I might get stuck with a wad of money or a gold watch."

Within the hour, Hook pointed to a network of timbers bridging an arroyo.

"There's a trestle, Pap."

Pap throttled down. The popper rattled like a thrashing machine as she coasted onto the trestle. Hook studied the terrain, a dry gulch maybe thirty- or forty-feet deep. Getting out, he walked the trestle to look for any signs of Elizabeth below.

"There," he said, pointing to a spot of color in the rocks. "Damn it. It's her, Pap. We'll have to back out and climb down over there."

Sweat ran into Hook's eyes as he worked his way through the rocks. Pap followed behind him in silence. What Hook found at the bottom caused his stomach to tighten. Elizabeth's remains were dashed across the rocks. Bloodied clothes and pieces of bone were scattered about as if they'd been tugged and pulled in a hundred directions. Even her leather purse had been dragged into the rocks.

Pap took out his bandanna and wiped the sweat that gathered on his forehead.

"Jesus, Hook," he said. "Something's been at her."

Hook knelt, studying the tracks that encircled the body. "Coyotes," he said. "The sons of bitches even tried to eat her leather purse."

"You figure she jumped?" Pap asked.

"There's no way of knowing. Things weren't going her way. Being lonely *and* sick is not a good combination."

Pap walked to where he could get a breeze and looked off into the desert.

"What do we do?"

"Take her in, I guess," Hook said.

"Shouldn't there be an investigation or something?" Pap said.

"We just did, Pap. Anyway, another night out here and there wouldn't be anything left to investigate."

When they'd finished, Pap cranked the engine. He moved his feet away from the bundle that lay on the floor between them. After lighting a cigarette, he looked over at Hook.

"You won't ever hear me complain about yard dogs again, Hook," he said. "Whatever they pay you, it ain't enough far as I'm concerned."

As soon as the body was secured in the baggage room, Hook contacted the sheriff to see when he would be out. After that, he searched out the car crew who were just finishing up the repair.

"When you switch 'em out, put the women's car next to the crummy, will you, boys?"

"Guess you figure the women need protection from the law, huh, Hook?" the foreman said, grinning.

"They need protection from the likes of you scabs, if you got to know," Hook said. "So maybe you could just do it and leave the reasons up to me."

He found Baldwin hunkered over his desk. Dark rings encircled his eyes, and the room smelled stale.

"The body's in the baggage room," Hook said. "I'll be turning it over to the sheriff later. By then that car should be ready."

Baldwin rubbed his face. "Andrea's pretty upset," he said.

"It could have happened to anyone," Hook said.

"I checked Elizabeth's records," Baldwin said. "She has a mother but there's no number. There hasn't been a visitor since she entered the asylum. She didn't have that much longer, you know. That tumor had already eaten half her brain stem away."

"Pretty sad business all around," Hook said.

"Look, Runyon, you just as well know. Someone has contacted the American Board of Psychiatry about that fire. The bastards are threatening to file a negligence charge against me. Now, with this, I don't know. I just don't know.

"And, frankly, I'm running damn short of funds. If I get hit with a violation, they could pull my license. I could lose everything. On top of that I've been feeling pretty flat, all exhausted. It's like the world's turned against me. All I ever wanted was to help people."

Hook rose. "I'm meeting the sheriff at three to turn over the body. I see no reason why we can't leave. If something comes up on the case, they can call ahead."

Baldwin nodded. "These patients have got to get settled in. This kind of upheaval is exactly what they don't need."

Hook had talked to everyone once more by the time the sheriff arrived. No one had seen anything. Santos had broken up a fight between two boys just as they had pulled up with the hotbox. He showed Hook the bruise on his arm where one boy had pinched him.

Neither Helms nor Frankie had heard anything out of the usual that night. They had sent Roy down to find out why the train had stopped. Other than that, the security ward had remained on lock-down throughout.

When the sheriff arrived, Hook took him down to the baggage room and showed him the remains.

"Jesus," he said, adjusting his crotch. "What the hell happened to her?"

"Besides the thirty-foot fall? Coyotes, I'd guess. I've heard the damn things will eat the tail right off a calf while it's being born."

The sheriff pulled the tarp back over the body and lit a cigarette. "How do you have it figured, Runyon?"

"The only logical explanation is suicide. She suffered from a brain tumor. Her nurse says that she had been especially depressed of late.

"She probably got out on the opposite side of the car when we pulled up on that trestle. Sometime during that time, she jumped. Nobody knew until another head count here at the depot."

"If you're certain about all this, I guess you'll be releasing the body for burial?"

Hook walked to the double doors of the baggage room and watched the inmates who were being loaded back onto the train.

"Yes, if I were certain," he said. "You think you might do me a favor, Sheriff?"

The sheriff shrugged. "I figure I might owe you one or two along the way. What is it you want?"

"An autopsy, just to make certain," Hook said. "And a criminal check on Frankie Yager."

"Right," he said.

"Oh, and one other thing. Would you make a call to the American Board of Psychiatry? See if you can find out who filed a complaint against Baldwin."

23

THE TRAIN PULLED out of Needles at sunset. Hook waited until they were well under way before entering the women's car. Seth looked up from his seat by the window.

"Got you set up next to the louse box," Hook said. "That way I can keep an eye on you."

Seth rubbed his chin, which had sprouted a noticeable beard.

"Something tells me I ain't the one you want to keep an eye on, Hook."

Hook could see Andrea at the other end leaning over the seat talking to Bertha. When she looked up, she smiled at him.

"Don't know what you're talking about, Seth. How goes it?"

"Well, I don't have those dreams," he said.

"That's good."

"Because I don't sleep no more, Hook. It's like being nibbled to death by ducks in here. I never thought I'd say this, but I'm damn sick of looking at that woman's nakedness."

"Ruth?"

He shook his head. "Me just sitting here minding my business, and there it is right in front of me. What's a man to do?"

"Did you ever consider not looking?" Hook asked.

"When's the last time you didn't look at a naked woman, Hook?"

"It's a point," Hook said.

"Some things are not humanly possible. Not looking is one of them, that's all I got to say."

"Where's your willpower, Seth?"

"Each time, I figure I'll just stare out the window or tie my shoe. But then I just got to look, like if I don't, I might die or lose my manliness.

"To top it off, I ain't had a smoke in days."

"Guess you could use a cigarette?"

"I sure could."

"A man could smoke in my caboose if he was my friend and if I took a notion to let him."

"I guess I'd do about anything for a smoke, Hook, even be your friend."

"Andrea might use a little break herself, you know, later on when the women here are asleep."

"Andrea don't smoke."

"Neither do you if I don't let you use my caboose."

"Once they're asleep, not much goes on anyway," Seth said.

"Go on back there and have yourself a smoke, my friend," Hook said. "I'll help Andrea watch things for a bit."

Seth checked his pocket. "I don't have matches, Hook."

"There's some next to the heating stove," Hook said.

Seth rose to leave. "About that girl, Elizabeth?"

"Yeah."

"I heard you found her."

"We found her."

Seth got to the door and turned. "I talked to her a bit at the cafeteria, Hook. She said she drank cranberry juice to make her tumor go away."

"I guess it didn't," Hook said.

"No, I guess not, but I sure didn't have her pegged as a jumper," he said, closing the door.

Hook worked his way down the aisle to where Andrea sat talking to Anna, who turned in her seat and threw her hands up when she saw Hook.

"It's that man," she said.

"Anna, just stop," Andrea said, shaking her head. "He's our friend."

"He's going to stab me with his hook," she said, scrunching down in her seat.

Lucy shifted her doll and looked up to see who had come to kill Anna.

"Esther stole all the toilet paper," Lucy said.

"Kill Esther," Anna said.

"Esther's been catching bugs under the seats," Lucy said.

Ruth stuck out her chest. "Seth's been looking at my breasts," she said.

"His hook would go clear through me," Anna said.

"Stop," Andrea said.

"He threw Elizabeth off the bridge with his hook," Anna said.

Andrea's eyes teared up. "It was my fault, Hook. I shouldn't have left her alone."

"Look, Andrea, you can't take responsibility for the whole world. It's too big and too awful. No one blames you for Elizabeth's death."

"I do," Anna said.

"Hush," Andrea said.

"I had your car switched next to the caboose," Hook said.

Andrea smiled. "I noticed."

"I let Seth go back to the caboose for a smoke. I'm thinking he might give you a break later if you'd like."

"I'd like," she said.

"Elizabeth's head exploded," Anna said.

Roy unlocked the door and let Hook into the security ward. Frankie peered over the top of his paper and then turned back without a word.

"Where's Doctor Helms?" Hook asked.

"Gone for meds," Roy said. "Wait too long, and it's a Paddy fight around here."

Hook moved along the aisle. Robert Smith sat with his head down, a string of saliva drooling from his mouth. Van Diefendorf snored, his head against the window.

"Are they being exercised?" Hook asked.

"We take them one at a time for a bathroom break in the supply car, walk them up and down a bit, but they don't seem to know one way or the other. That chlorine's mighty hard stuff."

"Tell Doctor Helms I need you down there with Santos. He's due a change off now and then."

"That suits me fine," Roy said. "That goddang Frankie hasn't muttered a word the whole of the way."

As Hook went out, he ran into Helms returning with her hands full of medications.

"If you need Roy, I guess we can manage," she said.

"Thanks," he said.

"Mr. Runyon, have you any idea how much longer it will be?"

"Not much longer, Doctor Helms, providing we can keep things underhand."

That night Hook lay in his bunk listening to the steamer draw down as her governor kicked in against the grade. Mixer lay at his feet, the clack of the wheels having driven him into a deep sleep.

Mixer traveled well, sleeping almost continuously while the train moved, but the moment the train stopped, he came alive to demand his run along the tracks. This arrangement worked fine so long as he didn't spot some unfortunate creature trespassing on railroad property.

When the knock came on the door, Mixer lifted his head.

"It's alright," Hook said, opening the door.

Andrea stood there, her arms folded against the cold that gathered between the cars.

"They're finally all asleep," she said.

"Hi," he said, pushing Mixer back with his foot.

Stooping down, Andrea gathered Mixer up. "It's alright," she said. "He must get lonesome in here by himself."

Mixer wagged from head to foot.

"Yes," Hook said. "He does."

"It feels wonderful just to be away for a moment," she said, standing.

"Could I fix you something? A drink? I've forty-year-old shine in the cabinet."

"No, thanks. Oh, can you see the train from the cupola?"

"Would you like to look?"

"I'd love to," she said.

They climbed the ladder, sharing the hard seat inside the cupola. Moonlight slid along the tops of the cars like a silver river.

"It's wonderful," she said. "Look, you can see the engine from here."

"I sometimes come up here at sunrise and have my coffee," he said.

Settling in against him, she took his hand, her fingers cool and delicate.

"Some life you lead."

"It suits me," he said. "When I'm on the move like this, my troubles never quite catch up."

"Except when they're on the move *with* you," she said.

"Well, it's a living, and it has its rewards from time to time."

She turned, the gray of her eyes lit in the moonlight. "The thing is, it doesn't fit you somehow."

"What do you mean?"

"I don't know, exactly, the books maybe, the collecting, all that reading."

"Just curious about things," he said. "Yard dogs aren't worth a damn without curiosity, you know."

"Well," she said, "I like that about you. I think I have you figured out, and then there's a whole different layer, the way you think, the way you see the world."

Hook tilted her chin up with his finger. "You mind if I kiss you?"

"I don't believe I do."

He brushed his lips against hers, and she melted into him. He held her, and they watched the moon arch through the sky.

"Hook," she whispered, "I'm glad you're here. I'm frightened sometimes about what might lie ahead."

He pulled her in close. "We're all a little frightened of the future, Andrea. But we have no choice but to step into it. It's the way of things."

She checked her watch in the moonlight. "I think my smoke break is up. I better get back."

"We'll arrange another," he said. "Seth's got a strong habit."

At the door, Andrea lifted her eyes. "Good night," she said.

Hook climbed down from the caboose at the Flagstaff depot and filled his lungs with the crisp mountain air. The peaks lifted into the blue, and the smell of pine steeped the morning. Mixer took off in a run, weaving in and out of the cars.

Hook walked up to the engine, where Frenchy was just coming down.

"Morning, Frenchy," he said.

"Told you this ole girl would make her across the desert," Frenchy said.

"How long a layover, Frenchy?"

"Going to grease the pig and give her a drink," he said. "Regular maintenance. Me and the fireman ran our trick out. We'll be hearing from the union soon enough."

"Maybe you can get this rust bucket there before I die of old age," Hook said.

Frenchy flipped the ash from his cigar. "At the rate you're going there ain't going to be any passengers left, anyway."

"Had you brought a decent train we'd been there by now," Hook said.

"Oh, sure. It's my fault. Sometimes I figure I'll just retire and move south."

"Give you a chance to visit with the wife more, wouldn't it?" Hook said.

"Oh, hell, she quit talking to me ten years ago."

"I'd like to stay and visit, Frenchy, but I got to make a call to Eddie."

Hook sat across from the depot operator and dialed the phone.

When Eddie came on, he said, "Division, Eddie Preston."

"Eddie, Hook here."

"Goddang it, Runyon, you know what time it is?"

"Some of us don't watch the clock, Eddie."

"Where are you?"

"Flagstaff and lucky to be here. The Mormons crossed the desert faster than this ole kettle."

"We need those outfit cars, Runyon. They got rip-track sleeping in a hotel, twenty hands drinking whiskey and eating steak. It's costing a goddang fortune. The big boys are not too happy. That makes me not happy. You see how it works?"

"Listen, Eddie, we've had a little trouble along the way."

"What the hell you talking about?"

"One of the inmates took a dive off a trestle."

"Oh, Christ. Hurt?"

"Dead, Eddie, and the coyotes had a little overnight party to boot."

"Oh, Christ, and where was railroad security when all this was going on?"

"Look, Eddie, this is not exactly a normal run you know. These people have problems. I can't watch them every second."

"I'm the one with the problems, Runyon. Now we have lawsuits. You know how the big boys hate lawsuits."

"I doubt it, Eddie. She didn't have any family that cared one way or the other."

"She?"

"Yeah."

"Let me know if anything comes up. Maybe we can get it headed off."

"Yeah, I will, Eddie."

"Listen," he said. "I get this call from Barstow about some goddang dog chewing up a city cop on railroad property. You know anything about that?"

"I don't know about dogs, Eddie, except maybe that one in Amarillo."

"Work on your sense of humor, Runyon, and call me when you get that work train freed up. Try keeping the goddang passengers inside the cars, will you?"

Hook pushed the phone back over to the operator, lit a cigarette, and looked out the window.

The phone rang, and the operator picked it up. "Who?

"Yeah, he's here. It's for you, Hook," he said. "Sheriff over to Needles."

"Hello, Sheriff," Hook said. "What did you find out?"

"That Frankie Yager fellow," he said.

"Is he clean?"

"No big stuff, Hook, breaking and entering, shoplifting, shit like that. He was booted out of the state university."

"What for?"

"Bogus application. Forged his grade point."

"I used to sign my own report cards," Hook said.

"You didn't threaten to kill the dean, though, did you?"

"They don't have them in seventh grade," he said. "Did Yager get time over it?"

"You know these goddang judges, Hook."

"Thanks," he said. "I thought I smelled something."

"And I checked with the American Board of Psychiatry like you asked."

"Yeah?"

"A Doctor Bria Helms had contacted them about Baldwin," he said.

"Thanks, Sheriff."

"There is one other thing."

Hook slipped his cigarettes into his pocket. "Go on, Sheriff."

"That autopsy came back."

"And?"

"That girl didn't die from no fall, Hook. Somebody strangled her."

24

As SOON AS they were under way, Hook asked Baldwin and Helms to meet him in the supply car. Helms sat down and folded her hands in her lap.

She lifted her chin. "I hope this is important, Mr. Runyon. It's time for medications, and we're quite shorthanded."

"I wouldn't have requested the meeting did I not think it necessary," Hook said.

"We've had another breakdown?" Baldwin asked, looking up through his brows.

"No breakdown," Hook said.

"Then what is so urgent?" Helms asked.

"Before I left Needles, I requested that the sheriff do a little checking on my behalf," Hook said.

"Checking?" Baldwin said.

"For one thing, I asked to have an autopsy conducted on Elizabeth."

Helms stood. "What on earth for?"

"Sometimes you get a feel," he said. "Turns out Elizabeth didn't commit suicide. She was strangled, dead before she went off the trestle."

"Good God," Baldwin said, dropping his forehead into his hands.

"Are you suggesting murder?" Doctor Helms asked.

"People don't strangle themselves," Hook said.

"But who would want to kill Elizabeth?" Helms asked.

"I also requested a criminal check on Frankie Yager."

"Frankie?" Helms said.

Hook rose and walked to the window of the supply car. Outside, the empty beauty of the prairie raced past. Frenchy had the bullgine wound tight.

"I have a responsibility here," he said. "When someone dies on my train, I take it personally."

"Yager has a background of petty thievery, and he forged his transcript. He also sent his dean a threatening letter."

"Oh?" Baldwin said. "I don't remember seeing anything about this when he applied with us."

"The usual background checks were done," Helms said. "None of this came to light."

"He most likely forged his application here as well," Hook said.

"Surely, you're not suggesting that Frankie had something to do with that girl's death?" Baldwin asked.

"At the moment, I have no proof of anything," he said.

"Well, it is railroad business," Baldwin said. "I see no reason to exclude anyone on this train from questioning."

"I must get back with the medications," Helms said. "Is the supply cabinet open?"

"Yes," Baldwin said.

Steadying herself against the pitch of the car, Helms counted out the meds. Her shoulders were bent forward of the rest of her body as if she carried a great weight. Hook decided he had no clear idea of her age.

She closed the door to the cabinet, paused, and then reopened it to retrieve pills from a green bottle high up on the top shelf.

When she got to the door, she turned, "I want it understood that my inmates must not be interrogated, Mr. Runyon. They are ill and not able to defend themselves."

"It's patient safety that concerns me the most, Doctor Helms. Perhaps you could ask Frankie to come to my caboose when you get back?"

Hook lay in his bunk dipping into Clarke's *Bloody Mohawk*, which he'd found under the seat in one of the outfit cars. His eyes had grown weary under the dim lantern light. Eddie had promised to upgrade the caboose with an electric generator, but it had never come to pass.

When he rose to put his book away, someone knocked at the door. He opened it to find Frankie Yager, his hair whipping from the wind that blew between the cars.

"You wanted to see me?" he asked above the clatter of the wheels.

"Come in," Hook said.

"It's time for bathroom breaks in the ward," he said, stepping in. "What do you want?"

"A few questions," Hook said.

"Look, Runyon, I got my hands full running them criminals back and forth to the john. You got something on your mind, maybe you could just get on with it."

Hook lit a cigarette, his match flaring in the black of Frankie's eyes.

"Alright," he said. "Turns out you weren't altogether honest about your history when you applied for a job with Baldwin."

"Ain't your business, is it?" he said.

"Shoplifting," Hook said. "Important stuff like that."

"You called me down here for that?"

"And then there's a matter of forging your transcript and sending a little thank you note to the dean."

Frankie scoffed. "No one ever proved that was me," he said. "Now, if you're through, I got to get back."

"I'm not through," Hook said.

Frankie squared his shoulders. "You are far as I'm concerned."

Hook put his cigarette out in the tray.

"Don't let this arm fool you," he said. "I'm not one of your boys you can push around."

"So what do you want from me?"

"About that girl that died," Hook said. "I'm not sure it was an accident, you see."

Frankie turned to open the door. Hook slammed it shut with his foot.

"I'm not finished," he said. "Turns out someone strangled her before throwing her off the trestle."

"I don't know anything about it," he said. "I've been up there taking that scum on piss breaks. Don't believe me? Ask Helms."

"Maybe you ran into Elizabeth on one of those breaks," Hook said, watching his eyes. "Maybe you decided to have a little fun and it got out of hand."

"And maybe I didn't," he said, his eyes darting in the lamplight. "Anyway, they said she had a tumor the size of a grapefruit, so what the hell difference does all this make?"

"And so you just helped her along a little?" Hook said.

Frankie lowered his arms and clinched his fists at his side.

"Maybe she likes freaks, Runyon. Maybe you had her all to yourself."

Hook reached for him, clamping Frankie's ear in his prosthesis, yanking him over. Frankie squealed, and his face turned red. Mixer growled, his hackles rising.

"I don't like you much," Hook said. "Go ahead and give me a reason to feed your fuckin' ear to the dog." Shoving him to the door, he said, "Now, get out of my caboose."

After he'd gone, Hook sat on the bunk listening to the clack of the wheels. Mixer rested his chin on Hook's knee and studied him, his brows peaking this way and that.

"I should have let you eat the son of a bitch," he said.

Hook poured himself a coffee, which begged for a dollop of shine. He read a little again, but he couldn't get the image of the girl's body out of his mind.

He blew out the lantern and turned on his side. He thought about Yager, his eyes, the smell of him, like stale bread.

The wail of Frenchy's whistle lifted as night closed over them. Hook dozed and awakened and then fell into a sound sleep, the weariness of the days washing in like a tide. Sometime in the night, he awakened again. This time the moon shined down from the cupola and cast shadows up the walls of the caboose.

He sat up, rubbing his face. Mixer groaned and curled up in a ball. Something didn't feel right, something adrift and unsettled. On nights like this, thoughts roamed through his head like lost ghosts, returning again and again to drive away his rest.

Finally, he rose and put on his prosthesis and then his sidearm. He'd take a walk through the cars, make certain all was well. Maybe then he could sleep.

The women were all asleep, Andrea as well, her coat folded under her head. He thought once to touch her face, but then resisted, unwilling to wake her. Seth, too, slept at the far end of the car, his legs drawn in the fetal position across the seat. He mumbled something in the darkness and then turned on his side, snoring softly.

He found Santos watching the moon through the window, his

boys all sleeping. They had adjusted to Santos's silence, finding in him an even hand.

Roy joined him for a quick cigarette between the cars, but neither spoke much as they smoked and watched the moon edge through the black sky.

Hook opened the door between supply and the security car, the wind whipping at his legs, the moonlight skimming along the tracks. When he reached for the grab iron to pull himself over, he spotted the figure slumped across the coupler, its arms dangling only inches above the tracks below.

25

Hook's heart chugged as he leaned down to pull the body back onto the platform. The ties flicked beneath him, and the wheels screeched under the enormity of their load. The body rose and fell on the coupler as it sawed back and forth between the cars.

He worked his arm under the torso and pulled with all that he had in him, but the body, still warm and malleable, slumped like a sausage, throwing him off balance. He snared the grab iron with his hook a second before being sucked into the chaos below. He maneuvered the body back onto the platform. Leaning on a knee, he caught his breath before turning it over.

Frankie Yager, or what had once been Frankie Yager, stared up at him with a singular blank eye. The other eye, having been gouged from his head, swung like a pendulum under the pitch of the car. A white liquid pooled in the vacant socket.

A crushing wound had opened the side of Frankie's skull, and there was the smell of butchery and body heat in the wind. Hook's stomach lurched, and he turned to clear his head. Frankie's ear had given way to the horror of the blow, settling down to where his jaw once hinged. The blow had drawn a macabre smirk across Yager's face, one that caused the hair on Hook's neck to crawl. Whoever had killed Frankie Yager had done so with zeal.

As he tugged the body back into the car, he struggled to make sense of it all. There were few on board capable of such a deed, and they were all in the security ward. He unholstered his sidearm and checked the clip. The killer could be anywhere, but if Hook could find him, the therapy would be quick and final.

He double-checked the safety on his sidearm as he approached the security-ward door. In all his years as a railroad bull, he'd not seen such brutality inflicted on a victim. To open a man's head in such a fashion must have taken repeated and violent blows.

He stood to the side, slipped his arm through the grab iron, and knocked on the door. The wind churned in a torrent about him. When he heard the knob turn, he moved into the shadows and steadied his arm against the car. He leveled his weapon.

Doctor Helms opened the door. Hook reached for her and pulled her to the side. She gasped softly. He glanced into the car behind her.

"You scared me to death," she said. "I was expecting Frankie."

"Frankie won't be coming," he said.

Hook stepped into the car. Moving down the aisle, he checked the restraints as he went. The men sat motionless and were unresponsive to his search. Most slept quietly in their seats. Helms followed behind him, the clip of her heels clicking on the wooden floor.

"Are you going to tell me what's going on?" she asked.

"Where's Smith?"

"Frankie took him on bathroom break," she said. "They haven't come back yet."

He could smell her in the darkness of the car, perfume mollified by time and travel.

"Frankie's dead," he said.

"What do you mean?"

"Murdered."

"Oh my God," she said. "Smith?"

"Looks that way. Smith may have jumped. With a little luck, he didn't make it."

"This is terrible," she said. "He's quite capable of anything. No one is safe with him on the loose. I told Baldwin we shouldn't have made this trip and now this."

"You heard nothing?" he asked.

"No, nothing. What are you going to do?"

"First, I've got to be certain he's not on this train. If he's jumped, there's little to do except wait until we reach Winslow. I'll alert the authorities there. I'll send Baldwin to help you here."

"Smith is a dangerous man," she said. "I told Doctor Baldwin . . . I told him men like this should never be released from their cells."

"Wasn't Smith sedated?"

"Yes, but it was time for his medication, and sometimes the doses have to be increased."

"Keep your doors locked. Don't open them for anyone but me or Baldwin. I'll alert the others to do the same. Is that clear?"

Hook started his search with Andrea's car. Andrea stood at the door, her hand over her mouth.

"Oh, no, Frankie? Are you certain?"

"Quite certain," he said. "And no one has entered here?"

"No," she said. "I've been awake ever since you walked through earlier."

"I thought you were asleep."

"I thought you might awaken me," she said.

"Don't open the door for anyone but me, Andrea. I've got to search out the train."

She took his hand. "I'll tell Seth," she said. "Hook, be careful."

"Don't worry. As far as I know, I have the only weapon on this train."

He alerted Santos and Roy; both had been sleeping. Just to make certain Smith hadn't managed to slip in, he searched under all the seats before leaving.

In supply, he found Doctor Baldwin sitting up in his bunk, his eyes huge in the darkness.

"Smith?" he said quietly. For a moment he only sat with his head in his hands. "This will be my end," he said. "This will be my end."

"If he's on this train, I'll find him," Hook said. "Meanwhile, Doctor Helms needs you in the security car."

Baldwin shook his head and sighed in the darkness.

From there Hook worked his way to the engine. The firebox door had been thrown open, lighting Frenchy's silhouette in the darkness. The smell of heat and oil wafted back from the engine. The bakehead leaned over the firebox, soot covering his face.

Hook waited for his eyes to adjust to the darkness, making certain that Smith hadn't ensconced himself in the cab, before alerting Frenchy.

"What the hell you doing?" Frenchy asked. "You out to get yourself killed?"

"We got a dead man aboard, Frenchy, and his killer might still be on this train."

Frenchy lit his cigar, the stub so short that he nearly burned his nose.

"What else is new?" he said. "Why don't you just let all them loonies loose, so I can turn this crawler around and go home?"

Hook dropped his legs over the water tank. "I figure he bailed, but I have to make certain. This guy is a dangerous son of a bitch, Frenchy. You boys don't take any chances."

Frenchy fished a new cigar out of his overalls pocket. "The only thing scares me is a goddang yard dog coming up on me in the night."

"Ask the bakehead what's the scariest thing he sees every day," Hook said. "He won't have to think long."

The bakehead grinned and pitched a little sand into the firebox to blow her out. Hook climbed back up.

"See you boys in Winslow," he said.

On top, he knelt down against the wind. The moonlight lit the roofs of the cars. They bobbed and weaved through the night like swimming sharks. From here he could see the caboose, the light shimmering in the cupola windows.

The probability of Smith having jumped was high, as were the chances that he now resembled raw hamburger somewhere back there in the desert. Hook found the prospect agreeable, though he remained ambivalent. There would be a hell of a lot of explaining to do once he arrived in Winslow. He'd have to call in the local authorities, something Eddie hated almost as much as paying overtime.

After securing Frankie's corpse in the end of the supply car, Hook made a final run through to make certain all were safe. Exhausted, he retreated to his caboose, where he took off his shoes and collapsed in his bunk. But he couldn't sleep. His body ached from running full throttle. He checked his watch. Hours had passed since all this had begun. He replayed the night in his head. Why, out of all those men, was it Smith who managed to overcome his sedative?

He searched out his cigarettes and climbed into the cupola. Frenchy's headlight beam faded into the first glow of dawn. The steam cloud boiled into the sky like a thunderhead, its edges tipped with the pinks and blues of sunrise. Soon enough daylight would break in all its glory.

He leaned back and lit his cigarette. He needed time to think. There were moments when a man had to act to save his life. But the real commerce of a yard dog came in the thinking, those quiet hours, the consideration of possibilities. While action might save a man's life, thinking solved his cases.

Sliding back the cupola window, he let the wind blow his hair. The morning smelled clean and clear as it could only at sunrise. The chug of the steam engine rose and fell like the lungs of a great beast. He shut his eyes, his thoughts drifting and pooling. Solutions more often arrived obliquely from the corners of reason, rather than through the glare of conscious thought.

When the arm encircled his neck, he knew instantly his failure. In that moment, Robert Smith yanked Hook's head out the window of the cupola, his arm around his throat, choking off his air. Hook glanced up to see the pockmarks, the deliberate blink of Robert Smith, the tongue working at the corners of his mouth, the gore of what had once been Frankie Yager still fresh across his front. Hook struggled to free himself, but his arms were trapped inside the cupola.

Smith screwed his thumb into Hook's eye to gouge it from its mooring. Lights exploded in Hook's head, and pain flowed down his spine. Smith laughed somewhere beyond the agony, a giddiness filled with pleasure and anticipation.

Hook's strength came from deep inside him, a wellspring issuing from some primitive lobe of his brain. He could taste iron and salt and knew that if he were to live, he must move now, or he would soon enough join Frankie Yager on the dunghill.

Darkness deepened about him, and he brought to bear the resolve that had borne him through the years of danger on the rails. He twisted his head sideways, his cheek tearing under Robert Smith's grip, and slipped his prosthesis through the opening above his head.

Unable to see, he shoved the prosthesis, long since an extension of body and brain, into Robert Smith's cheek like a fishhook. He twisted and yanked and knew that he had found his mark. Blood sprayed across the window. Smith's legs slid off the caboose, but he held on against the plummeting wind, his grin frozen and grizzly.

Hook covered his eye against the rudeness of Smith's thumb,

the pain having narrowed to a singular point inside his head. Smith still clung to the cupola, his knuckles white, his arms trembling, his legs dangling over the side.

Hook leaned out the window, the roof of the caboose slick with blood. Robert Smith looked up at him through his arms, his cheek loose and flapping in the wind. When Smith let go, he disappeared in a whisper, leaving behind only silence and a world reeling with the anguish of his madness.

Hook climbed down from the cupola and lit the lantern. Mixer stretched and glanced up.

"Thanks for nothing," Hook said.

Hook looked in the mirror. Red gathered in the white of his eye, and the abrasion on his cheek seeped into his whiskers.

He went out on the caboose porch and lit a cigarette. The first rays of the morning sun lit the desolation in reds and golds, and high in the blue, buzzards gathered for the morning hunt.

He sat down on the steps, considering what to do. He could alert the others, but for what purpose now? Soon enough they would be in Winslow, and there was little anyone could do until then.

Frenchy blew his whistle to announce their approach to the depot and the La Posada Hotel.

Mixer joined Hook and pushed his head under Hook's arm.

"So now you come," he said, pulling him in.

He'd tell Baldwin and the others, then make his report. Some effort would be made to recover Smith's body. Though by that time the vultures would have taken care of the most of it. One thing was certain, neither Frankie Yager nor Robert Smith would be giving up any information from here on out.

There were a good many loose ends, things he didn't understand, not the least of which was how a drugged inmate managed to kill Frankie Yager and nearly blind one railroad yard dog in the doing.

26

HOOK BROKE THE news to Helms and Baldwin shortly after Frenchy sided the bullgine within walking distance of the Winslow depot. Helms sat emotionless as Hook related the last few moments of his encounter with Robert Smith. Baldwin's face darkened, and he shook his head slowly back and forth.

"What happens now?" Helms asked.

"I've got to talk to Frenchy," Hook said. "This business with Yager and Smith is going to take some time to clear up."

"You do realize we are sitting here with twenty, make that nineteen, of the most dangerous men in the country?" Helms said.

"I do understand. Believe me. But these things have to be dealt with. We'd have the law down on us for sure if we let it ride until we reached the fort."

Hook turned to Baldwin. "What do you think, Doctor?"

Baldwin looked up through his brows. A dullness had entered his eyes as if he had moved beyond reach.

"Doctor Baldwin is under some stress," Helms said.

"Very well," Hook said. "I'll talk to Frenchy and get back to you."

The news of the deaths had quickly spread the length of the train. Hook found Frenchy checking the side rods on the engine. His overalls strap had twisted over his shoulder, and his cigar had long since wilted into a cold stub.

As Hook approached, Frenchy stood and flipped his cigar onto the tracks.

"Hell, Hook," he said. "You ought match them eyes up, then you could look like a goddang raccoon."

"Thanks for the sympathy," Hook said. "What's the matter with this piece of junk now?"

"Side rod's slapping," he said. "Bushing's probably wore out. I'm going to run her into the shop for a look-see."

"Jesus, Frenchy, I've got problems back there."

Frenchy stuck his hands in his pockets and looked down line.

"I'd say that's an understatement, but then that's why you make the big money, Hook."

"You figure we're tied down for awhile then?"

"Depends," he said. "Me and the fireman are overdue for a rest. We're going to have to get some sack time. I can't keep my goddang eyes open. We have an accident, there'd be hell to pay."

"Meanwhile, what am I supposed to do with those inmates, Frenchy?"

"Why don't you just throw a few more off the caboose? That way we wouldn't have nothing to worry about."

"Things are getting pretty stressful back there."

"I ain't your supervisor, thank God for favors, but if I was, I'd say put them folks up in the La Posada Hotel right here at the depot. It's a damn nice place."

Hook walked to the front of the engine, her boilers warm against him in the morning chill.

"I'm not sure Baldwin has the funds for a hotel, but I can't keep those people locked up in those outfit cars much longer."

"Well, if I was asked, which I ain't been, I'd have to say this side rod is a danger, and I had to shut things down for reasons of safety to the passengers. That would pretty much make this stop the railroad's problem. I figure they'd have to pick up a good share of the tab."

"Thanks, Frenchy. I guess you'd make a pretty good supervisor at that."

"Hell," he said, pulling a grease rag out of his pocket, wiping his hands. "I'll just put in for a pay raise."

"I better go call the Winslow sheriff and get the paperwork under way. Maybe he will spare a few men overnight to relieve my security people. Things are wearing thin."

Hook found pay phones in the lobby of the La Posada and called the sheriff, who agreed to pick up Yager's corpse and send someone out to search for Robert Smith. When Hook asked for a few men to help out the night watch, the sheriff said that the city didn't pay overtime. But he would give it some thought if the railroad could reimburse them the man hours.

Afterward, Hook called Eddie Preston. He lit a cigarette and cracked the door of the phone booth as he listened to Eddie rant. In the meantime, Doctor Helms came into the lobby and went into the end phone booth.

"The sheriff's agreed to give us a little relief here for the night, Eddie. My people are exhausted."

"So let him," Eddie said.

"Thing is, he wants the railroad to reimburse the city."

"What? Without the railroad, his town wouldn't even exist," Eddie said.

"Frenchy said the side rod's shot on the engine. This is the railroad's responsibility. I'll tell the sheriff you okayed it."

"Look, Runyon," he said. "I got an opening for security in the Chicago train station. All you'd have to do is run in drunks and keep the whores out of the waiting room."

"Thanks for the confidence, Eddie," Hook said.

"I've got a new man coming on line. He could make those runs, and he's got an education."

"What he doesn't have is seniority, Eddie. I'll have the union up your ass if you try to bump me."

"Lose any more of those inmates, I'm going to have to, Hook, one way or the other. And then there's this business with the disciplinary board."

"What business?"

"They said someone would probably have to pay for the truck."

"That truck was a pile of crap, Eddie."

"You could lose your seniority over this, Hook. It isn't a goddang birthright, you know."

"I'm having a little trouble hearing, Eddie. I'll have the sheriff send in a reimbursement order."

When he stepped out, Helms was just coming out of the booth.

"Oh, Mr. Runyon," she said.

"Well," he said. "Looks like we'll be staying over here at the La Posada."

"Another delay? You do realize that I can't keep these men medicated forever. Serious side effects could develop. In any case, we are hardly prepared to handle criminals in a hotel."

"I've arranged for some help with the local sheriff's office."

"Doctor Baldwin can scarcely afford hotel rooms for these inmates."

"The engine's been canned with a bad side rod. Frenchy thinks the railroad will pick up the slack for hotel rooms."

"One more glitch in a disastrous trip," she said.

"We'll have to make the best of it. I'll arrange to have the security ward at the back of the hotel. We'll get food delivered. The others can eat in the restaurant."

Helms lifted her chin to look through the bottoms of her glasses. "I guess we have no choice then, do we?"

"I'll tell Doctor Baldwin."

"No," she said, shaking her head. "Let me tell him. I'm afraid Doctor Baldwin has become quite despondent."

While Hook completed paperwork at the sheriff's office, the inmates were moved into the La Posada. Four off-duty officers were assigned to assist through the night, giving the others a chance to clean up and get some rest.

By the time Hook returned, most everyone had showered and fallen asleep in the luxury of their beds. Hook, too, preferring the privacy of his caboose, soon slept soundly for the first time in days.

When he awoke, the sun had set. He checked his face in the mirror. The swelling had receded, but a black smudge had formed on his cheek. He walked Mixer and then went to search out Andrea.

The La Posada, in grand Spanish hacienda style, invited guests by way of a veranda that led into the dining area. A majestic fireplace and stairwell were the focal points in the room, giving it a castlelike feel.

He found Andrea coming from the kitchen, where she had just completed arrangements to feed the women in the main dining area. She wore a simple pink dress, her hair pulled back with an ivory comb.

"You look wonderful," he said.

Andrea fanned out her skirt and curtsied.

"Thanks. And the nap didn't hurt either. We're about ready to eat. Maybe you could join us?"

"Great," he said.

"I've already ordered the women's dinner. Why don't you order for yourself while Seth and I bring them down?"

The women arrived looking clean and rested. Had he not known better, he would have thought them members of the local Sorosis Club.

Bertha hooked her arm through Seth's and smiled at Hook as she came down the stairs. Seth, freshly shaven, had slicked back his hair like a carnival barker. He shrugged and lifted his brows at Hook as Bertha guided him to the far end table.

Ruth and Esther took up places near the kitchen, while Anna and Lucy sat near the window, as far away from everyone as they could get.

"There," Andrea said. "That wasn't so bad, was it?"

The waiter, a young man in his early twenties, served up plates of mashed potatoes, green beans, and fried chicken.

Hook looked at Andrea over his glass. She sat erect and poised, her eyes the color of a spring storm cloud.

"Are you staying in the hotel?" she asked.

"Caboose," he said. "Quiet, you know."

"Yes," she said.

"How are the accommodations?" he asked.

"The women are absolutely giddy. Esther took three showers."

"Maybe you could get away a little while tonight?" Hook said. "There will be deputies to help through the night."

Andrea paused to sip her water. He could see the burn scars still there on her hands. She smiled over at him.

"Would it be safe? I've heard you lead a dangerous life."

"Well, there's Mixer," he said. "He's a terrific guard dog when he's not napping."

Hook pushed back his chair and took up his coffee. The waiter exited the kitchen wearing his white jacket, his arms stacked with dishes of apple pie à la mode. He set down Ruth's dish and turned to leave, when Lucy threw her doll on the floor and commenced pounding her head on the window.

The waiter froze. Ruth stood, opening her blouse.

"I have nice breasts," she announced.

The waiter, fear on his face, looked over at Hook.

"Want to see them?" Ruth asked, pushing them forward for a more suitable viewing.

The waiter jumped back, his dishes crashing onto the tile floor.

Anna stood. "It's the hook man," she screamed.

Lucy banged the window with her head, the glass thundering and trembling.

"Oh, no," Andrea said.

Struggling to escape, the waiter slipped in the apple pie and ice cream and sprawled onto the floor.

"There aren't any bugs down there," Esther said.

The chef stuck his head out the door, his hat bent at an angle.

"What bugs?" he asked. "We don't have bugs. We had it sprayed. Good God," he said. "Who is that naked woman?"

Andrea pushed back her chair. "It was a very nice dinner, Chef. Thank you. I'll take them back to their rooms now."

"I'll tell the manager about the bugs," he said. "The son of a bitch said he had it sprayed."

The sky filled with stars, and the moon slid high overhead by the time the knock came on the caboose door. Hook opened it to find Andrea gazing up at the celestial display.

"Come in," he said.

"Hook," she said. "Let's sit out here on the steps. The evening is spectacular, and I'm a bit wound up from dinner."

"Sure," he said. "I'll let Mixer take a run. He hasn't killed anything in several days now."

They sat on the steps shoulder to shoulder.

"I'll be so glad when this is over," she said. "When do you think we'll get there?"

"A couple of days, if we don't have more trouble," he said.

"We're all exhausted, and I'm worried about Seth, too."

Hook slipped his arm about her shoulders. "What about him?"

"His dreams," she said. "They're awful for him sometimes, and then he worries about his wife, too."

Hook lit a cigarette. "Seth worries about that scar of his. Thinks his wife won't be able to tolerate it."

"That's ridiculous," she said.

"Things like that can worry a man," he said.

Andrea leaned in against him. "I'm worried about when we get there, Hook, a strange place and all. I don't know if we'll ever get things back to normal."

Hook leaned back on the step, crossing his legs at the ankles.

"Helms thinks Baldwin is acting a little strange," he said.

"Strange?"

"Despondent, you know, like he's thinking about something else all the time. I've noticed it myself. I think Helms doesn't trust his decisions."

"He's one of the most stable men I know," Andrea said. "Excluding you, of course."

"I've been accused of many things," he said. "Stability isn't one of them.

"Doctor Helms tells me that patients can adjust to their sedatives, that the doses sometimes have to be increased to maintain the effect. She thinks that's how Robert Smith managed to overpower Frankie."

"A lot of it depends on how agitated they are."

"Robert Smith was about as agitated as anyone I've come across in a while," he said.

Andrea moved in close. She snuggled into his shoulder like a small bird. Her breath was warm against his neck, and his groin stirred. Her hand rested on his leg like a small, hot iron.

"I've missed you," she said. "So many miles with nothing to do but think."

He lifted her chin, kissing her, her mouth hungry and searching.

"Andrea," he said, catching his breath. "We could go inside. I mean, if that's what you want."

"I want," she said, slipping her hands inside his shirt. He started to get up, but she took his arm, pulling him back. "But not inside," she said. "Here."

"Are you sure? Someone might see?"

"Yes," she said. "Afraid?"

"A little."

She leaned over, whispering in his ear. "Me, too."

Her breath seared into his core, her legs ivory in the moonlight, and his head whirled at the prospects. She rose over him like a warm ocean wave, dropping her head, moaning, clutching the caboose grab iron. And when the head beam of a freight train swept out of the darkness, she neither paused nor hesitated as it bore toward them, its whistle screaming in a blast of heat and steam.

When Andrea had gone into the darkness, Hook leaned against the wall of the caboose to smoke, the day's heat ebbing from the iron porch beneath him.

Whatever misery had been wrought and whatever might lie ahead, he would never forget his stay at the La Posada.

27

Hook FOUND FRENCHY backing the steamer into the coupler of the supply car. Frenchy climbed down the ladder and searched his pocket for a match.

"You look a sight better today than yesterday," Hook said. "But then sleep can only do so much."

Frenchy unwrapped his cigar and slid it under his nose. "Least my eyes match up," he said.

"You get that side rod fixed?"

"In a fashion," he said, snapping his match to life on his overalls button. "They ain't big on replacing parts on these ole buckets, given they're headed to salvage soon enough anyways."

"Kind of like old engineers," Hook said.

Frenchy lit his cigar, the flame of his match lifting and falling, a cloud of smoke encircling his head.

"So," Frenchy said, blowing out his match. "I'm checking out with the operator this morning, see, and he says, 'Did you hear about what happened at the restaurant last night?' And I says, 'No, I been up there in the sleeping rooms making up for listening to that lying bakehead all week.' And he says, 'Those mentals out of Barstow had a riot and broke up all the furniture.' And I says, 'Why would they do that?' and he says, 'Because of them bugs coming out of the kitchen.'"

"That so?" Hook said.

"And I says, 'Bugs?' And he says, 'Yup, cockroaches the size of saddle horses. The chef quit this morning. Says he won't work in no goddang café with bugs.'"

"You been drinking Mexican beer again, Frenchy?"

"So then I stop by the kitchen to see if the operator had it right. He gets things mixed up now and then."

"I noticed that," Hook said.

"And there was the chef madder than ole Billy. And so I says, 'What's the matter, Chef? You still mad about them bugs?' And he says, 'What bugs? I'm mad about that goddang dog.' And I says, 'What dog?' And he says, 'The one snuck in here this morning and ate up five pounds of my breakfast sausage.'"

"That's a mighty sad story," Hook said.

"Guess you wouldn't know anything about that dog, would you, Hook?"

"I hate a sneaking dog," Hook said.

"We'll be pulling out here pretty quick," Frenchy said. "You got that bunch loaded up?"

"Loaded," he said. "What's the schedule?"

"Albuquerque, then Amarillo. Layover there for service and then on to Oklahoma."

"Maybe we can make some time then, huh, Frenchy?"

"You want to make time, you should have booked the Chief, Hook. And then we got that spur off the main line. It's forty miles of rusted iron and weeds. Hell, there ain't been nothing but a doodlebug over that track in twenty years. There's nothing but a short crossing loop outside town, no yard office, no turnabout, and there's a creek trestle the size of the goddang Grand Canyon to boot.

"Even if we make it, which seems unlikely, I'll have to back this kettle all the way back to Tangier. That means I can't see nothing, so I might find a farmer and a couple of cows stuck to the caboose when I get back."

Hook found Mixer lying on the caboose porch. He peeked at Hook over the top of his stomach, which resembled the world globe that once sat on the teacher's desk in Hook's third-grade classroom.

"Damn ole thief," Hook said, pushing him through the door. Mixer groaned and stretched out in the corner.

Hook signaled all clear before climbing into the cupola. The smears of blood down the side of the caboose had covered with dust and dried. As soon as the train made speed, he'd do a turn through to make certain they had everything under control.

Hook watched the countryside open up like an oil painting as they chugged down the alley. Birds swarmed in the cobalt sky like schools of fish, and the sparkling air filled his lungs.

Whatever burdens had accrued faded now, and the hopes of a new place and time emerged. Each departure brought with it the promise of renewal, the chance to change. For it not to be so, to live always in a single place, would be to bury a man alive under a lifetime of mistakes.

When the train had made speed, Hook circulated through the cars. Andrea and Seth were occupied with Esther, who had taken Bertha's seat, having decided that it was larger than her own. Esther hung onto the armrest with both hands, determined not to be ousted.

"Morning," Seth said, prying Esther's fingers loose. "You'll never know how much I appreciate you getting me this job, Hook."

"You need a change, Seth, they could use a hand in the security car. Course smoke breaks are a little hard to come by."

Andrea smiled over at Hook and winked. "We live for our smoke breaks around here, don't we, Seth?"

Seth grinned. "Something tells me my smoke breaks are not as exciting as Hook's."

"I'll talk to you later," Hook said to Andrea.

He found Doctor Baldwin in the supply car digging through the files. Baldwin looked up when Hook came in. Deep lines pulled at the corners of his eyes.

"Doctor Baldwin," Hook said.

Baldwin stacked the files on the corner of his desk.

"I've been going over these personnel files again. I could find nothing to suggest that Frankie Yager might have been a risk. His credentials are all in order."

"Yes," Hook said. "I believe that's what Doctor Helms indicated."

Baldwin rubbed his face. "The complexity of the human mind is at once our greatest asset and our greatest weakness, Mr. Runyon. In the end we know so little about how it functions."

"Things will work out," Hook said.

"I do hope you're right. I'm afraid my energy has hit bottom. I can barely concentrate it seems. For all practical purposes, Doctor Helms has been keeping the security ward together on her own. I don't know what I'd do without her.

"And now Winslow is asking for immediate payment for the meals and the damages incurred by the patients. They're telling me the railroad has declined to pay for the hotel.

"And when I called ahead to report our arrival at Fort Supply, I'm told the town has refused to turn on the utilities at the fort without an advance deposit.

"The fact is, I'm all but broke, and there's been no movement on the insurance problem. On top of that, the mayor has asked that we reconsider locating in the community. They are fearful of the inmates. People are often afraid of what they don't understand."

"We'll soon be there," Hook said. "Once you're settled, things will calm down."

"Yes," he said. "Perhaps you're right. I do hope you're right, Mr. Runyon."

Hook took Mixer for a quick spin at the Albuquerque depot while Frenchy watered the pig, and they were soon on their way to Amarillo. The land leveled out as they steamed into the staked plains of West Texas. No boundary existed between sky or land. A man alone might wander endlessly in the featureless landscape with no way different from the other.

Amarillo first appeared as a dot, a single point in perpetuity, and then as a cluster of buildings huddled on the horizon.

Rather than risk another calamity in the Harvey House, Hook arranged for sandwiches and coffee to be delivered to the cars, assuring the manager that if the railroad didn't reimburse, he would personally do so.

From there, he cut between the depot and the Railway Express Agency to get back to his caboose. He'd gone only a few yards when three men stepped out.

All three wore uniforms and police badges. The tall one, whose gray hair had been carefully groomed, rested his hand on his sidearm.

"You Hook Runyon?" he asked.

Hook looked them over. The visit clearly wasn't social.

"That's right," Hook said. "What can I do for you?"

"I'm the chief of police," he said. "You could surrender your sidearm for a start."

"I'm the railroad dick," Hook said. "What's the problem?"

"Your sidearm first," the chief said. "If you don't mind?"

"You're on railroad property," Hook said.

"I got a warrant for your arrest," he said. "You surrender the weapon, or we'll be forced to take it."

"That could be an uncomfortable situation," Hook said.

"It's your call," the chief said, nodding to the other two, who circled out.

"Okay, Chief," he said, reaching for his weapon with two fingers. "Maybe we can straighten this out."

"Down at the station," the chief said. "More comfortable there."

"I might miss my ride," Hook said.

"We'll give the operator a call from the station," he said. "You got nothing to hide, you'll be on your way."

"Alright," Hook said.

Once at the station, they took him into the interrogation room, a closet-sized space with a single table and no windows. After they'd read him his rights, the chief pulled up a chair and offered him a cigarette.

"Thanks," Hook said. "What's this all about, Chief? I usually find myself on the other side of the table."

The chief lit their cigarettes and leaned back. "I guess we all wind up on the wrong side of the table now and then, Runyon."

"I don't mean to rush you, Chief, but I got a trainload of mental patients waiting back there."

"They found that Robert Smith fellow strung out over five miles of track, Runyon. Fact is, appears there's bodies strewn all the way from Barstow to Amarillo."

"That's all been cleared up, Chief."

"Not quite all," he said.

"We received a call from Barstow just this morning," he said. "A body turned up under the bridge there. Looked like critters had dug it up, they said."

"Can't quite see what that has to do with me, Chief."

"There was a quart jar with a set of dog tags in it. This feller's name was Ethan Berger. Don't suppose you recognize it?"

"A vet we hired on at Baldwin," Hook said. "He never returned after he came down sick."

"This Barstow cop says he was attacked by a one-armed man under the bridge and nearly killed, a railroad bull who frequented the jungle there. He figures that this soldier's death might be connected to that railroad bull somehow."

"That's how he figures it, does he? I whipped that son of a bitch even up, and he's still sore, that's all.

"Look, Chief, Ethan was just a lonely vet living in the jungle. He died from what was probably food poisoning and complications from a belly wound he got in the war. Being Jewish, he needed to be buried within twenty-four hours. I figure the others helped him out a little, that's all."

The chief pushed back his chair, took out his comb, and ran it through his hair.

"That's quite a story."

"The truth often is," Hook said.

"Especially since there was a cross found right there by the grave. A cross would be Christian, I believe."

"I don't know about a cross, Chief. I wasn't there. But I know who was. I hired all those boys out of that jungle to help transfer insane-asylum patients to Oklahoma. They're out there in that train as we speak. I figure they could fill in the details if you'd bring them in."

The chief squashed his cigarette out in the ashtray and stood.

"Alright," he said. "We'll go pick them up. Meanwhile, you can have a rest back there in the tank."

"You best take some men with you to watch those cars," Hook said. "If not, you'll have your hands full. There's nineteen of the meanest sons of bitches this side of Arizona out there, and there's nothing between them and your boys here but a couple pills a day."

———

Hook sat on the bunk in the drunk tank and considered how he'd gone from lawman to inmate in a single hour. A cockroach with antennas the size of a patrol car's raced across the floor and under his bunk.

When he heard voices in the office, he stood up, straining to hear.

"Take a look at that man in there, boys," the chief said. "Tell me if you know him."

Seth stepped to the door and looked in at Hook.

"I ain't sure, Chief. He looks a lot like one of them insane criminals we got on the train. What do you think, Roy?"

Roy peeked in. "You sure he ain't a hysterectomy?" he said.

Santos joined Roy, grinning over his shoulder. "Un hombre loco," he said.

"Look it there," Seth said. "He's got one arm just like ole Hook."

"How'd you like me to choke you to death with it?" Hook said.

"Sounds like Hook, don't it?" Seth said.

"Gentle as a milk cow just like ole Hook," Roy said.

"By God, I believe that *is* Hook," Seth said.

The chief let Hook out and brought him into the room with the others.

"You boys through having your fun, maybe you could tell me if this man had anything to do with Ethan Berger's death?"

"Like we told you, Chief," Seth said. "Hook wasn't nowhere around when Ethan died. Ethan came down with poison sickness he picked up at Baldwin Insane Asylum. Said he'd rather be dead under a bridge than alive in an army hospital.

"We'd all been on the front together in Germany, and Ethan had no family except us. We were his brothers, you might say. He asked us to bury him if he died. He died, and we did."

"How is it he had a cross on his grave, him being Jewish and all?" the chief asked.

Santos shrugged. "Un converso?" he said.

"That Barstow cop claims Runyon here jumped him when he

wasn't looking, beat him up, committed assault and battery. Is that how it happened?"

"I admit he don't look like much of scrapper," Seth said, "but Hook here fought him even up. That cop figured him for an easy mark what with him having one arm. It's a mistake he came to regret."

The chief sat down at his desk and looked over his papers.

"Well, there were no indications of homicide. I figure you boys got no reason to lie about your friend's death. But unlawful disposition of a body is a misdemeanor."

"Who's she?" Roy said.

"We buried plenty on the front," Seth said. "No one ever complained then."

"Look, Chief," Hook said. "Without these boys to help, that train isn't going anywhere. Finding accommodations for all those inmates would be a considerable challenge. Maybe we could let this thing go. We'll be on out of state and out of your hair in a few hours."

The chief stood. "I guess I know where to find you if something comes up," he said.

"Thanks, Chief," Hook said. "Now if I could have my sidearm?"

Outside, Hook lit a cigarette and looked at Seth, Roy, and Santos, who were all grins.

"You bastards might want to work on your memory some," he said, walking off. "Lest you forget who's paying the bills around here."

28

As THEY LABORED east, the sun flared into the thin sky and sent the temperature soaring. Within a few hours, the outfit cars sweltered. The inmates fanned themselves and pushed wet hair from their faces.

Hook made the rounds, handing out encouragement. Andrea dabbed the sweat from her forehead with her sleeve and smiled. But the trip had turned hard. The car stank of bodies and of the old bridge planking that had been used in the floors. The drinking water, the temperature of blood, tasted of chlorine and fishpond. A cadre of flies swarmed at the doors of the latrines.

Hook found Doctor Baldwin in the supply car. He lay on the bunk, his arm dropped over his eyes. He rose slowly when Hook entered.

"Oh, Mr. Runyon," he said. "I'm not feeling well. I've left Doctor Helms on her own, I'm afraid."

"What's the problem?" Hook asked.

He sat up on the edge of his bunk, his head sagging.

"To tell you the truth, I've been getting worse. Maybe it's this heat. My energy has just evaporated. I can hardly hold up my arms at times."

"We're coming up on the last leg," Hook said.

"It's the strain of it all," he said. "Everything has just fallen apart, and I can't get it pulled back together. Sometimes a man can stay on too long, I think. It's difficult to know when that time has come."

"You're doing fine, Doctor Baldwin. Anyone can have a run of bad luck."

"First, we lost Frankie, and now I've fallen ill. We simply must get some help."

Frenchy's whistle rose and fell like a dirge as they moved into the vastness.

"I don't know if I could find anyone," Hook said. "There's nothing but small Texas towns ahead: Panhandle, White Deer, Pampa. From there we move into a remote corner of Oklahoma, where the pickings are even slimmer. These men are ranchers. They come to town rarely and leave as soon as possible."

"We must find someone," he said. "Everyone is worn out, and tempers are short. Frankly, I fear we can't maintain control."

"I'll give it my best," Hook said. "We'll have to water the engine at Panhandle. I'll see if I can find someone. In the meantime is there anything I could do for you?"

"Perhaps a couple of aspirin," he said, rubbing his temples. "I'm blind with a headache."

"Andrea has some," Hook said.

"There in the medical cabinet," Baldwin said. "It's unlocked."

Baldwin groaned as he lay down once again. Hook balanced himself against the wall of the car as he searched through the cabinet. A green bottle sat on the top shelf and, behind it, a tin of aspirin. He took two and started to close the door. Pausing, he took the cap off the green bottle and smelled it. Taking one of the pills, he dropped it into his pocket.

"Okay," he said, pouring a glass of water. "Here are your aspirins. I hope you get to feeling better."

Baldwin nodded, downed the aspirins, and folded back into his bunk once again.

Hook went to the security-ward car, where Doctor Helms met him at the door, her hair hanging in wet strands about her face.

"I've got to have help," she said. "There's no one to take these men to the bathroom. In fact, I haven't gone myself."

"I'll send Roy from the boys' car," he said.

Hook sat in the cupola for a smoke after having helped Santos with the boys for several hours. They'd all been watered and walked and were settled in for a rest.

The wind blew hot through the open window, and sweat trickled from behind his ears. The horizon stretched into infinity, not a tree or bush or bump. Soon they would exit the staked plains, an event capable of lifting one from despair.

Roy had joined Helms but not before filing a complaint. It was, he said, like charging Normandy Beach with a water pistol. But in the end, he went.

Frenchy sounded the arrival of Panhandle, a speck in the distant prairie. The water tower stretched into the sky in a feeble attempt to mark a landscape silenced in monotony.

Hook changed his shirt and combed his hair. The wear of the trip lingered in his eyes.

When they came into the depot, he let Mixer out for a run and alerted Frenchy to his plans for finding help. The operator, a cola between his legs and a bag of peanuts in his hand, listened to Hook.

"Looking for what?" he asked.

"Someone to help us transport mental patients to Oklahoma."

"I think they got all they need," he said.

"It's a paying job," Hook said.

"Does it require sitting a horse?" he asked, pouring his mouth full of peanuts.

"Hasn't so far," Hook said.

"Ain't no one here be interested then," he said. "I guess you could check the Texan Hotel down the street. There's some ole boys nailed to the porch down there."

"Thanks," Hook said. "Don't let Frenchy leave without me."

"Oh, no sir," he said. "We don't want no stranded yard dog in town."

Hook found them on the front porch, just as the operator had said. One fellow, looking somewhat like a pelican, loaded his jaw with loose-leaf tobacco. The other man wore overalls stiff with dirt. His hat sidled over an eye, and his glasses were cloudy with scratches. A red bandanna hung out of his back pocket.

"Mental patients?" the pelican said, squinting up an eye.

"Pay's good," Hook said.

"No sir," he said. "I got calves to be worked. They already got nuts the size of bell clappers."

"What about you?" Hook asked the other man.

"No sir," he said, hooking his thumbs under his overalls strap. "Last time it rained, river took out my gap. I got wire strung out for a mile."

Hook put his foot up on the porch and looked down main street.

"Wouldn't know anyone else might be interested, would you?"

"No sir," the pelican said. "We ain't had much experience with mentals around here, if you don't count the county superintendent."

"Well, thanks anyway, boys," Hook said. At the curb, he turned. "When *was* the last time it rained?" he asked.

The guy in overalls dropped his hands in his pockets and rocked back on his heels as he thought it over.

"Be two years ago next month," he said, grinning. "Give or take a week."

By the time Hook got back to the depot, Frenchy had the pig greased and watered and was busy tending to the side rod. Hook circled the depot.

The waiting room smelled of stale cigar smoke and was completely empty. He ducked into the restroom, splashing water on his face. What he wouldn't give for a cool shower and a rare steak, chased down with a cold glass of Mexican beer.

When he exited onto the platform, he whistled in Mixer and pitched him into the caboose. Steam shot out the engine, clouding into the dry heat.

Hook pulled up on the grab iron and gave Frenchy the green. Frenchy waved back and stuck his head behind the drive wheel for a final check. When Hook turned to light a cigarette, a woman stepped up behind the caboose.

"Hi," she said.

"Hello," Hook said. "What you doing out here, lady?"

"My name's Oatney."

"We're fixing to pull out anytime, Oatney."

She wore a cotton blouse opened far enough to reveal where the Texas sun stopped and the white cleavage of her breasts began. A turquoise stone, hanging from a silver chain, lay like hidden treasure between the mounds of her breasts. The ravages of the Texas sun had taken its share of Oatney's youth.

"You come through often?" she asked.

"Not so much," he said. "You best get back, lady. Sometimes Frenchy doesn't know forward from backward."

"Gets lonely on the road, doesn't it?" she said.

"I got my dog," he said. "Move on your way, lady."

Oatney dropped her hands on her waist and peeked around the side of the caboose.

"Looks like the engineer's tied up," she said. "That caboose looks right cozy. How about inviting me in?"

"That would be against regulations," Hook said.

"Well now, who's telling?"

"I see," he said, searching for a cigarette.

Oatney pulled up on the step. Taking one of his cigarettes, she leaned in for a light, letting her hand linger on Hook's. Turquoise earrings dangled from stretched lobes.

"What happened to your arm?" she asked.

"Careless woman," he said.

"I could make your trip a lot more pleasant, railroader."

"That so?" Hook said. "At what price?"

Oatney smiled, tracing the edges of her mouth with her tongue. "Ten dollars," she said.

Hook reached for his billfold, pulling out his badge.

"Soliciting on railroad property is against the law, Oatney."

Oatney's eyes narrowed. "A yard dog?" she said, backing down the steps. "I'll be on my way."

Hook grabbed her by the wrist and cuffed her up. Frenchy blew his whistle.

"Damn it," Hook said.

The engine bumped ahead, slack rattling down line, snapping the caboose. Hook guided Oatney inside.

"Guess you'll be riding to White Deer, Oatney. We'll fix you up with a stay when we get there."

"Come on, Mister," she said. "Let me go."

Mixer sniffed Oatney's shoes. Deciding that she was one of them, he wagged his tail.

"That's sure an ugly dog," Oatney said.

"Careful what you say in front of him," Hook said. "He's got a sensitive nature."

The train gathered speed out of Panhandle, settling in across the level plain.

"Sit down, Oatney," he said. "It's a fair ride to White Deer."

"Maybe you could take the cuffs off, Mister," she said. "There's nowhere I can go."

Hook took out his cuff key and released her. "If you're thinking about jumping, you might want to reconsider. You'd roll for a mile in that bedrock. We'd be hard put to find what's left."

"Thanks," she said, rubbing her wrists.

"And there's three carloads of mental patients that direction," he said. "You see the problem?"

"What's all the books?" she said.

"They came with the caboose," he said. "Listen, Oatney. That is your name?"

"Yes. Don't you like it?"

"It doesn't matter if I like your name or not. You do realize you're in trouble here?"

"Look, Mister . . ."

"Hook," he said.

"Hook is your name?" she asked.

"You were saying?"

"I do what I have to. I've got no one to open my doors or pay my bills. It's me for it and has been for a good long while now."

"What were you doing in Panhandle?" he asked.

"I came back to help my ex-husband die," she said.

"Right," he said.

"He was afraid. He asked me to come, so I did."

"And what were you doing before you came back?"

"Like I say, I've been taking care of myself the only way I can."

"Turning tricks?"

"That's right. You read all these books?"

"Someone left them."

"What's the dog's name?"

Hook sat down on his bunk. "Mixer."

"That's his name?"

"He likes to fight."

Oatney leaned forward to tie her shoe, her hair, thick as wool, spilling about her face.

"I'm nonviolent," she said, looking up through her bangs. "I'm a Buddhist. Perhaps Mixer just needs more attention."

"Mixer could never be a Buddhist. He loves violence. Anything that gives him attention, he kills.

"What did your husband die from?"

"I don't know," she said. "I didn't ask."

"If you loved him so much, why did you leave in the first place?"

"I didn't say I loved him. I said he asked me to come back and help him die.

"Why do you collect books?"

"I like their permanence," he said.

"May I have another cigarette?" she asked.

Hook gave her a cigarette and lit it. She leaned back against the wall. Oatney reminded him of earth, the tan of her skin.

She studied the end of her cigarette. "Will they put me in jail?"

"Probably, for a little while."

"I have to make a living. It's the only way I know how."

"I know," he said. "You hungry? I have a stick of salami."

"I'm a vegetarian."

"They don't have vegetarians in Panhandle," he said.

"Not anymore," she said. "Do you read the books?"

"Most of them, but I've been busy transferring these mental patients to Oklahoma," he said.

"Why?"

"They had a big fire. A lot of them died."

"How sad. Where are their families?"

"Most don't have any. We've lost two of our employees to boot."

"You don't have carrot sticks, do you?"

"No."

"I was sentenced to thirty days in Amarillo once. I got nits and lost big patches of my hair," she said.

"You should try a different line of work," he said.

"I could give you a blow job," she said.

"It's too bumpy," he said. "You ever work as a nurse or orderly?"

"I *did* an orderly one time."

Hook went out on the caboose platform and watched the track disappear behind them. When he came back in, Oatney was looking through his 1937 edition of Kenneth Roberts's *Northwest Passage*.

"Oatney," he said. "How would you like a job?"

"I thought you said it was too bumpy."

"I mean a real job, working for the Baldwin Insane Asylum?"

"No jail?"

"No, but you'd have to work with mental patients. You up to that?"

"I've dealt with every pervert between El Paso and Pampa," she said.

"Fine. I'm taking you to see Baldwin. Let me do the talking."

After introducing Oatney to the others, he took her to the supply car, where they found Baldwin fast asleep.

Hook shook his shoulder. "How's the headache?" he asked.

Baldwin rubbed at his face. "Better," he said.

"Doctor Baldwin, this is Oatney. I found her in Panhandle. She has agreed to help us out."

"I see," he said, sitting up. "And have you worked with mental patients before, Oatney?"

"Her experience is in research," Hook said. "We are very lucky to have found her."

"Wonderful. And what do you research?" he asked.

"Deviant sexual behavior," Hook said.

"Interesting. Well, we certainly have our share of that. Have you ever worked with violent patients?" he asked.

"On occasion," Oatney said.

"I thought I might put her in the boys' car since Roy is helping out Doctor Helms."

"Yes, yes. I suppose I should take a look at your credentials, Miss . . ."

"Oatney," she said.

"I'm afraid we didn't have time for all that, Doctor Baldwin, and our needs were pressing," Hook said.

"Yes, well, another time. Welcome aboard."

"Thank you," Oatney said. "If you ever need a . . ."

"We really must be on our way, Doctor Baldwin," Hook said. "I'm sure the boys will be delighted with our choice."

29

THE BOYS FOUND Oatney to their liking, as did Santos, who blushed when Oatney dropped her arm around his neck. The boys made goggle eyes and rushed to do her bidding. Oatney, too, flourished in giving them maternal attentions.

Helms only shrugged. "At least now I can go to the bathroom," she said, turning back to her work.

As they left Pampa behind and moved into Oklahoma, the heat rose with each passing mile. The sun scorched overhead, and the flat plains gave way to red gullies and mesquite. Sagebrush cropped from the plains like puffs of smoke. Paddle cactus sprang from the cracked earth, and prairie dogs guarded their holes, watching the skies for danger.

The whistle stops grew smaller and farther between. Listless with heat, the inmates slept in their seats and made trips to the water for drinks.

Somewhere in the midst of all the isolation, Frenchy slowed to a stop. Hook climbed down from the caboose and made his way forward. Frenchy leaned out over his elbow, his cigar parked in the corner of his mouth.

"It's the spur," he said. "Can you throw that switch up there?"

"I'm a yard dog, Frenchy, not a switchman. I only got one arm to boot, or hadn't you noticed that, either?"

"Well, there ain't a goddang switchman within a hundred miles," he said. "I'd do it my own self except you ain't a goddang engineer either, are you?"

"Why don't you see if that bakehead's still alive. Maybe he could climb down and do it."

"I got to have my fireman building fire, Hook. Just throw the goddang switch."

Hook worked at the switch. Clogged with dirt and debris, it took all he had to get it thrown. Sweat dripped off the end of his nose.

"Anything else?" he hollered up at Frenchy.

"It's a slow go from here on out," Frenchy said. "I hope this ole bullgine stays astraddle the track."

"You need any driving advice, just let me know," Hook said.

"Oh, sure. I'll be right back to the caboose for that, alright."

"And give me time to walk my dog, Frenchy."

"We'll just hold up the goddang train so's you can walk your dog," Frenchy said. "I'm sure the railroad wouldn't mind."

"I could put a rope around his neck and walk him out the back of the caboose at the rate this ole bucket moves," Hook said.

They eased off down the spur at walking speed. The cars waddled along like ducks, heat waves spiraling up from their roofs.

Hook checked on everyone and then went to the cupola to have a smoke. He opened the window, letting the hot air out. Clouds gathered on the distant plain, a bank as blue as an ocean wave, and the smell of moisture rode in. Mesquite stretched into the hills, their leaves of lace, their limbs like skeleton fingers reaching up from their graves.

By late afternoon, the heat had stifled all conversation, and the thump of the wheels wormed into their heads. Hook checked on Santos and Oatney to make certain all was well. He needn't have worried. The boys followed Oatney everywhere, and Santos grinned from the back of the car.

He took another trip to the cupola to have a smoke. The cupola served as sanctuary, provided his need for a moment's privacy. Without it, they would have him cuffed and sedated in the security ward along with the rest.

Ahead, a red ravine cracked open the earth like a wound, splitting the countryside in half. Frenchy slowed, the caboose bumping and hauling as he brought her down.

The train eased over the rim, and the air cooled about them, smelling of damp and leaves. The scorched earth gave way to cedar trees, post oak, and elm. Grapevine, searching for sunlight, climbed skyward on the limbs. The trestle reached across the chasm like a giant Tinkertoy.

As they pulled onto the trestle, Hook looked out the window to see the stream below, a silver line twisting up the canyon. The bullgine thumped and churned, and steam rose skyward as she started the ascent on the other side. Black smoke boiled upward obscuring the treetops. Hook lit a cigarette, hoping the while that Frenchy knew what the hell he was doing.

A third of the way up, the train commenced to tremble like a man hefting an enormous weight. The engine hissed and rolled, and her stroke drew down. When she stopped, she sighed, and Frenchy threw the brakes.

For a moment, she hung in the stillness. The backward slide commenced slowly at first, the screech of the brakes filling the canyon, and then like a giant roller coaster, she gained momentum, racing backward toward the trestle with the full weight of the train at their back.

Hook stood, his heart thumping as they shot onto the trestle at breakneck speed. The trestle trembled beneath them, and bits of debris plummeted into the canyon below. As they rose up the opposite slope, she slowed once again, rolling forward until she came to a stop at the bottom.

Hook dabbed the sweat from his forehead and climbed out. Frenchy walked the trestle toward Hook, rubbing his neck with his bandanna. Andrea and Seth and the others stuck their heads out the doors.

"What the hell was that all about?" Hook asked Frenchy as he approached.

Frenchy searched for a cigar. He cupped his match and lit it before speaking.

"We can't go forward or backward or in between," he said.

"What do you mean?"

"I mean we're stuck," he said. "She don't have the muscle to get out of this ditch. Simple as that."

Andrea came down onto the step. "What's the matter, Hook?"

"Frenchy says we're stuck, meaning this ole smoke pot can't get us out of this hole."

"What will we do?" she asked.

"Well, now," Hook said. "You'll have to ask the engineer here. He's the expert on driving."

Andrea looked at Frenchy.

"Well," Frenchy said. "We can't get a pusher out here. So, we either lighten the load, or we figure on living out our days in this here canyon."

"What do you mean lighten the load?" Hook asked.

"Uncouple a few of these cars," he said. "I'll run the others in to the crossing loop. Come back for the rest."

"And which cars had you figured on abandoning?" Hook asked.

Frenchy dropped the ash of his cigar onto the track.

"The last two, Hook. Even a goddang yard dog ought figure that one out."

"The caboose and the women's car?"

"That would be the last two by my count, wouldn't it?"

Hook walked to the edge of the ravine and back. "You're going to leave me and these women out here in the middle of nowhere? And for how long?"

"Well, now, I can't be certain about that," Frenchy said. "Given no more breakdowns, it shouldn't take all that long."

"You do realize we don't have food, and the water won't last in this heat?"

"The longer I stay and listen to you cry, the longer it's going to be before I get back, Hook."

Hook pitched a rock into the canyon. He never heard it hit bottom.

"You told Baldwin?" he asked.

"I'm telling *you*," he said. "Baldwin is your job."

Baldwin only nodded before collapsing back in his bunk. Hook closed the door and went out to watch Frenchy uncouple the cars. After setting the hand brakes on the caboose and the women's car, Frenchy climbed into the engine cab and brought up a full head of steam.

He goosed the bullgine, filling the canyon with her roar, and made a hard run across the trestle. Her drivers churned, slipping and catching against the rails as they made for the hill ahead. And when he'd topped the rim, Frenchy hung his arm out the cab, waving until they disappeared from sight.

The silence of the prairie pressed in about them as they listened to the whistle of the engine somewhere in the distance.

Seth unloaded the women and moved them to the far end of the trestle and under a giant elm. Hook carried out water and whatever food he could scrounge from the caboose. Mixer ran the tracks in search of something to kill, finally curling in the shade of the outfit car for a nap.

By dusk, they'd settled in under the tree and built a fire for company. Thunderheads had grown throughout the day's heat and now boiled skyward like giant cotton balls. Seth dragged in logs for sitting on.

"How long you think it will take Frenchy to get back?" he asked Hook.

"Did you ever try to get a straight answer out of Frenchy?" he said.

"Couldn't be any harder than getting one from a yard dog," Seth said.

Andrea combed the nettles out of Ruth's hair and rebuttoned her blouse, which was one buttonhole off. Anna, concerned about the wilderness at her back, sat as far away from Hook as she dared but close enough to still enjoy the protection of the fire. Lucy sat cross-legged and rocked her doll, humming something obscure the whole time. Esther had spotted an ant den and worked at it with a stick.

Hook lay on his side, watching the thunderheads clip across the sky. Soon the sun dropped behind the canyon wall, and a cool dampness settled in about them. Lightning flickered from deep in the heart of the storm, and thunder rumbled off. Seth poked the fire, and embers lifted upward on the column of heat.

"I'm sure hungry," he said. "I wonder how long Frenchy's going to be?"

"Stop, Seth," Hook said. "There's nothing to eat."

"We could eat that dog," Seth said.

"Go ahead and try," Hook said.

"Esther's digging ants," Ruth said.

"Don't start," Andrea said.

"I don't want to eat dog," Lucy said, rocking.

Hook took out his pocketknife to sharpen sticks to heat up the salami he'd found.

"He's going to kill me with his knife," Anna said.

"No he's not," Andrea said. "He's fixing sticks."

"I don't like to eat sticks," Lucy said.

"God," Andrea said.

Ruth stood. "I have nice . . ."

"Ruth," Andrea said. "You say that again, we'll roast *you* over the fire."

Hook gave his knife to Andrea to cut up the salami. She passed the pieces around until they were gone. Darkness fell, and heat lightning sputtered here and there in the distance.

"Are there Indians at the fort?" Bertha asked.

"No," Hook said. "There used to be long ago."

"Are they all old now?" Esther asked.

"Very old," Hook said. "There's no need to worry. You have Seth to protect you."

"They cut Seth's face open," Esther said.

"Bertha puts her hand in Seth's pocket," Lucy said.

"No I don't," Bertha said.

The first splashes of rain slapped the ground around them, and a burst of cold wind swept through the canyon.

"I think it's going to rain," Hook said. "We better get inside."

No sooner had he spoken when the sky opened. Wind whipped the fire and sent embers flying into the night. Wet and shivering, they all crowded into the car. At first only a few scattered hailstones pinged the roof, but within moments the stones drove in from the sky as big as fists. The women held one another and covered their heads with their arms. Gusts of wind rocked the outfit car, driving rain through the window cracks and onto the floor.

The car pitched and rolled under the gusts of wind, and lightning lit the canyon in fluorescent light. Seth sat at the end of the car, his jaw clinched. Each time a clap of thunder rolled down the canyon, he jumped, covering his head with his arms.

All night the storm raged, wave after wave rolling across the plains. Not until dawn broke did the wind subside. As they climbed from the car, the sun broke to a clear sky. Birds chirped high in the treetops, and squirrels leaped from limb to limb like acrobats.

Seth built the fire, and they all gathered about to dry out. The sun lit the canyon in orange, and the smell of the campfire cheered them all. When they heard the chug of Frenchy's steamer breaking in the distance, the women giggled and locked their arms.

Hook and Andrea walked down the tracks for a moment together while Seth loaded the women into the car. They sat on a fallen tree and breathed in the rain-cleaned morning.

"We'll soon be there," Andrea said. "And there's much to be done. Oh," she said, reaching in her pocket. "I forgot to give you your knife back."

"Thanks," he said.

"We've not nearly enough help yet," she said. "And who knows what condition the facility is in."

"Baldwin is doing poorly," Hook said. "He's not handling the pressure well."

"There's always Doctor Helms, I suppose," she said. "She's quite efficient."

He dropped his knife into his pocket. "Oh, wait," he said. "I took this pill from the medicine cabinet in supply. I thought maybe you could identify it for me?"

Frenchy's engine labored into sight. Black smoke boiled skyward as she steamed in backward toward them.

Andrea turned the pill in her hand. Picking it up, she nibbled at its corner.

Glancing over at him, she shrugged. "It's just a sugar pill, Hook, a placebo."

30

DOCTOR HELMS STUCK her head out of the security-ward car as Frenchy backed into the crossing loop outside Fort Supply.

"Finally," she said to Hook. "Do you have any idea how hot it is in here?"

"Some," Hook said. "What about transportation to the fort?"

"None," she said. "That would make too much sense, wouldn't it?"

"Then how do we get all these people there?"

"That's Doctor Baldwin's department, or should be."

"Look, Doctor Helms, my job is finished here."

"Well," she said, looking down the tracks, "I suppose we could walk. You can see the fort. You do understand that these men have been under sedation a long time. I would hate to think how the railroad would fare if one should escape."

Hook pursed his lips. "One did escape as I recall.

"I'll talk to Frenchy."

He followed Frenchy back to the engine.

"We're going to have to walk in, Frenchy. There's no transportation."

Frenchy squinted up at the sun. "Good planning. How long you figure it will take?"

"Most of the day. I can't be sure."

"They're hollering for these outfit cars, Hook. They got a crew put up in a hotel. We got to get back soon."

"You think this ole can will make that grade over the trestle?"

Frenchy fished a cigar out of his pocket. "Well, she'll be some lighter without passengers, but I can't be sure. We can split the load like before if we have to."

Hook shaded his eyes with his hand. Fort Supply loomed in the distance like a haunted castle. The town spread out at its base. Already the heat quivered up from the tracks, and the buzz of locusts rose and fell about them.

"It's walk or turn them loose," he said.

"There's enough trouble in this world without yard dogs and mentals running around loose," Frenchy said. "Me and the bakehead will catch a wink in the supply car. We are overdue anyway. But I can't wait forever."

"Thanks," Hook said. "I'll get back soon as I can. Check on Mixer, will you? I wouldn't want him to overheat."

"Oh, hell no, we wouldn't want anything to happen to that goddang killer dog."

On the way back, Hook found Oatney sitting on the step of the boys' car. She'd unbuttoned her blouse against the heat. Perspiration shined on her forehead and in the depths of her cleavage.

"We going to sit here and die or what?" she asked.

Hook gave her a cigarette and took one for himself. He leaned over to light it and could feel the heat from her body.

"We're going to walk them in," he said.

"Walk?"

"It's not that far," he said. "Help Santos get ready, and we'll gather up down there at the caboose."

Oatney leaned back on the step, her bosoms rolling like ocean waves.

"It isn't safe, Hook," she said. "Those men are dangerous."

"I know," Hook said. "But we can't leave them here. Anyway, it isn't so far."

From there, he searched out Andrea.

"Couldn't they have lined up transportation?" Andrea asked.

Hook kicked his foot up on the car step and placed his elbow onto his knee. Despite the heat, Andrea's eyes snapped with energy.

"To tell you the truth, Baldwin isn't hitting on all cylinders," he said.

"What do you mean?"

"Just out of it."

Andrea locked her hands behind her head and looked out at the fort. Her lean stomach peeked from under her blouse.

"He's been under a lot of pressure, I guess." She stretched and slipped her hand into Hook's. "You are going with us, aren't you?"

"It's not my business now, you know. But Frenchy said he'd wait."

Andrea smiled. "Things will be alright with you along."

"Let's hope. Tell Seth to move to the end of the train. We'll strike out from there."

At the top of the steps, Andrea turned. "I'll miss our smoke breaks," she said.

"Yeah," he said. "Me, too."

First came Seth and Andrea with the women, all carrying their supplies and blankets. The heat beat on the women's bare heads, and sweat trickled down their cheeks. Bertha walked next to Seth, her arm looped through his. Lucy snapped her fingers and swung her doll by its hands.

"We're here," Andrea said, "in a fashion."

"Where are the Indians?" Bertha asked.

"There aren't any," Andrea said.

"Did they die of old age?" Esther asked.

"Yes," Andrea said.

"They cut Seth's face," Esther said.

Just then Doctor Helms came from down the line. The men shuffled along behind her, their hands cuffed. Roy and Doctor Baldwin brought up the rear. Baldwin's arms drooped at his sides, and his head hung down.

Now and again, one of the men would stop as if he'd forgotten something, forgotten perhaps what the next move should be. They gathered at the side of the tracks away from the women. Sweat ringed their necks and underarms.

Oatney and Santos assembled on the opposite side with the boys. Oatney had taken the lead, and she now stood with one foot propped on the rail, her arm spiked on her waist. Her silver necklace shimmered in the sunlight. She reminded Hook of some exotic Indian princess instead of a rail hooker.

"Okay," Hook said, waving his arm above his head. "Here we go."

They headed for town, looking like some bizarre circus parade, the women circling about, the boys quiet with anxiety, the men hobbling along like zombies.

As they approached the main part of town, Hook spotted a crowd gathered near the gas station. The man who stepped out wore a full gray beard and leaned forward at the waist. He held up his hand for them to stop.

"What's the problem?" Hook asked.

"My name's Herbert Crumling. I'm mayor of this here town. This is Nadine," he said, pointing to a woman in her fifties, who was studying Hook from a distance. "She runs the drugstore and pharmacy. Shorty over there owns this filling station. These other folks are concerned citizenry."

Shorty pushed a greased-stained ball cap to the rear of his head. His two front teeth were yellow with nicotine, and the mole on his nose looked like a dead spider.

"Concerned about what?" Hook asked.

"About these here people," Crumling said.

"We're moving into the fort," Hook said. "There's going to be a new hospital in town."

"Now," the mayor said, hooking his thumbs into his waistband, "that's what we wanted to talk about. We had a town meeting, you see. Fact is, we've concerns about these folks, given the general nature of things, if you know what I mean."

Andrea looked at Baldwin, who didn't respond. She stepped forward.

"That facility has been purchased by us for a mental institution," she said. "We've every right to move in."

Ruth started to say something, and Andrea took hold of her arm.

"You may have a right," Mayor Crumling said, "but it can be uncomfortable living where you ain't welcome."

"It's a forty-mile drive for medications," Nadine said.

The men behind Nadine grumbled their approval and stirred about. Andrea glanced over at Hook, alarm on her face.

Shorty stuck a toothpick in his mouth. "Same with gas. Don't know if I can keep enough on hand to take care of my regulars and that looney bin out there, too."

Hook lit a cigarette and looked back over at the inmates. They were silent, their eyes trained on him. He turned back to the citizens of Fort Supply.

"By the looks of things, times might be a little hard around here," he said.

Shorty nodded his head. "The dang highway passed us up. I can remember when this town hopped. I trucked in gas twice a week."

"We're three short on the town council," the mayor said. "Ben Hadley and Ross Dicks fought over trash rates for three years. Now, folks have to haul it to the dump their own damn selves."

"Don't know if you folks have thought about it," Hook said. "But this hospital will be hiring all kinds of help: cooks, guards, groundskeepers, even orderlies. There's likely to be a pretty good boost in tax revenue, too."

"They be hiring local?" Shorty asked.

Hook looked over at Baldwin. "That's been our intent all along," Baldwin said.

"Give us a couple days to settle in," Hook said. "We'll post a notice at the post office for interviews."

Mayor Crumling glanced over at Shorty and Nadine. "Well, now," he said. "We're a friendly enough town and wouldn't want you to think otherwise."

"I can see that you are," Hook said. "And we certainly appreciate it. We've been wondering about the utilities out to the fort."

"They're on city hookup," the mayor said. "Shorty here doubles up on working the utilities."

"We haven't had a chance to get money down just yet," Hook said.

"Don't worry about that," Crumling said. "I figure you ain't going nowhere. We'll have them on by day's end tomorrow."

"Thanks," Hook said. "It's a comfort to know we're moving into such a fine town. We'll be interviewing for jobs soon."

As they moved out, the citizens parted way, gawking at the mentals, figuring which job might best fit their needs.

As the procession approached the fort, they came into a long drive bordered on both sides by large elms. All the buildings were of red brick with faded white veranda porches. An old guardhouse stood solid against the elements, perhaps the best structure on the grounds. Most of the cells had been located on the second floor. To the far side was the ordnance sergeant's quarters and the officers' quarters. The barracks were three, two of which leaned dangerously to the north.

Doctor Helms approached Hook. "The obvious choice for the security-ward is the guardhouse. Perhaps you and the others could help me get them settled?"

"Alright," Hook said.

Andrea and the others waited in the shade while Hook, Roy, and Doctor Helms moved the men into the upstairs cells of the guardhouse. Baldwin sat in the shade of the porch, his face pale and his eyes listless.

Though the place smelled of dust and rat droppings, the guardhouse had weathered well. The iron doors slid shut with a clang, and, when the last man had been locked in, Doctor Helms found an old chair downstairs and sat in it.

"I'll take them off the heavy meds now," she said. "I can handle things by myself from here. We'll work at cleaning the place up later."

"We'll go help the others," Hook said.

"Yes," she said, wiping her brow with her dress tail. "Put me in the officers' quarters; Andrea and the other orderlies can stay in the ordnance sergeant's quarters. The remaining inmates can be housed in the barracks."

"What about Doctor Baldwin?" Hook asked.

"I'll take care of him in my quarters. His medications need attention."

Hook nodded for Roy to follow him.

"Mr. Runyon," Doctor Helms said. "When things have settled down, I really must talk to you about Doctor Baldwin. I'm afraid some difficult decisions have to be made."

"Doctor Helms, my duties are related to railroad security. The conduct of your institution is really not under my authority. Frenchy says he'll leave me at track's edge if I don't wind things up pretty quickly."

"Doctor Baldwin has slipped even farther into depression, you see. If there's no improvement . . . Given no other alternative, it looks as if I'll be taking over."

"I'll go help the others, Doctor Helms, and be on my way."

He found Andrea and the girls nearly asleep under the elms. He took them to the quarters, where they searched out rooms and made beds as best they could. Transoms over the doors were the single source of fresh air in the sweltering rooms, and the women fanned themselves against the heat.

Santos and Oatney took the boys to the upper floor, where Oatney spent an hour digging the remains of an owl's nest from out of the chimney.

When all had at last settled down, Hook searched out Andrea. Cobwebs clung to her clothes, and a black smudge decorated the end of her nose. They moved around the corner of the barracks to talk and take refuge from the sun. Sagebrush and prairie grass stretched to the sky behind them.

"Frenchy is waiting on me," he said.

Andrea's eyes welled. "You're going to leave now?"

"Andrea, would it surprise you to know that Doctor Helms has contacted the American Board of Psychiatry about Doctor Baldwin?"

Andrea paused. "They don't always agree about things. Sometimes Doctor Baldwin lets his emotions influence his decisions. Doctor Helms is all business all the time."

"I better go now," he said.

"Will I see you again?"

"Yes."

She leaned into him. "But when?"

"As soon as possible."

"It's scary here alone," she said. "So far away from everything."

"I'm sure Seth and the others will be here, for a while at least."

He tipped her chin up with his finger and kissed her.

"You be careful, Andrea."

"I'll be careful. Hook," she said, taking his hand. "Come back soon."

Frenchy had the bullgine up and the cars coupled by the time Hook got there. Frenchy climbed down from the cab to check the side rod. "It's about time," he said. "I didn't sleep a wink in that goddang supply car. That bakehead snores like a trip-hammer, and it was too hot to die."

"I'll be in the bouncer," Hook said. "Try not to run this steam pot into the gorge, will you?"

"Oh, sure, sure," Frenchy said. "I sure as hell need your advice, don't I?"

"Did you water my dog?"

"He humped my leg the whole time. Why don't you get the poor son of a bitch a friend?"

"Maybe you ought to take a bath once in a while."

"I intend to if I ever get back to civilization."

Frenchy climbed up on the ladder, leaning back. "What about that stuff in the supply car?"

"What stuff?"

"All them dang records of Baldwin's."

Hook looked down line. "Damn," he said. "They didn't take their records?"

"Given their planning skills, they ought go into law enforcement," Frenchy said.

Hook lit a cigarette and watched the buzzards circle in the blue.

"Frenchy," he said. "Without that caboose on, you figure you could make that grade the first run?"

"Guaranteed," he said. "What the hell you up to, Hook?"

"Move those records into the bouncer, Frenchy, and uncouple her from the train. I'm staying here."

31

HOOK WATCHED THE train disappear into the prairie, black smoke lifting into the blue. When it had faded, the silence pressed in. He let Mixer out of the caboose and waited as he sniffed and marked out his territory.

"Come on, Mixer," he said. "I've got to call Eddie."

He found a pay phone at Shorty's filling station and broke out a dollar's worth of change. Lighting a cigarette, he waited for Eddie to answer.

"What do you mean you are still there?" Eddie asked.

"Frenchy couldn't make the grade with the bouncer on," Hook said. "And I knew what a hurry you were in to get the outfit cars rolling."

"Goddang it, Hook, couldn't you have left the caboose and come back with the train?"

"Hell, Eddie," he said. "You wouldn't leave *your* house behind, would you?"

"I don't know what you're up to," Eddie said. "But Topeka's got that hearing scheduled in a couple weeks. You damn well better be there for it."

"The Chief doesn't run out here, Eddie. How am I supposed to get there?"

"I suggest you catch a bus, walk if you have to, but if you don't show up for that hearing, you can check in your card. There's not a damn thing I can do for you."

Hook dropped his cigarette on the floor and squashed it out with his foot. Mixer looked at him through the door of the phone booth.

"Alright, Eddie, I'll catch a bus out, but don't blame me if the pickpockets move in while I'm playing footsie with the disciplinary board."

When he stepped out of the booth, Shorty waved him over to the station.

"Jeez," he said. "That's an ugly dog, even for these parts."

"He has a winning personality," Hook said. "When do you figure to have the water on out to the fort?"

"Well," he said, burying his hands in his pockets, "them lines out there ain't been used in quite a spell. You might have leaks sprouting up here and there."

"I'll leave all that to the experts, Shorty," he said. "I'm just a goddang yard dog and not a very good one at that."

"Yes sir," Shorty said, clamping a cigarette between his teeth. "The pressure's up, and the fort's downhill. Don't see a major problem."

"You should think about applying for a maintenance job out there."

"Yes sir. I've been giving that some thought, alright. Pumping gas ain't what it used to be."

Andrea laid her broom down and covered her mouth with her hands. Her eyes lit up, and a smile spread across her face.

"Hook, what are you doing here?" she asked.

"Frenchy wasn't sure he could make the grade with the caboose on, so I decided to stay behind."

"Wonderful," she said. "You'll be staying here awhile, then?"

"Eddie's insisting I make the hearing in Topeka. In the meantime, maybe I can help out."

"I can use all the help I can get."

"Let me check in with Helms, and I'll be back."

Hook found Doctor Helms going into the guardhouse, and he followed her in. Anguished sounds emanated from the cells, and molten eyes peered through the bars. Van Diefendorf, his skin as translucent as a newborn, stared out from under his blond brows. Without the effects of the chloral hydrate, the evils had reared up from out of the darkness.

The heat seeped from the thick walls, and the rooms stank of perspiration. Van Diefendorf paced back and forth, the wildness apparent in every jerk and pause. He turned about, rubbing at his crotch, his tongue darting from his mouth like a wild animal.

"I thought you left?" Doctor Helms said to Hook.

"Frenchy didn't think he could make it up the grade with the caboose."

"I see," she said, taking up her chair. She crossed her legs, long and cylindrical, and the white of her thighs darkened under the folds of her dress.

"I'll be taking a bus out, first chance," he said. "How's Doctor Baldwin?"

Before she could answer, Roy came in with his arms loaded with blankets.

"Lordee, the law is here," he said.

"It's only the unlawful fears the law, Roy," Hook said.

"It's only the unlawful knows how fearful the law is," Roy said. "I thought you'd be on your way to civilization by now."

"Soon," Hook said. "How are you doing?"

"Thing is," Roy said, pushing back his hat, "I'm getting used to these boys, and that's a right scary thought."

"Maybe you have a lot in common."

Roy dropped the blankets in the corner. "That's just it. Me and these boys see eye to eye on a good many things, including our estimation of yard dogs."

Hook turned to Helms. "About Doctor Baldwin?"

"He's in the officers' quarters," Helms said, adjusting her skirt. "Doctor Baldwin is not doing well, as you know."

"I'll stop by," Hook said. "Maybe cheer him up."

Doctor Baldwin lay in a makeshift bunk, his arm drooped over his eyes.

"Doctor Baldwin," Hook said.

At first Baldwin didn't answer. But then he groaned and turned onto his side.

"It's you," he said, wiping at his face with his hand. "For a minute, I thought we were still on the train."

Hook knelt at his side. Baldwin smelled of sweat and sick. "How are you feeling?"

"I can't get enough sleep," he said. "I'm worn out."

"Is there anything I can do?"

He pulled himself up on an elbow and then lay back down. "Nothing," he said. "Doctor Helms brought me soup earlier. How's the transfer going?"

"We'll have utilities on soon. In the meantime, everyone is trying to get the place cleaned up. This fort has been empty for a good many years."

When he looked over, Baldwin had fallen asleep, so Hook slipped on out.

Andrea had sent Seth to grub out the ordnance sergeant's quarters, and she had put the women to sweeping out rooms in the barracks. Santos, Oatney, and the boys had nearly completed their cleanup and were picking up stray limbs from the sidewalks.

Hook helped Andrea set up the bunks that Helms had located in the supply shack. The heat mounted throughout the day, and a hot wind blasted in from the southwest. Years of dust had settled into every cranny, and scorpions scurried about, their pinchers raised in defiance. Spring storms had loosened boards from porch roofs and scattered them about the grounds.

After Helms managed to get credit at the local bank, Roy walked to the village, where he bought a truck from Shorty to bring in groceries from the nearby city of Woodward. He returned with sacks of potatoes, slabs of bacon, and a dozen crates of eggs. Much to Helms's chagrin, he'd purchased three five-gallon cans of milk, which were already tainted from the heat by the time he returned.

At noon they ate egg sandwiches and swilled tepid milk. By that afternoon their lips cracked from the dryness, and their eyes burned against the hot winds.

Andrea and Hook took a break under the shade of an elm while the girls finished up the cleaning.

A scream suddenly issued from out of the barracks, and they both stood, looking at each other.

"Oh, Lord," Andrea said. "Something's happened."

When they reached the barracks, they found Seth bent over Anna. Her wails reverberated in the barren room and sent chills down Hook's spine. He knelt next to Seth.

"What's happened?" he asked.

Seth pointed to the porch board that was firmly attached to the bottom of Anna's foot. The nail had exited between her toes, and blood pooled on top of her foot.

"Oh my God," Andrea said.

"He stuck me with his hook," Anna wailed.

"We'll have to get it out," Andrea said.

"I can't stand hearing a woman cry," Seth said.

"He's killed me," Anna wailed. "Oh, oh, oh."

"How do we get it off?" Hook asked.

"Put your foot on the board, and I'll pull her leg up," Andrea said.

"I think I'm going to be sick," Seth said.

"Go call a doctor, Seth," Andrea said.

"The hook did it to me," Anna cried.

"Okay," Hook said, placing both of his feet on the plank. "But do it fast."

"Yeow!" Anna screamed. "It hurts. It hurts."

Andrea took hold of Anna's leg and on the count of three yanked her foot free from the board.

Anna slumped onto Hook's shoulder. Together, Hook and Andrea dragged her into the officers' quarters. When they came in, Baldwin lifted onto an elbow but then turned back to his sleep.

By the time the doctor and Seth arrived from town, Anna's toes had swollen into a strut, and red streaks shot up her leg. The doctor, a man in his fifties with glasses thick as milk bottles, administered injections. He took a pill from his stock and peered up at them.

"Puncture wounds can turn nasty," he said. "It's hard to say where that nail's been. I'm sending an ambulance out to pick her up, so we can keep a watch on her for a few days."

He closed his bag and walked to the bunk where Baldwin lay. After a few moments, he went to the door. Hook followed him out.

The doctor turned. "About that man in there?"

"That's Doctor Baldwin, owner of this place, and he hasn't been doing well."

"So I can see."

"Perhaps you could take a look at him while you're here?"

"Well," he said.

"He's been under considerable stress," Hook said. "He isn't coming around like he should."

"Sure," he said. "I guess I can take a look."

Andrea and Hook waited on the porch steps. When the doctor came out, he sat down on the railing. He took off his glasses and wiped them clean with his handkerchief.

"I can't quite make it out," he said. "There's some confusion and malaise, and his heartbeat is irregular. The odd thing is that his body temperature is low." He slipped his glasses back on and folded his handkerchief into his pocket. "There's no obvious underlying cause that I can see."

"What should we do?" Andrea asked.

The doctor picked up his bag. "I would recommend a few days in the hospital. We could run some tests. Perhaps it's nothing more than stress, but I think it prudent to check it out. I'll have the ambulance pick up both him and the girl."

"Thanks, Doctor," Hook said. "I'll inform Doctor Helms."

"What?" Helms said, peering over her glasses. "And who is supposed to run things around here in the meantime?"

Hook shrugged. "The same person who's been running things all along, Doctor Helms. Doctor Baldwin has hardly been able. Anyway, the doctor felt it necessary."

Helms walked to the window, which was covered with hand-forged bars.

"I should have been consulted," she said.

"I had no idea you would object to his medical care," Hook said.

"That's not the issue. There were a great many things to consider. This place doesn't run itself, you know."

"Perhaps it *was* inconsiderate."

"The fact is, I think it's time that Doctor Baldwin be removed from his responsibilities so that we can move on with things."

"Perhaps with medical attention, he will improve?"

She turned. "I simply don't have the time to attend to this institution and address Doctor Baldwin's personal problems."

Hook reached for the door. "I told the locals a job interview schedule would be posted."

"And so it will be," she said.

"Oh," he said, "the personnel records were left behind in the supply car. I have them stored in my caboose."

"See that they are delivered. We'll need them for the interviews."

Hook closed the door behind him.

When the water and electricity came on later that afternoon, a shout went up from the barracks. Baths were in order, and clothes were washed and dried. The women scurried about with their hair stacked on their heads and towels under their arms. And as evening fell, the locusts hummed in the cool, and the inmates laughed from their rooms.

When the hot winds had abated, Hook and Andrea walked about the old fort. Shadows stretched from the ancient buildings, and ghosts from the past whispered in the treetops. Mixer roamed out, sometimes disappearing from sight, only to race back from the prairie at full speed, his tongue lolling from his mouth.

At the far side of the grounds, they came upon a spring. Water bubbled up from its sandy bottom and spilled into the rocks below. They sat on the bank and put their feet into the frigid waters. Andrea leaned against him and laughed, her toes curling with the cold. Her hair shined in the red of sunset.

As dusk fell they walked through the fort cemetery, the old headstones leaning with age. They read names long since forgotten to the years. Andrea knelt at each, running her fingers over the time-worn letters. At a young corporal's grave, she paused for the longest moment, counting the years between birth and death. They walked on through the evening then to find Hook's caboose, still sitting on the crossing loop.

Hook lit the kerosene lantern while Andrea settled in among his books. She picked them up, thumbing through their pages, stacking them to the side.

"This is the first time I've been away from the women for days," she said. "I didn't realize how exhausting it's been."

"You've done a great job," he said.

Andrea leaned back, her face aglow in the soft light of the lantern.

"I was doubtful of you at the start, you know," she said.

"Why so?"

"Railroaders enjoy a rowdy reputation, especially yard dogs."

"And now?"

"Now I know why."

Hook slipped down on the floor next to her, the first stars of evening winking through the windows of the cupola.

"I'll make it up to you," he said.

He turned the lantern down, and she nuzzled into him, her fingers falling cool and delicate on his ear. He kissed her mouth, the soft pockets of her throat, her heartbeat tripping beneath his lips.

Slipping from their clothes, they pushed aside the books. "Hook," she whispered, her voice like a warm spring rain in the coolness of the evening.

Afterward, they lay together. They dozed and then dressed in the dim light of the lantern. Hook smoked and whistled Mixer in from the darkness.

Andrea buttoned her blouse and combed her hair back with her fingers.

"We really must be getting back," she said. "They will be wondering."

"I nearly forgot," he said. "Helms wants the personnel files brought to the guardhouse."

"Files?"

"These," he said, sliding the box over. "They were left in the supply car."

Mixer stepped into Andrea's lap, and she pushed him back. "Look, it's Doctor Helms's personnel file."

Hook opened the first page of the file. "It says here she graduated with an undergraduate degree from Moorehead State University, *summa cum laude*."

"With honors, of course," Andrea said.

"Should I go on?"

"The files are confidential, Hook."

"And I suppose we mustn't break the law?" he said.

"No," she said, putting the file back into the box. "We mustn't."

32

THE LOCALS SHOWED up for the interviews in force, a line stretching from the guardhouse to the fort gate. The mayor and Shorty led the way. By the end of the day, the Baldwin Insane Asylum was once again fully staffed, albeit with people who didn't have a clue what awaited them.

Santos and Roy asked Hook if he could arrange for them to stay on. Both Oatney and Seth were undecided. Seth did not sleep well, sometimes not at all, roaming about the fort like a lost ghost. Oatney, on the other hand, found her job less exciting and less profitable than what she was accustomed to.

Hook spent his days with whatever needed to be done. While arranging rooms in the barracks, he discovered a complete set of fort records dating back to the end of the Indian wars. Looking for a place to store them, he discovered a door under the stairwell that led into a basement room.

Working his way down the steps, he pushed away the spider-webs that crisscrossed the stairwell. Silence reigned behind the thickness of the stone walls. A forged ring with a single skeleton key hung on the wall next to the door.

Dank, cool air drifted up from the darkness, and crickets leaped about like popcorn. He shined his light around, finding two cells, each no larger than a crypt. Hand-forged bars enclosed the cells, and iron beds hung by chains from the walls. Graffiti filled every available space, and black mold grew from between the stones.

Such a place could have had only one purpose, to punish. Even now in all its neglect and dilapidation, it reeked of loneliness and grief.

He stacked the boxes on one of the bunks and made his way back up. Once outside, he dusted the webs from his front and breathed in the sun-warmed air. In a hundred years so little had changed. Upstairs, men still sat in closed cells, their soulless eyes like pools of stilled water, and the guardhouse still stood indifferent to the pain it bore within.

A week in, Doctor Helms returned from the hospital with Anna, whose toes had turned green as copper patina. Anna's eyes widened when she saw Hook. She hunkered behind Doctor Helms and then moved into the group of women who greeted her with restrained enthusiasm.

Hook put out his cigarette. "How did you find Doctor Baldwin?" he asked.

"Quite the same, I'm afraid," Helms said. "His condition appears more mental than physical, though the doctor is determined to administer every possible test."

"Well, if that's what's needed."

"I'll be assuming his duties, though for all practical matters, I've assumed them for some time now. It's quite perfunctory at this point."

"But unfortunate for Doctor Baldwin," Hook said.

"We are fully staffed now, so I see no reason that you should have to stay on longer, Mr. Runyon.

"Training sessions will be starting for the new staff. I've asked Andrea to assist with the security ward. She'll be quite busy."

"I have to be in Topeka in a few days," Hook said. "I'll be catching the bus out. Roy and Santos have asked to stay on. I hope you can find room for them."

"I see no reason why not. And what about Seth and Oatney?" she asked.

"I don't know. I'll find out," he said.

Oatney and Seth sat under an elm drinking from a pitcher of springwater. Oatney had unbuttoned her blouse, and perspiration glistened between her breasts.

"Helms asked what your plans are," Hook said. "She says you can stay on if you've a mind to."

Seth tipped up his glass. Water dripped from his chin as he drained it. He rolled over on his side and hooked his arm under his head.

"My plans are a bit unsettled," he said.

"You want the job, it's yours," Hook said. "If you don't, she'll hire out a local."

"I've been thinking on it," he said. "I've been thinking maybe I ought give Tulsa another go."

"This time you could knock on the door," Hook said. "Let your wife make up her own mind."

"What if she says no?"

Oatney took off her shoe and poured sand from it. "Maybe you should think about her instead of yourself for once, Seth."

Hook nodded. "It's easy to build things in your mind, Seth, things that don't exist anywhere else."

"I was just so damn scared of what I'd see on her face."

"Men are scared of everything," Oatney said. "Scared that they won't be brave enough, or that their dicks are too small, or that they won't rise to the occasion. Scared that they can't stay in the game or that someone will play it better. Scared that they will be loved or that they won't be loved. I swear I don't know how the species ever got started in the first place."

"It's women like you makes us that way," Seth said.

"If you men knew what we know, you'd blow out your brains," Oatney said.

Seth looked over at Hook.

Hook shrugged. "It's like standing naked in a cold shower, isn't it?"

"I'm thinking I might give Tulsa another run," Seth said. "If I stay here with this woman much longer, I'll be sitting in the corner rocking."

Oatney pulled her skirt above her knees and fanned herself.

"I'm figuring on leaving, too," she said. "I can't stand the quiet and the thought of the world moving on without me."

"What about you, Hook?" Seth asked.

Hook lit a cigarette and wiped his forehead with his sleeve. The wind blew hot as scalding water out of the southwest.

"I've got to go to Topeka. Division wants to kick someone around. I'm up."

"When you leaving?" Oatney asked.

"There's a bus to Wichita," he said. "I figure to be on it."

"Wichita," she said. "My kind of town."

Seth got up and walked to where the shade ended, and the sun beat down on the parched earth. He rubbed at the scar on his face.

"Count me in," he said, turning. "I can catch a bus to Tulsa from there."

Andrea, who was preparing medications in Doctor Helms's office, pushed the hair from her face with the back of her hand and looked up at Hook. She had tanned to a deep brown from the prairie sun, and the tips of her hair were bleached.

"When will you be back?" she asked.

"Soon," he said. "Soon as possible. Will you keep an eye on Mixer?" She moved against Hook. "You *will* come back?" she asked.

"Yes."

"I'll miss you."

"Listen," he said, taking her chin. "Keep your eyes open."

"For what?"

"I've been following a trail that always comes back to water. There's no beginning and no end. Call it an old yard dog's intuition, but things don't feel right."

"Alright," she said. "How long will you be gone?"

"That depends on the hearing," he said. "I'll call."

Hook bought tickets from a lady who looked remarkably like Bette Davis. Then Hook, Seth, and Oatney waited on the bench outside. Seth had shaved and slicked back his hair, and Oatney had applied a fresh run of lipstick.

They drank colas and smoked cigarettes, and, when the bus sent a cloud of dust up in the distance, Oatney dropped her arm over Seth's shoulder. She looked back at the fort.

"I'm going to miss those boys," she said.

"Not as much as they'll miss you," Seth said.

Hook took an inside seat in the bus and dropped the window against the staleness. Moving from one place to another had always represented a beginning for him, a chance to start anew. But this time a knot drew tight in his stomach. Leaving Andrea behind did not sit well with his conscience.

A lot of people died in that fire in Barstow, unexplained even now, and then Elizabeth and Frankie were killed on his watch. He didn't believe in coincidence. Not that it was impossible, but he'd placed enough bets to know that odds mattered.

The bus traveled north through the Cherokee Outlet, a land

void of all but the occasional ranch or the town drawn by little more than a railroad track or water well or dirt intersection. People sat in the shade to watch the bus roll in, a point marked in lives otherwise vacant.

Seth slept in his seat, rest that had eluded him in the night hours at the asylum, and he snored quietly. Oatney studied the landscape and dug objects from her purse. The bus driver, a man who wore sunglasses, checked his passengers through the mirror and ate peanuts from a bag he kept on the dash.

When they came into the Wichita station, they waited for their luggage to be unloaded and then stood about as if looking for instructions. Finally Hook checked the schedule, Oatney having yet to decide her destination, and reported that Seth had a two-hour layover and that he had one.

Seth and Oatney were waiting in the coffee shop.

"What are we going to do in the meantime?" Seth asked.

"Well," Oatney said. "There's always church services."

"Or we could have a drink," Hook said.

"I went to church once," Seth said. "I prayed not to get shot in the war. I'm voting for a drink."

Oatney applied a new layer of lipstick and dropped the tube into her purse.

"Well, I'm voting for church services. But it's two to one, so I guess I lose."

"We could have a cocktail in the bar," Seth said.

"Or a fifth for half the price," Hook said.

"But where would we drink it?" Seth asked.

"In a patch of sunlight," Hook said. "It's a fine day to enjoy nature."

"Who's going to go get it?" Oatney asked.

Hook held up his prosthesis. "I'm disabled."

"And I have night terrors," Seth said. "And a Purple Heart."

"And I'm screwed again," Oatney said, gathering up the money.

Oatney returned with a fifth of whiskey in her purse. They hung their luggage over their arms and convened in an alley down the street.

Hook unscrewed the cap and gave it the sniff test. "Like taking the gas cap off a John Deere tractor," he said, handing the bottle to Oatney.

Oatney took a pull, her eyes tearing. "I prefer church," she said. "Though we are all called upon for sacrifices now and again."

Seth tipped the bottle. Wiping his mouth with his sleeve, he shook his head.

"Like being hit with a Mauser shell," he said. "Only more so."

Hook took his turn. "I'm not one to drink without the blessings of nature about me," he said.

Seth lit a cigarette and sat down on his luggage. Oatney hiked her leg on the curb, bracing her arm on her knee.

"I think I was here once," she said.

Hook leaned against the wall, which now sidled a little to the north.

"It's a well-known fact that a bottle of whiskey can evaporate by as much as a third on a hot day in Kansas."

"Put your thumb over it," Seth said.

Hook held up his prosthesis. "I don't have one."

Seth took the bottle. "It's a goddang shame a man can't provide a thumb when it's called for."

"I knew a man in Fort Worth had a thumb long as a thunder lizard," Oatney said.

"Thunder lizards don't have thumbs," Hook said.

"Neither do yard dogs," Seth said.

By the end of the hour, the empty bottle sat between them on the curb. Hook watched his bus pull in.

"Guess it's time," he said. "See you folks down line."

"So long," Seth said.

Oatney gave him a hug. "You ever want a job, let me know."

Hook sat on the seat behind the bus driver, who had a dot of shaving soap behind his ear. As the bus pulled out, he could see Seth and Oatney still sitting on the curb. Seth gave him thumbs up as the bus pulled away.

33

H<small>OOK STOOD UNDER</small> the hot shower washing away the grime of the bus. The board had set the hearing for ten in the morning. He'd hardly had time to consider the possibilities. He'd done his job as best he could, but sometimes things happened in the field that couldn't be understood from behind a desk.

He sat on the edge of the bed and watched a neon light flick on and off across the street. A siren eased away in the distance. He dialed the operator and asked for the fort. With luck, they would have the phones up by now.

Roy answered. "Baldwin Asylum," he said.

"This is Hook, Roy. I want to talk to Andrea."

"Hook who?" he asked.

"How many Hooks do you know?"

"Too goddang many," he said.

"Damn it, Roy, go get Andrea."

"She's showing Shorty how to keep that inmate in cell two from biting off your finger when you give him meds."

Hook paused. "How do you do that?"

"Push his cheek in between his teeth with your finger. Works like a goddang charm."

"Go get Andrea, Roy."

"Right," he said.

Andrea came on the line out of breath. "Hi," she said. "You made it?"

"Made it," he said.

"What about Seth and Oatney?"

"Yeah. We all made it. Oatney decided to stay in Wichita.

He rubbed at the stubble on his chin. He'd have to shave before the hearing.

"Doctor Baldwin's doctor called," she said. "He wants to talk to you."

"Me?"

"He said it was urgent."

"Baldwin's still in the hospital?"

"No visitors. I think he has something contagious."

"I will be here after the hearing."

"I miss you," she said.

"I'll be back soon."

"Breaking in these new people has me worn out," she said. "They keep thinking things should be rational."

"They'll get over that. I'll call after the hearing. You can call me, too, if you take a notion," he said, giving her his number.

"I will," she said. "Good luck. I'll be thinking of you."

They held the hearing in a room the size of an outhouse. The supervisor sat at the head of the table, flanked by three men with notepads. Hook took his seat at the end, placing his prosthesis in his lap.

The supervisor cleared his throat. "Thank you for coming, Mr. Runyon. I assume you know why you're here?"

Hook nodded but waited while the supervisor read the charges.

"You understand the seriousness of these allegations?"

The other men turned to their notepads.

"Yes," he said, wishing he could have a cigarette.

"You understand that another Brownie could force your dismissal?"

"It's true I didn't get the truck cleared of the tracks. I was in pursuit, and it was dark. That bo had been cracking sealed cars up and down the line. He needed to be apprehended. Had I taken time to check on your truck, he would have been long gone. Having him on the loose would have cost Uncle John a hell of a lot more than that worn-out truck."

The man on the left said, "It might have been an entire work train derailed. Had you thought about that?"

"There's a time for thinking in this business," Hook said. "But it's rarely when in pursuit."

"We understand the nature of your work, Mr. Runyon, and that there's a certain element of risk involved. The problem here is that the foreman claims he could smell alcohol on you that night."

"That bo had been drinking Thunderbird down at the livestock pens."

The man on the supervisor's right laid down his pencil.

"You're denying you had anything to drink that night?"

"I'm not saying I don't have a drink off duty now and then. But I don't drink on the job, not ever."

"Is there anything you'd like to add?" the supervisor asked.

Hook looked at the blank pad they'd placed in front of him. "You have to understand that in this job, there's a trade-off between risk and success. There's never one without the other. A man unwilling to risk when it's called for will never catch a bo or stop a thief."

The supervisor said, "Is that your defense?"

"That's the truth."

"Thank you, Mr. Runyon. Now, if you'll wait outside, we'll consider the facts and then let you know our decision."

Hook smoked a cigarette and walked the hall. He'd never really thought that much about what he'd do if he wasn't a railroad bull. As far as most jobs went, having only one arm closed a hell of a lot of doors. Though he had a bent for books, his education was minimal. With his beat-up mug, he doubted there would be many openings in Hollywood. Maybe he'd just go on the bum again. He knew that world best of all, knew how to survive when others couldn't.

When they called him in, the supervisor asked him to take a seat.

"We've considered your case, Mr. Runyon. We believe that there is insufficient evidence to charge you with drinking on the night in question. That portion of the allegations will be dismissed.

"However, it's clear you were negligent with company equipment; consequently, your continued employment with the railroad will be contingent on reimbursement for the truck. Your first payment is due immediately.

"Now, before you respond, I want it understood that you are walking a thin line here. It's only the exemplary way you solved the case in the Alva POW camp a time back that allows us to be this lenient.

"Is there anything you'd like to say?"

"No," Hook said.

"Good day, then. I trust we'll not be hearing from you again."

Hook lay in his bed and considered the injustice of having to pay for a wrecked truck. The first payment had taken a sizeable chunk out of an already-meager budget. He barely had enough discretionary funds to buy a few books. He should have told them what they could do with their truck, the problem being that he loved this damn job. In another life he would have been a gypsy or desert nomad. A life on the rails came as close to that as he could get.

When the phone rang, adrenaline shot through him like electricity. He found the phone hidden beneath a stack of clothes.

"Hello."

"Mr. Runyon?"

"Yes," he said. "This is Hook."

"This is Doctor Anderson."

"Who?"

"Anderson. Doctor Baldwin's physician."

"Oh, yes."

"I'm phoning you as an objective third party and, frankly, because of your association with the justice system. You see, I have decided to quarantine Doctor Baldwin."

"Doctor Baldwin has a contagious disease?"

"Not exactly," he said. "This has been a very perplexing case."

"I don't understand."

"I've run every test I can think of and have been unable to diagnose his problem. I don't quite know how to say this, but I suspect that he might be addicted to chloral hydrate."

"Doctor Baldwin?"

"It's commonly administered to mental patients and can be addictive. Doctor Baldwin's symptoms are compatible with this sort of addiction, and it would be readily available to him. He strongly denies it of course. A quarantine should force the issue."

Hook listened to the buzz on the line, or was it in his head?

"His condition hasn't improved?"

"To the contrary. I suspect he still has access to the drug. That's why the quarantine."

"Thank you for calling, Doctor. I'll keep in touch."

When he awoke, he was still in his clothes, and the morning sun had edged into the window. He'd spent a long time in the night trying to put Baldwin's situation into some kind of perspective. Baldwin's situation just didn't fit what he knew about addiction, which was admittedly limited. He knew a hell of a lot more about winos than doctors taking chloral hydrate.

He showered and ordered a pot of coffee and a newspaper from room service. A used bookstore had a fifty-percent sale advertised in the paper. Maybe he could work it in. One of the things he'd learned in the detective business was that when he came up against a wall, it was almost always better to walk around it.

He'd have to be selective with his book buys, which wasn't his style, but he had damn little money left and no way of transporting a bunch of books around.

After his coffee, he called Eddie at Division.

"Division," Eddie said.

"Hook here," he said.

"You make that board hearing, Runyon?"

"Yeah," he said. "I'm paying for their goddang truck."

"Where are you now?"

"In Topeka, Eddie. That's where the hearing was."

"Don't put that hotel room on the company dime, Runyon."

"I wouldn't think about it, Eddie."

"We got problems out of El Paso," he said. "Mexicans been hopping freighters north. Immigration is raising hell."

"I'm tied up here, Eddie. I'll catch the bus back to Fort Supply."

"Why can't you just hop a reefer train to El Paso?"

"Cause my caboose is sitting in a goddang pasture at Fort Supply."

"You're lucky they don't can you, Runyon."

"Send one of your new boys to El Paso. It would be damn good experience."

Eddie cleared his throat. "I did. They found him in the desert with his jaw broke. Now the little prick is suing the company."

"Tell Frenchy to come get my bouncer. He can connect me up with a reefer going south."

"This ain't your goddang private railroad, Runyon."

"You want me in El Paso or not, Eddie?"

He could hear Eddie puffing on the other end of the line. "I'll see if I can get something, but there's a shortage of equipment, you know."

"Believe me, I know."

"And I want you ready to go when it gets there."

"Sure, Eddie. I'll be ready."

Hook dressed and checked with the front desk about the location of the bookstore, which turned out to be within walking distance from the hotel. He needed time to think, and nothing provided that like a little book scouting.

The store, located next door to a Woolworth's, turned out to be well stocked. It smelled of mold and paper, and the proprietor, an old lady with thinning hair, peered at him.

"We don't take trade," she said.

"Just browsing," he said.

"No charge for that," she said. "Though we'd be knee-deep in cash if we did."

He worked his way through the stacks on his knees so he could scout the bottom shelves. Within a couple hours, he'd found a half-dozen titles, realizing that even those were too many to lug about. Finally, he settled on *The Heart Is a Lonely Hunter,* by Carson McCullers. Not only was it a fine copy, but he had yet to read it. Perhaps it would take some of the pain out of the bus ride home.

The old lady pointed him to a restaurant down the street. "It don't look like much, but the food's good," she said. "You come back. I don't get many men readers."

The waitress, thickened a little about the waist and wearing horn-rimmed glasses, slid the menu in front of him.

"Special's meatloaf," she said, taking her pencil from behind her ear.

"Is it good?" he asked.

"No, hon, it's awful. That's why we put it on special."

He couldn't afford to eat out after paying that fine, but a person had to live a little.

"That's what I'll have," he said.

"A man who knows his mind," she said, slipping the receipt book into her pocket. "The apple pie is terrible, too."

"With cheddar," he said.

When the meal arrived, he pushed back and waited as the waitress set the dishes in front of him. Steam rose from the meatloaf, which had been stacked to dangerously high levels and then topped with a red sauce. Brown gravy pooled in the mashed potatoes, and a slab of butter melted on the sourdough roll. There were green beans; a helping of corn, buttered and heavily peppered; and a serving of coleslaw swimming in cream.

When he'd finished, the waitress brought him a slice of Amish apple pie topped with a slab of cheddar cheese. She poured him black coffee, looking at him through the steam.

"How was it, hon?" she asked.

Hook dabbed at his mouth with his napkin. "Just awful," he said.

She smiled and swept off to the next table.

That night he read awhile and then dozed. When he awoke, he sat up and leaned back against the headboard of his bed. The day's distractions had cleared his head, like opening a window curtain and letting the sun shine in.

He lit a cigarette and talked himself through the scenarios. The one consistent element from the beginning had been Frankie Yager. There had not been a single incident in which he couldn't have been directly involved. He figured Andrea was right. Frankie Yager wasn't a planner. But now he was dead, and the bad luck continued.

And why hadn't anyone caught Frankie's bogus employment application at Baldwin?

He reached over and dialed the phone. Andrea answered. "I've been waiting," she said. "What did they say?"

"I have to pay for their truck. The railroad needs the money."

"That's not so bad, then," she said. "I mean, it could have been worse."

"Listen, Andrea, I wonder if you could do me a favor?"

"If I can."

"You know those personnel files that were in my caboose?"

"Yes. Doctor Helms has them in the guardhouse for the interviews. Why?"

"Do you think you could get at look at Helms's file?"

Pausing, she said, "I don't understand. We agreed that we shouldn't."

"I know," he said. "But things have changed."

"I'd do anything you ask, Hook. What am I looking for?"

"That's just it," he said. "I don't know."

34

ANDREA THOUGHT ABOUT Hook's call all night long. She sensed alarm in his voice, or at least urgency. On the other hand, just working the security ward had put her on edge. Dealing with the criminally insane presented enough challenges in itself. Add trainees and a new director, and all the ingredients for a nervous breakdown were in place.

Doctor Helms, having taken over the director's position, had cranked up the rules, making the work even more difficult. At times her intractability sent Andrea's blood pressure soaring. She required an absolute schedule on meds, both timing and quantity, which defied the obvious: mental illness by its nature lacked predictability. Half the time patients were either overmedicated or manic.

Andrea didn't doubt Helms's intelligence, but she scored a minus two on the sensitivity scale. All and all, Andrea had begun to doubt if she could continue working there. Hook would be moving on. This much she knew. It was in his nature. One day they would come for his caboose, and he would leave on it. Staying here alone and working would be problematic. She was increasingly uncertain whether she could do so.

One of Helms's better decisions, born of a need to spread the experienced personnel among the wards, was to move Roy to the women's ward and Santos to the boys' ward. Both had taken on their responsibilities with enthusiasm. Santos demonstrated an uncanny ability to control the boys. His nonverbal calm suited them, and they searched him out at every opportunity.

Roy, on the other hand, went from woman to woman, chattering and talking and cajoling. The women found him endearing and most often tried to please him.

After lunch, she sought out Roy, who had just finished eating with the women. Bertha sat nearby gazing up at him, while Ruth and Anna giggled over the pictures in an old army-issue pamphlet.

"How's it going?" Andrea asked, sitting down on one of the bunks.

"Depends on how you look at it," he said.

"From a professional point of view?"

"Things are under control," he said. "We've had no riots or upheavals in the last twenty-four hours."

"That's good," Andrea said. "How about at the personal level?"

"Now that's a different story altogether. Bertha here followed me into the bathroom. It's right disconcerting to have someone crawl under the stall while you're amidst your business, if you know what I mean.

"Ruth over there stood on the landing of the upstairs floor to watch the new employees come in for interviews."

"Doesn't sound so bad," Andrea said.

"Not unless you consider the fact that she was stark naked at the time.

"Anna swears Hook visited her in the night, hung her on a cross, and drove a nail through her foot."

"Pretty calm then?" Andrea said.

"About as calm as it gets. I keep thinking sooner or later something unusual might happen."

Andrea gazed out the window. From here she could see the fort cemetery and, beyond, the spring where she and Hook had walked. Mixer waited in the shade for her to come out. He followed her everywhere she went since Hook left.

"You thinking to stay on for a while, Roy?"

Roy shrugged. "I can't be certain. It's as good a life as a man like me has come up with so far," he said. "What about you?"

Andrea studied her fingernails. "I left everything I own behind. I thought I was doing something important here, that it would be worth it, but now I'm not so sure. I've been thinking I might go home."

"Since Baldwin fell sick?" he asked.

"Doctor Helms is competent, but she can be distant and . . . Oh, I guess I'm being foolish."

"Andrea, that's the one thing you're not."

"I have this feeling that she doesn't care like she should."

Roy nodded. "Like everything comes from a page in her head and that it has been written by someone else?"

"Exactly. This work is too difficult to do just for money. With Baldwin I felt like what I did mattered."

"And now you don't?" he said.

Andrea squinted up an eye. "I guess what I can say is that now I'm not sure. Anyway, thanks for listening to me, Roy."

"I'm getting real good at listening," he said.

That afternoon Andrea stopped in at Doctor Helms's office, a cell she'd secured for such purposes on the first floor of the guardhouse. For the last few days Helms had been busy interviewing locals, and now she sat behind her desk poring over one of the files.

"Excuse me," Andrea said.

Helms slipped the file folder back into the cabinet behind her.

"Yes, what is it, Andrea?"

"About Van Diefendorf," she said. "He's very agitated, and we've not been able to get him to eat. I thought a pill might help calm him."

Helms folded her hands in front of her. "Mr. Van Diefendorf will eat when he's hungry enough. He can wait for his medications like the others."

"It's just that he has bad days," Andrea said.

"Anything else?" she asked.

"No," Andrea said. "Nothing else."

"Very well, then. Oh, I'll not be here this evening. I'm to check on Doctor Baldwin. If you have problems, you can reach me at the hospital."

"Yes," Andrea said.

Helms stood and smoothed her skirt. Her hips were wide and open, a pelvis capable of bearing litters of children. For her to be childless struck Andrea as incongruous.

"And I've been getting reports that Ruth has put herself on display again. If this behavior doesn't stop, I'll have her isolated."

"She's quite compulsive, you know," Andrea said.

"Then it will be up to us to control her, won't it?"

"Yes, Doctor. I'll have a talk with Roy."

"And while you're at it, ask him to stop smoking on duty. It's unacceptable," she said. "Now, if there's nothing else?"

Andrea waited until the meds were given and the second shift had settled in before she went back to her room. The sun shimmered on the horizon, bolts of orange and red striking into the clabbered sky. From her window, she watched Helms pull out of the gate on her way to see Baldwin.

Shadows slid from beneath the buildings like black spirits, and the sounds of evening rose from out of the prairie. She put on her jacket and made her way across the compound. The moon popped onto the horizon like a cork and commenced its ascent into the black sky.

The guardhouse lights were off, the madness upstairs sedated and silent. Andrea stood on the porch, her heart tripping in her ears. She was a caretaker, a nurturer. Breaking into someone's office went against her instincts. There was only one person in the world she would do this for, and he had called.

Easing the door open, she waited for her eyes to adjust. Moonlight lit a patch on the floor no larger than a man's hand. Helms's perfume lingered in the stillness, and her reading glasses lay on top of a file folder on her desk. Her coffee cup sat on the cabinet behind.

Andrea paused, listening, the only sounds an occasional distant cough from the cells above. Opening the filing cabinet, she thumbed through the names until she found Helms's personnel records. Taking them out, she held them under the patch of moonlight and read the pages, then slipped each back into its exact location.

Several moments passed before she rose again and opened the files. This time she went to the back and pulled Frankie Yager's folder. She read it through and then read it again. She picked up Helms's phone and dialed the number Hook had given her.

When Hook came on the line, there was sleep in his voice.

"Hook," he said.

"This is Andrea," she said, her voice hushed. "I've just gone through Doctor Helms's personnel file."

"What did you find?"

"She graduated with a 3.9."

"That's all you found?"

"Her recommendations are impeccable."

"I was hoping for more."

Andrea dropped the phone against her neck and then placed it back to her ear.

"There is one thing," she said.

"Yes?"

"She did her residency in Fergus Falls."

"Fergus Falls?" he asked. Andrea waited for Hook to process the information. "Isn't that where Doctor Baldwin had his practice?"

"Yes," she said.

"Helms never told you this?"

"No," Andrea said. "She never talks about her past."

"Odd," he said. "I mean, wouldn't you have mentioned something?"

"It's not Helms's style," she said.

"You're right about that."

"There is one other thing," she said.

"Yeah?"

"I took a look at Frankie Yager's file while I was at it. He worked at Fergus Falls, too."

"At the same time as Helms?" he asked.

"Yes. In fact, one of his employment recommendations is from Doctor Helms herself."

"I'll be damn," Hook said. "They knew each other before?"

"Looks that way."

"I don't know what all this means," Hook said. "Maybe nothing."

Andrea studied the shadows that had edged up the wall of Helms's office.

"Hook, I don't think I can work here much longer. With Helms in charge, all the joy has gone out of my job. It's like working in a prison. I'm not cut out for this."

"I got a call from Baldwin's doctor," he said.

"How's Doctor Baldwin doing?"

"He has been quarantined because his doctor thinks he might be addicted to chloral hydrate."

"Doctor Baldwin? He doesn't even drink coffee, Hook. Nobody I know leads a cleaner life."

"His doctor says it wouldn't be the first time. Doctors have access. Things like this happen."

"But why the quarantine?"

"He thinks that Baldwin might still be getting the drug, that he hasn't come around as he should, that a quarantine might flesh things out."

Andrea fell silent. A coyote's call quivered up from the prairie. The pack joined in then, their yips pitched and frantic.

"Helms is there now," she said.

"At Baldwin's?"

"Yes."

"And where are you?" he asked.

"I'm still in her office," she said.

"Get out of there," he said. "They're not going to let her see him. She could be on her way back."

"When are you coming, Hook?"

"Soon, and thanks, Andrea. Thanks for everything."

After Andrea hung up, she sat at Helms's desk, her hand on the phone. Hook sounded concerned. Her experience had been that it took considerable trouble to disturb Hook Runyon about anything.

She went back to the files and replaced the personnel folders. After that, she double-checked to make certain she'd left no telltale signs of her having been there.

She closed the file drawer and then reopened it to retrieve an overstuffed folder from the very back of the drawer. She read through the papers. When finished, she rubbed at her face and then put the file back into the drawer.

The moon slid behind a cloud, plunging Helms's office into darkness. Something thumped from beyond the door. Chills raced down her spine, probably just an inmate in one of the cells above.

Gathering up her courage, she took a deep breath and stepped into the blackness.

35

Hook HUNG UP the phone and lit a cigarette. He shouldn't have asked Andrea to break into those files. She'd put herself at risk for him. Why hadn't he just left with Frenchy? Why did he always set an upstream course?

Eddie was probably right. The business with the Baldwin Insane Asylum had little to do with him or the railroad at this point. But how could the fiery death of all those people be ignored? And what about the two people who had died on his watch, one of whom had been strangled and thrown off a bridge by an unknown assailant? Sooner or later he would be called in as a witness in Elizabeth's death. What troubled him most was that he didn't know any more now than he did the day they went out for her body. Any way it was cut, he couldn't walk away from it even if he wanted to, not if it cost him everything.

After squashing out his cigarette, he lay down on his side and watched the neon light flash on and off through his window. Why hadn't Helms mentioned that she'd known Yager in the past? She'd certainly had the opportunity to bring it up when Baldwin questioned her about Yager's credentials.

And then what about Baldwin, who had been at Fergus Falls himself? And why had his drug habit suddenly come to the forefront? He'd been perfectly fine in Barstow. On the other hand, Hook knew all too well how dead habits could resurrect in unexpected moments.

Turning over, he closed his eyes against the light. Tomorrow he would go back. The truck payment had nearly cleaned him out of cash, and then with the meal and the book. Maybe he would just hop a freighter to Wichita. He could buy a bus ticket from there to Fort Supply.

By sunrise he'd checked out of his hotel and walked to the Topeka yards. He knelt in the sunflowers just below the switch point. Their pungent smell rose about him thick as syrup in the morning air.

Adrenaline rushed him as he waited for the train. Sometimes the past beckoned him, the thrill of a moving train, the knowledge that, once rolling, nothing or no one could stop it. Besides all that, this was a hell of a lot faster, and, frankly, he was concerned about getting back to Andrea.

The train slowed at the grade, chugging and huffing, black smoke boiling into the blue. Hook spotted an open boxcar coming down line. He broke into a trot, and as it came up, he threw his bag in, latched on, and hoisted himself up.

As luck would have it, the car was empty. The train drove into the countryside, gaining speed, the clack of the wheels now indistinguishable one from the other. He lay back, resting his head on his bag.

Unknown and unreachable, he clipped across the land. At this moment, no troubles could touch him, no woes could find him. Freedom reigned. Dropping an arm over his eyes, he slept, and in that sleep was all the peace a man could ever want.

He awoke to a cold blast of air whipping into the car. He looked out to see black clouds moving in. In this country, summer squalls could sweep in from nowhere, race across the plains like a buffalo stampede, and then disappear. He struggled to close the door, but rust and dirt had long since clogged its track.

A bank of dust boiled upward at the storm's lead, debris sweeping into its vortex. It moved across the plain toward him, and when the gale hit, a blast of rain and pea-sized hail screamed into the open car. Moving into the corner, he buried his head in his arms, his ears stinging from the assault. The squall passed as quickly as it came, a pale rainbow arching skyward.

Taking off his britches, he hung them over a nail that protruded from the wall. Shivering, he dumped his bag in a heap. He hopped from foot to foot, searching for a dry pair of pants. Just then the train whistle signaled a slow stop.

"Damn it," he said, grabbing his pants off the nail. "How long did I sleep?"

Sticking his head out the door, he could see the Arkansas River looping into the city limits of Wichita.

The train slowed as she moved into town. He waited, calculating the moment to jump. Bail too soon, and he'd have a long walk to the bus station, too slow, and he could wind up in Oklahoma City. When the moment came, he pushed off. He hit the bedrock standing up, but the momentum propelled him forward. He rolled down the right-of-way like a Texas tumbleweed.

Gathering himself up, he dusted off and watched the train shuffle off down the tracks. Hopping a freighter hadn't been the brightest idea he'd had lately. Maybe he was getting too old. There was a day he could have taken that jump without a hitch.

He looked at his clothes, wrinkled and dirty, his shirtsleeve torn. Only then did he realize he'd left his bag on the car and a half carton of cigarettes to boot.

"Goddang it," he said, kicking at the bedrock.

It took him nearly an hour to get to town and another hour to find the bus depot. He washed up best he could in the restroom and combed the nettles out of his hair. As he approached the ticket agent's window, he reached for his billfold and found it missing. It must have fallen out in the boxcar.

"Damn it to hell," he said. "Now what?"

The woman next to him took her child by the elbow and guided him away. At the ticket window, Hook explained his problem.

"You're a railroad bull?" the ticket agent asked, glancing over at the girl behind the desk.

"That's right," Hook said. "The railroad will reimburse you for the price of the ticket."

"Let me see your badge."

"I told you that I lost it."

"Why don't you take the train?"

"The train doesn't go there, not on a regular basis, I mean."

"Look, Mister, you better move along. Loitering in the bus station is not allowed."

Hook went out on the sidewalk and sat down on the curb. Some days it didn't pay to take the first breath. He fished a crumpled cigarette out of his last pack and lit up. Now what the hell was he supposed to do? He was broke, hungry, and anxious to get back to Andrea. Any sane person would have made arrangements to ride in on a passenger from Topeka. But not him. He never did what was easy, not if he could manage to make it hard.

At what point he became aware of the woman on the corner, he couldn't say. But something familiar caught his eye, the way she stood with her arm cocked on her waist. He squashed out his cigarette and worked his way closer. She turned, the sunlight striking her profile.

"Oatney?" he said.

She looked over at him. "Could be, Mister. You got a sawbuck?"

"Oatney, it's me, Hook Runyon."

Oatney shaded her eyes against the sun. "I'll be damn. I thought you were a bus bum looking for a freebie. Jeez, Hook, you look like hell."

"Yeah," he said. "I'm headed back to Fort Supply. Lost my stuff bailing off a freighter."

"You were bumming a freighter?"

"Yeah, I know," he said.

Oatney pushed the hair back from her eyes. In spite of impending old age, she looked pretty good.

"You hear from Seth?" she asked.

He shook his head. "Look, Oatney, you wouldn't have a twenty to get me back, would you? My billfold's on its way to San Antonio."

"Just started the day, Hook. Leave my money in the room. These bastards will steal all you have.

"Here comes a cop. He's been circling all morning."

Hook turned to leave, but the patrol car pulled at an angle in front of him. The cop who stepped out looked like someone from a silent movie. He wore sunglasses, his hat pushed back on his head, and his mustache had been blackened with mascara. He placed his baton across Hook's chest.

"Hold on," he said. "You ain't going nowhere."

"What's the problem?" Hook said.

The cop turned to Oatney. "Come on over here, Missy. Don't you know that prostitution is against the law in Kansas?"

"Just talking to my friend," she said. "Is that against the law?"

"Let me see some identification," he said.

"I left my purse in my room," she said.

"She's telling the truth," Hook said.

"And who are you?"

"I'm a railroad detective," he said, "a yard dog."

"Now who would have thought?" he said. "So you would have a badge?"

"I lost it in a boxcar this morning."

"I see," he said. "It's right hard to keep track of anything nowadays, ain't it?

"And what were you doing in a boxcar, I wonder?"

"Hitching a ride."

"A railroad detective bumming a ride? Christ," he said, "you people think I'm an idiot?"

"We don't know you that well," Oatney said.

"The both of you get in the car," he said.

The next morning, Hook and Oatney stood in front of Judge Hampton as he read over the charges. He pushed his glasses up on his forehead and squinted down at Oatney.

"Madam, do you understand that prostitution is illegal in Kansas?"

"She wasn't selling *anything*, Judge," Hook said.

"Shut up, you," he said.

"Two days in jail," he said, "and a ten-dollar fine."

"I don't have ten dollars," she said.

"Four days," he said.

"Judge," Hook said, "I'm railroad detective."

"And I might be Abe Lincoln," he said, "was there a fool big enough to believe it. Soliciting prostitutes in our fair city is not something we abide. Add in trespassing on railroad property, and you've also earned two days and ten dollars."

"I lost my billfold, Judge."

"And I my patience. Make that four days in our facility. I trust this is the last I'll see of either of you. Take them out, Deputy."

The day they got out, Hook waited for Oatney in the stairwell of the courthouse. "Oatney," he said from the shadows.

Oatney paused, staring into the dim light. "Hook?" she said.

"Yeah," he said.

Oatney joined him. "You've aged ten years, Hook. Jesus, I hardly recognized you."

"It's the beard," he said, "and the fact I haven't slept for four days."

"Or bathed either by the smell of you. The judge here is a real dick," she said.

"Listen," he said. "I've got to get back to the fort. Could you spot me a little money?"

"Got a smoke?" she asked.

"No," he said.

"Jesus, Hook, you don't have a smoke?"

"Well, will you?"

"I've been thinking," she said. "I kind of liked those folks, you know. They took up with me and no questions asked."

"It's hard to be uppity when you are in an insane asylum," he said.

"Maybe I'll just go back with you. You think Doctor Helms would hire me?"

"If she doesn't, you can stay in my caboose," he said.

"Alright," she said. "I've money in my room, but no freebies. I've my principles, you know."

36

Hook AND OATNEY boarded the bus just at dusk. Oatney had sprung both for the tickets and a carton of Luckys, which they had divided before leaving her room. By the time they'd reached the city limits, darkness had fallen, and the prairie sky blinked with a million stars.

Soon Oatney slept, her head falling against Hook's shoulder, her hair brushing his ear. He wondered at her strength and her softness, how they coexisted, how in her world she could still manage a smile and face the day. She never railed against injustice or succumbed to the malice and hatred due her. Had she been a man, her spirit would have long since flickered away like a spent candle.

Andrea, too, had such strength. Men, in their determination to control and change their world, refused what they knew intuitively: their flashes of bravado paled against the smoldering strength of the women around them.

By the time they pulled into Fort Supply, the moon had ridden from sight, and the darkness before morning claimed all in its spell.

They climbed from the bus and stood in the chill. Hook lit a cigarette and rubbed the tension from his neck.

"Where do we go from here?" Oatney asked.

Hook looked out at the fort, where the first morning lights were just winking on.

"I'll take you to the caboose," he said. "You can catch up on your sleep while I check things out."

"You ain't expecting a freebie, are you?"

"No freebies, Oatney."

"'Cause if you were, I might make an exception in your case."

"Thanks, Oatney, but Andrea and I are kind of close, you see."

"Sure, I understand. You change your mind, let me know, hon. Oatney can make you forget your worst days."

"Thanks, Oatney. I'll remember."

"You think Doctor Helms will take me back?" Oatney asked.

"She's nothing if not practical," Hook said.

"And if she doesn't?"

"You can ride out with me when they pick up the caboose."

Oatney slipped her arm through his. "Seems like that's where we started. Sometimes I feel like a mouse in a maze."

"You may be in a maze, Oatney, but you'll never be a mouse. Come on, it's not such a far walk from here."

The caboose sat in the morning dawn like a red matchbox. They were nearly upon it when Mixer bolted out from underneath the wheel carriage and raced toward them with his tail wagging.

Hook ruffed his head and pulled his ears. "What you doing out here, boy?" he asked.

"I thought you said Andrea was taking care of him?" Oatney said.

"Yeah," he said.

"Maybe he got lonesome for the caboose."

"Maybe so," he said, unlocking the door. "Make yourself at home. I'm going on to the fort."

"You don't think the yard dog will pick me up for being on railroad property, do you?" she asked.

"I hear he's a mean son of a bitch," he said. "But this time I'd say you're pretty safe." Dropping down onto the tracks, he looked back up at Oatney. "I've a paycheck coming soon. I'll get that money back to you."

"Who's worried?" she said. "I got your caboose."

Mixer followed at his heels as Hook made his way to the fort. Now and again he would range out with his nose to the ground in hopes of stirring up some trouble. As they passed the guardhouse, Mixer marked the porch step and then again at the entrance to the women's ward.

Roy met Hook at the door, his hair disheveled, sleep in his eyes. "I'll be damn," he said. "It's the yard dog."

"Hello, Roy. You sleeping with the ladies now, are you?"

"I've an orderly room in the back," he said. "Price is right, though you're never quite off duty."

"Just blew in," Hook said. "Oatney followed me back. Said she hadn't gotten enough of this place."

"That's great. Don't mind me saying so, but you look like hell, Hook."

"So I've been told."

"You drinking busthead again?"

"Spent a little time in the Wichita hoosegow. Case of mistaken identity," Hook said.

"Least you didn't lose your arm this time," Roy said, searching for his cigarettes.

"Much as I enjoy standing here on the porch explaining my life to you, I need to talk to Andrea."

Roy lit his cigarette. "Well, hell, Hook, why didn't you speak up?"

"I just did."

"She ain't here."

"Not here? Where is she?"

"I don't rightly know."

"Is she working the security ward?"

"No, she ain't."

"Goddang it, Roy."

"She left, Hook."

"Left?"

"Andrea went home."

Hook rubbed at his neck. "She told you that?"

"Well, not exactly. She said she didn't think she could work here much longer, and first thing I know, she's up and gone."

"When did she leave?"

"Well, I don't know exactly, do I, 'cause she didn't say."

"Why wouldn't she say, Roy?"

"She didn't say, Hook. Christ almighty, that hoosegow didn't do much for your personality, did it?"

"Did she say anything about leaving Mixer behind?"

"No, she didn't. But *everybody* I know would leave that crazy mutt behind given the chance."

"It doesn't fit, Roy, her just taking off like that."

"Maybe she was sore, Hook. She'd been training over in the security ward. That's enough to drive anyone crazy."

"Did Helms say why she left?"

"Helms doesn't tell me squat, Hook. Anyway, I've been thinking about leaving my own goddang self. Helms has chewed on my ass until I can't keep my britches up anymore. Last time, she accused me of stealing sugar out of the cafeteria."

"Did you?"

"Not out of the cafeteria."

Hook stepped off the porch. Dawn had broke, lighting the headstones in the old fort cemetery.

"Andrea mentioned leaving when I talked to her on the phone," he said. "But I didn't expect her to just take off."

"You know how women are, Hook. It's either rain or shine. Speaking of which . . ."

"What? You been cooking again, Roy?"

"There's just enough gypsum in that springwater to keep a man regular," he said. "Maybe you'd like a sample? Taxes are paid."

"I quit drinking, Roy, and would suggest you do the same while your liver's still intact."

Roy dropped his cigarette on the porch and smashed it out with his shoe.

"God gave me a liver as is necessary for having a drink now and then," he said.

"You'd of thought he'd given you a brain, too," Hook said.

"A brain ain't required for drinking, though a liver is. You'd do well not to question the decisions of your Maker."

Roy pushed the cigarette butt off the porch and into the bushes.

"Helms gets hysterectomy when I smoke," he said.

"Where *is* Helms?" Hook asked.

"Most likely having breakfast with the criminally insane over in the security ward. She's got that Shorty doing orderly duty. Says he has the right temperament for working with them inmates, him being a mechanic and all."

"What does that mean?"

"If it don't work, just whack it with a goddang hammer until it does," he said.

"You sure Andrea didn't leave any word for me, where she was going, a phone number?"

"I know it's hard to believe," Roy said, "you being such a charmer and all."

"Thanks," Hook said. "Maybe I'll just report you for stealing sugar."

Roy opened the door. "Something tells me my secret is safe," he said.

Mixer followed Hook to the guardhouse. He dropped down at the front door and put his head between his paws.

"I'm going to talk to Doctor Helms," Hook said. "Don't kill anything while I'm gone."

As he climbed the steps to the upstairs cells, the wails and cries of the demented rose up. When he opened the door, the smell of urine and sour wafted over him. The inmates watched him from behind their bars, the humanity in their eyes extracted in some cruel joke of nature. Left behind were but cold remains and empty shells, life reduced to skin and bones and emptiness.

Van Diefendorf, who had been placed in an isolated cell near the end of the long hallway, sat on his bunk, wearing nothing but his underwear, his body as white as paper. A network of veins coursed beneath his translucent skin. As Hook walked by, Van Diefendorf rubbed his hands together and watched him through blond brows that sprouted from above his eyes.

Shorty sat on a high stool at the end of the hallway with his arms folded over his chest. He wore a uniform, apparently of his own making, since the color of the shirt and pants didn't quite match. Straitjackets hung on a row of nails behind him, and an axe handle leaned against the wall.

"Shorty," Hook said. "Is Doctor Helms around?"

"She's fixing meds in the back," he said. "Keep these animals tamed for a few hours."

"Who's doing the plumbing around here, what with you taking over guard duties?"

"Plumbing's alright, given the lack of opportunity for more fruitful work, I suppose. But since this here insane asylum came to town, I've found my real calling. Doctor Helms says I have a knack for orderly work. These here inmates may have done their dirty deeds out there in the world, but in here they damn well know Shorty's the boss, that much I can tell you."

Just then Doctor Helms came down the hall, a tray of meds in her hands. She set it down and focused in on Hook through the bottoms of her glasses.

"Mr. Runyon," she said. "I thought our business had ended. Did we fail to reimburse the railroad properly? I'm afraid Doctor Baldwin had stopped attending to business. I've kept all the receipts."

"I would have heard from Division had there been a problem with the payment," Hook said. "I wonder if there's some place private we might talk?"

"My office is downstairs," she said. "But I don't have a great deal of time. Since Doctor Baldwin's illness, my duties have doubled, as you might guess."

"Your office would be fine."

He followed her down the stairwell to her office, the cool breeze coming up the stairs.

She pulled her chair up to her desk and folded her hands in front of her.

"Now," she said. "I've told you everything I know about Elizabeth's unfortunate accident. Do the police need yet more?"

"This is not about Elizabeth," he said, "though the case remains open. It no doubt will until all the evidence is in."

"Has it occurred to you, Mr. Runyon, that Elizabeth may not have died had the railroad provided us with proper transportation and security?"

"Until I know more details, I can't make those kinds of assumptions, Doctor Helms."

"Yes, well. Would you mind getting to the point? I've work to do."

"Two things, actually. First, Oatney has returned. She's staying in my caboose. Do you think there might still be a place for her here?"

Helms pushed her chair back. "I'm aware of Oatney's past, of course. Folks do talk, even in here. But then none of us is perfect. I *could* place her in the women's ward. There are times when a woman's hand is needed. However, she should understand that if she leaves again, she'll not receive another opportunity."

"Thanks. I'll tell her."

Helms clasped her hands and tapped her thumbs together. "You did say you had *two* things?"

"It's about Andrea, actually," he said.

"Andrea quit, Mr. Runyon. I'm surprised no one has told you."

"I'd heard," he said. "She didn't say where she was going?"

"Home, I presume."

"Back to Barstow?"

"Andrea's departure was quite abrupt."

"I don't understand why she left," Hook said.

"Nor I, Mr. Runyon. Perhaps Andrea's dedication to Doctor Baldwin prevented her from working under my leadership. In any event, she found it impossible to continue her employment here.

"Now, if there's nothing else?" she said.

"Have you heard from Doctor Baldwin?" he asked.

"Doctor Baldwin is still in the hospital," she said.

"When will he be coming back?"

"That's unclear. Though Doctor Baldwin is physically improved, he continues to exhibit signs of stress. I've agreed to serve as director until he is fully recovered.

"I really must be going, Mr. Runyon."

Hook stood. "Do you expect to hear from Andrea?"

Helms lifted her chin, bringing Hook into focus. "Frankly, Andrea left our employment without notice or explanation. I should think that recommendations could not be expected.

"If you'll excuse me. Surely you must have important crimes to solve somewhere on your railroad. Good day to you, Mr. Runyon."

37

OATNEY SMILED AND gave Hook a squeeze. "I'll be working with the women?" she asked.

"Yes, and you'll be with Roy," he said. "More locals are hiring on all along as well."

"Thanks," she said. "And thanks for letting me sleep in your caboose."

"You can sleep in my caboose anytime," he said.

"So where's Mixer?" she asked.

"He hung back. I can't get him away from the compound. I think he misses Andrea."

Oatney slipped her shoes on. "I figure he's not the only one."

Hook lit a cigarette.

"Helms says Andrea left in a hurry. She says they won't be able to recommend her for another job since she left without giving notice."

"Doesn't sound like Andrea," Oatney said. "The only way out of here would be by car or bus. You could check with the lady who sells bus tickets. Maybe she would remember."

The woman behind the bus ticket counter glanced up from reading the comics and took a drag off her cigarette. Hook studied her face through the cloud of smoke. He hadn't the faintest idea why he'd thought she looked like Bette Davis. One eyelid drooped slightly, and creases notched her lip line. Her teeth were nicotine stained, and there were splotches of coffee on her blouse.

She looked at Hook's prosthesis and then up at him. "You leaving again, Mister?"

Hook leaned against the counter. "I've a question," he said.

She tapped the ashes off her cigarette. "I *heard* you was a yard dog," she said.

"Did a girl with glasses and freckles buy a bus ticket out of here, maybe to Barstow?"

"Look, Mister, I've been selling tickets out this window for twenty-five years. You think I can remember a girl with freckles?"

"You remembered me," he said.

"Some folks you just remember."

"It would have been recently, the last few days maybe."

"I don't think so," she said. "She might have come through with those ladies from the First Baptist. They were headed to church camp, giggling like eighth graders. She could have been here then. Who knows?"

"Thanks," he said.

She turned back to her comics. Peeking over the top of the paper, she said, "Sometimes folks go to Woodward to catch the bus. Lot more connections. Maybe she caught a ride over with someone. It's not that far, you know."

When Hook passed the guardhouse on the way to the women's barracks, Mixer, who had been asleep on the porch, came out to greet him. He wound his way through Hook's legs, his tail swinging back and forth like a metronome.

"You okay, boy?" Hook asked, rubbing the backs of Mixer's ears. "There's food at the caboose."

Mixer answered by shaking from head to tail and then going back to his spot in the shade.

Hook found Roy leaning against the door of the women's ward. Roy scratched at his head as he thought.

"Someone might have taken her over," he said. "There's folks going back and forth all the time. In fact, I got a load of groceries to pick up today. I'd figured on waiting until my shift ended."

"How about going now?" Hook asked.

"Well, Oatney's here. I guess she could manage. She's got all those women in the bathroom stuffing socks in their bras."

"What?" Hook said, shaking his head.

"Oatney says it does more for lifting a woman's spirits than a diesel-powered dildo."

"I'd appreciate a ride to Woodward soon as possible, Roy."

"You ain't going to be packing heat, shooting up train robbers and such, are you?"

"I hadn't planned on it," Hook said.

"Wait here," he said. "I'll get my list."

The old truck rolled out in a cloud of blue smoke. At thirty miles an hour, the front wheels began to wobble. At forty-five, the side windows rattled in the doors, and dust rose up from the floorboards. By the time they came into the bus station, dust covered Hook's pants, and his clothes smelled of gasoline.

The ticket agent looked up through the window bars and sucked at a tooth.

"None with freckles," he said. "Saw one with a wart on her lip the size of a quarter."

"Thanks, anyway," Hook said.

From there they went to the store and bought four sacks of white flour, two twenty-five-pound sacks of sugar, and ten pounds of sweet butter.

On the way out of town, Hook said, "Would you mind stopping by the hospital, Roy?"

"You sick, Hook? You been looking a little pale."

"It's from gasoline fumes and tall tales, Roy. No, I'm not sick. I want to talk to Baldwin's physician."

Roy cut left and lumbered the two blocks to the hospital. "I've been hauling inmates over from time to time," he said.

"I shouldn't be long, Roy. Have yourself a smoke."

The nurse told him that Doctor Anderson was just washing up after a tonsillectomy and that Hook could wait in the hall and probably catch him.

Anderson came out combing his hair back with a comb. The blood splatters on the cuffs of his white coat still looked fresh, and he smelled of ether.

"I don't know what the medical profession would do without tonsils and ovaries," he said.

Hook explained who he was.

"Yes," Anderson said. "You're the rail detective. Perhaps you'd care to step into my office."

The doctor slipped off his coat and adjusted his tie.

"So how's the young lady with the foot wound?" he asked.

"Anna? They tell me she's doing fine," Hook said.

"Ah, yes, Anna. I'd forgotten her name. She said you tried to kill her with your hook."

Hook smiled and held up his prosthesis. "Anna's an elusive victim," he said.

Anderson nodded. "And an imaginative one."

Hook said, "I came over for supplies and thought it a good opportunity to check on Doctor Baldwin's condition."

Doctor Anderson wet his finger and rubbed at one of the blood splatters on his cuff.

"I guess you hadn't heard. I released Baldwin a few days ago."

"No. I didn't know."

"He was quite anxious to get back to his work, and there was little more that I could do for him here."

"I don't believe he's shown up at the asylum yet," Hook said.

Doctor Anderson twisted his mouth to the side. "I was ambivalent about releasing him, but in good conscience I simply couldn't keep him here longer."

"It's odd he hasn't returned," Hook said.

"Doctor Baldwin didn't share his plans with me, but perhaps he decided to take a short vacation before going back to work."

"Perhaps," Hook said. "His illness came on rather suddenly the first time. I hope he's not had a relapse. Are you still convinced that drugs were involved?"

"I have to be careful here, Mr. Runyon, patient confidentiality and all. Frankly, I can't be certain about the diagnosis. Our lab is quite primitive here, so determining the cause was difficult at best. Still, it was a reasonable diagnosis given his symptoms and his access to drugs."

"I see."

"There were other complicating issues as well. I have a responsibility to both treat and protect my patients. But sometimes the two principles are contradictory. One has to weigh one's options and then decide. It's difficult territory. Doctors much prefer facts to ethical contradictions."

"It's the same with detective work," Hook said. "There's the book and then there's reality. Personally I've found common sense to be the best course in such situations.

"I do admit that sometimes it doesn't pan out so well. Leaving a truck on the tracks to apprehend a hobo seemed a reasonable course of action at the time."

"Excuse me?"

"Just a little disagreement with the railroad on procedure."

Anderson smiled. "After Doctor Baldwin's confinement, he improved markedly, but I was also compelled to treat his symptoms, which over the course of time subsided."

"From the medical treatment?"

"That's the dilemma, isn't it? He was anemic and complained that he had trouble attending. I gave him medications. In the end, the treatment may have corrupted the purpose of the confinement, which was to isolate the cause. But as a doctor, I was duty-bound to relieve his situation."

"You diagnosed and treated Doctor Baldwin, and he improved as a consequence. How is that a problem?"

Doctor Anderson picked up a pencil and tapped his desk with the eraser.

"I felt intuitively that Doctor Baldwin was under the influence of drugs. This is something patients rarely own up to, particularly doctors. I thought by isolating him, I could, through the process of elimination, determine the source of the symptoms. As it turned out, I could not make those distinctions."

Hook rubbed at his shoulder where the harness cut. Its constant weight sometimes gave him a violent headache.

"Could you be more specific, Doctor?"

"I was unable to determine if Doctor Baldwin's improvement was the result of our medical intervention or his inability to obtain drugs. Nor could I eliminate the nagging possibility that his improvement might be due to the absence of outside interference."

Hook looked up. "You mean someone else could have been supplying him the drugs?"

"That's one of two possibilities," he said.

Hook stood and studied Doctor Anderson's face. "Or could have been giving him the drugs without his knowledge?"

"Yes, Mr. Runyon," he said. "That's the other possibility."

38

THEY RELEASED DOCTOR Baldwin several days ago," Hook said to Roy.

Roy looked at him over his shoulder. "Where did he go?"

"Don't know," he said. "Baldwin didn't leave a forwarding address. Maybe he had a little thinking to do."

Roy pulled out on the highway and brought the truck up to a mild lope. As they rattled along, Hook lit a cigarette and thought about what Doctor Anderson had said. Was it possible that someone else had been giving Baldwin drugs without his being aware of it?

There were certainly any number of people who had access to drugs, almost anyone under the employ of the asylum. Security was lax at best. Many times he'd seen the medical-supply cabinet unlocked.

For that matter, drugs were available in other places as well. If access defined the crime, if there was a crime, even Andrea could not be eliminated.

The real question, the one that had eluded him from the beginning, was, Why? It made more sense if Doctor Baldwin was procuring the drugs himself. He had access and an addiction that needed feeding. But that failed to explain the other calamities that had befallen the asylum.

"You're sure quiet for a yard dog," Roy said. "You have gas?"

"Jesus, Roy, you ever censor yourself before you say something?"

"You got to hear words before you know if they're proper," he said. "Anyway, that was sure enough a pained look you had on your face."

"I'm worried about Andrea," he said.

"Why don't you just call her, Hook?"

"It would be impossible for her phone to be connected this soon."

Roy rolled down the window and hiked his foot up on the clutch pedal.

"Couldn't you call the Barstow police?" he asked. Hook looked over at him.

"No," Roy said. "I suppose not."

By the time they pulled into the fort, the sun had dropped. Roy turned on the dock lights and backed in the truck. Hook helped carry in the supplies. When he went out to get the last twenty-five-pound bag of sugar, it was gone.

"Where'd the sugar go?" he asked Roy.

"I carried it in already."

"You did?"

"Yeah. I was working while you were smoking. It ain't no wonder you're a yard dog. You wouldn't last ten minutes in a real job.

"About that girl, Hook," he said, leaning against the fender of the truck. "I figure she's on her way home. Things were pretty sour around here with Helms. Andrea wasn't one to put up with it."

"Thanks for the lift," Hook said.

Hook stopped by the guardhouse to report to Helms what he'd learned about Baldwin's release. Mixer met him at the steps.

"You still here?" Hook asked.

Mixer went to the corner of the porch, circled a couple of times, and lay down.

The lights were out downstairs, and Helms's office door was open. Hook made his way up the stairs and knocked on the door. Animal sounds came from the cells, sounds made by creatures whose lives consisted of little more than a cell and a bunk and the misery within.

Shorty opened the door. His shirt was unbuttoned to expose a hairless chest. A gold chain with an agate pendant hung about his neck.

"Doctor Helms left several hours ago," he said. "She had some kind of meeting."

"You're here alone?" Hook asked.

"Just me," he said. "But these bastards are locked up and I ain't."

"Just remember these folks are insane, Shorty. They aren't stupid."

"Stupid enough to be here," he said. "Anyway, I have my axe handle back there to do the talking if it comes to it."

"You haven't seen Doctor Baldwin, have you?"

"He's in the hospital over to Woodward," Shorty said.

"Thanks," Hook said.

At the bottom of the stairs, Hook paused. Moonlight shined through Helms's office window and across her desk. He could see her telephone and, next to it, her coffee cup. A stack of papers had been set to the side.

Eddie would be fuming by now, wondering why he hadn't called. Eddie could heat up fast when someone challenged his authority. If Hook got another Brownie, he could end up sleeping on a gunnysack under a bridge.

He slipped into Helms's office and sat down at her desk. The moonlight fell over his shoulder. Helms's scent lingered in her office like funeral flowers. He looked out the window for any signs of her. She would not approve of his using her phone.

He picked it up and called Eddie.

"Hello," Eddie said.

"Hook here, Eddie. Just wanted you to know that I'm back."

"Do you ever call during work hours, Runyon?"

"Some of us work longer hours than others."

"What the hell is going on with you, Runyon?"

"What do you mean, what's going on? I'm working security for the railroad and giving them back my goddang paycheck for a wrecked truck."

"I get a call from Wichita police," Eddie said, "something about them picking up a yard dog for soliciting a hooker, and I'm thinking that might be Runyon they're talking about. But then they say this yard dog was bumming a Santa Fe freighter, and I'm thinking, Christ, even Runyon ain't dumb enough to hobo on the railroad where he works."

"It isn't what it seems."

"It never is," he said.

"Look, I'll be winding this thing up soon. You still need me down at El Paso?"

"Hell, Runyon, Mexico is empty. They all rode the train to Chicago."

"I got a few loose ends, Eddie. The railroad doesn't like loose ends."

Eddie paused on the other end. "Frenchy says he can get something out there in a matter of days."

"Thanks, Eddie."

"Course, if you got something against legal transportation, you could always hop a freighter and ride the rails down to El Paso, maybe pick up a hooker or two along the way."

"You're a hell of a supervisor, Eddie. I'll be ready."

Hook sat in the darkness. The last time he'd talked to Andrea she'd been in this office on this very phone. He turned his chair around and looked at the filing cabinets that sat under the windows.

On impulse, he opened the files and leafed through them. He pulled Helms's and Yager's personnel folders. The details Andrea had given him were spot on. Helms's academic career could only be described as stellar, and her recommendations for Yager glowed, were without reservations, and left nothing to be read between the lines.

He reached for a cigarette, hesitated, remembering what Roy had said about Helms's objections, and put it back into the pack.

He pulled over the file lying on the desk. It was marked "personal." He thumbed through the sheaf of papers. In it he found Helms's old research papers, monthly bank reports, letters, a photograph of a young Helms standing next to a man, his arm around her shoulders. She leaned away, her face absent of emotion. Hook realized that the man next to her could be no other than Frankie Yager.

He started to close the folder when he spotted a yellowed newspaper clipping near the back. Several of the creases had given way from having been folded and refolded many times. He turned to let the moonlight fall on the article.

RELEASED INMATE MURDERS LOCAL FAMILY

Last night at eleven P.M. Moorhead police responded to a call reporting a fire at 1207 Fifth Street. Upon their arrival, they found the home of John and Martha Helms fully engulfed in fire. All attempts at rescue failed, the heat having driven the police back. Both John and Martha Helms, overcome by smoke, perished in the inferno.

It was not until they searched the grounds that they discovered Bria Helms, sixteen-year-old daughter of John and Martha Helms, hiding in the storage shed behind the home.

Bria Helms managed to report to the police that a sound had awakened her in the night. She got up to find that a man had entered the house through a window.

Fearing for her life, she fled to hide in the shed. Helms reported that the man exited through the back door, removed his clothes, and watched as the house was destroyed.

Though Helms could hear the screams of her parents as they were consumed by the fire, she was unable to assist them. When the assailant heard the police siren, he quickly dressed and escaped into the darkness.

Bria Helms's description led to the arsonist's arrest a short time later. He has since been identified as Bertrand Van Diefendorf, a pyromaniac who had committed a similar crime a few years earlier.

An interview with Doctor Theo Baldwin, the psychiatrist in charge of the criminally insane ward at Fergus Falls, revealed that Van Diefendorf had pleaded insanity to the previous crime, subsequently escaping punishment.

Doctor Baldwin and his colleagues had only recently found Van Diefendorf competent to rejoin society. Baldwin expressed sympathy for the family but maintained that a broken mind could not be held responsible for its deeds, regardless of how reprehensible they may be. He said that no matter how long it took, someday he would present Van Diefendorf as a functional member of society.

Having no other relatives to assume guardianship, Bria Helms has been placed in the custody of the state. Van Diefendorf will most likely be returned to Fergus Falls Insane Asylum to resume treatment.

Hook leaned back in the chair. At last his search for "why" may have come to an end. Revenge had driven crime since the beginning of time, and Bria Helms must surely have had need to avenge the death of her parents.

But then Yager could just as easily have been the one responsible. He'd had opportunity in every situation: the fire, Elizabeth's plunge from the trestle, even the food poisoning.

Hook took out his pack of cigarettes again but then set it aside. He drummed his fingers on the desk. The destruction of the asylum had continued after Yager's demise. In the end, only one person remained who might want it destroyed.

Hook took the photograph from the folder and studied it again. Yager's infatuation with Helms showed in his face, the way his arm drooped over her shoulders. Perhaps he had been no more than her dupe, an instrument of her retribution.

Once Helms knew that Hook had exposed Yager's past, she could have arranged Yager's death. Maybe she had withdrawn Smith's medication or replaced it with the placebo, allowing Smith the full force of his aggression against Yager. Hook had seen her take the green bottle from the cabinet that very day. In the end, maybe Bria Helms just didn't like getting her hands dirty when it came to killing people.

But could she have nourished such hatred for such an extended period of time? Could anyone? She would have had to overcome her situation, both parents gone, and she little more than a teenager at the time. There would have been an education to complete, and then she would have had to pursue Baldwin halfway across the country to destroy him.

And what about Yager, a man of limited intelligence and appeal? She would have had to recruit him; given him whatever price he'd required to carry out her plan; and, in the end, have him brutally murdered. Why hadn't she just killed Van Diefendorf at the outset? There had been ample opportunity. And through all this, she would have placed herself in danger of discovery.

Could Bria Helms have held all this together over the years to destroy everything that her nemesis had tried to build?

Hook turned and studied the moon, which had climbed into the blackness.

It would never have been enough for Bria Helms to simply destroy the sick mind that had set the fire. She would have had to destroy the principle behind it and the man who had sworn to once again turn madness loose upon the world.

And then the question came to Hook like a jolt of electricity. If Bria Helms had discovered Andrea's involvement, would she retaliate with the same deliberate cunning as she had with the others?

His heart beat in his ears at what he knew to be the answer.

Lights flashed in the window. Closing the file, he stepped into the darkness and squeezed behind the door.

The click of Helms's footsteps were singular in the night.

She paused. He could smell her perfume in the stillness and knew she must be standing in the office doorway.

And then she turned to climb the stairs. Hook waited until he heard the door close. Outside, a breeze swept through the trees, and shadows danced in the moonlight, illuminating his pack of cigarettes still lying on her desk.

39

HOOK SLIPPED THROUGH the darkness to the front door of the guardhouse. He had to find Andrea, and he had to find her soon. Maybe he should have followed Roy's suggestion and called the Barstow police, but he'd put himself on the wrong side of the law there. He could contact Eddie Preston, ask him to do it, but then he'd have a lot of explaining to do.

At the door, Hook looked out the window. The barracks' lights were out, and things had settled in for the night. Mixer still slept on the porch, curled in a ball just outside the door.

Hook turned the knob and eased open the door. Mixer rose, sniffed the air, and darted between Hook's legs into the guardhouse.

"Damn it," Hook said under his breath.

He peered into the dark, trying to spot Mixer before he alerted the whole damn fort.

"Mixer," he whispered. "Come here, boy, you son of a bitch."

Damn that dog. He was going to get a cat, a big fat one that slept twenty-three hours a day.

And then the scratching came from out of the darkness, as if Mixer were trying to dig a hole in the floor. Hook stepped back indoors. He couldn't leave him in there.

He followed the sound through the darkness. Suddenly, Mixer touched his hand with his wet nose and then disappeared once more to dig at the floor.

Hook paused at the stairwell. Looking up, he could see the door at the top of the stairs, a thin line of light seeping from under it. If Helms came out now, there would be no explaining.

"Damn you, Mixer," he whispered. "I'm going to chain you to the caboose."

When Hook reached out to snag him, his prosthesis clanked on the hinge of the door that led under the stairs. He stopped, his heart thudding in his ears. Maybe that was it. Maybe something or someone had been taken down there. Maybe Mixer had known it all along. Hook checked his P.38 and clicked off the safety.

The second he opened the door, Mixer disappeared down the steps. Hook edged along in the darkness, the smell of damp and mold in the air. At the bottom, he paused, listening.

"Hello?" he said. Silence rang in his ears. "Hello? Anyone here?"

A voice came from the darkness. "Hook? Oh, Hook, is that you?"

"Andrea? Jesus, Andrea, what are you doing down here?"

The explosion in Hook's head came as a flash of light, a white-hot point sizzling in the darkness. And when he came to, he lay on the floor, a sticky mass oozing from above his ear. He groaned and tried to move, his stomach seizing. He reached for his sidearm. It was gone.

Through the bars of his cell, he could see Bria Helms sitting on a bench next to the stairwell, the kerosene lantern on a stand, its flame dancing on the ceiling of the chamber. Shorty's axe handle lay across Helms's lap, and in her hand she clasped a skeleton key on a ring.

In the cell next to Hook, Andrea sat on the bunk, her hair matted, her eyes sunken and weary. Doctor Theo Baldwin sat in the corner on the floor, his legs pulled into his arms. He watched Hook over the tops of his knees. Baldwin's beard had darkened with growth, and his eyes were drawn. The air reeked with the stink of sewage.

Neither Baldwin nor Andrea spoke or acknowledged Hook's presence. Helms rose to hang the key on its peg next to the door. She spoke then, her back toward them, as if speaking to herself.

"Even though my charge is unfinished, all things must end, even this," she said. "I would have followed this evil philosophy to its ruin." She turned, her eyes afire with lamplight and hatred. She locked them on Baldwin. "I would have pursued you to the finish, Theo. I would have destroyed all that you are and that you have."

With that, she left, closing the door behind her. Hook struggled to stand. His ears rang, and his head whirled. Andrea reached through the bars, touching him.

"Helms came from behind in the darkness," she said. "There was no time, nothing we could do."

"What's going on, Andrea?" he asked, leaning against the bars.

"She caught me going through the files," she said. "I'm lucky to be alive. I didn't think I'd ever be found."

Baldwin pulled himself onto the bunk. He buried his face in his hands.

"I realized I'd been drugged," he said. "I also realized that it might be Bria. I came back to confront her. She told me about her parents and about how her life had been ruined. She confessed to having Andrea imprisoned. I demanded that she show me." He looked up at Hook. "I'm a foolish man, Mr. Runyon. First thing I knew, I'd been locked in the cell with Andrea."

"No more foolish than me," Hook said. "What do you think Helms will do?"

Baldwin peered at him through the lamplight. "Her anger is

consuming and irrational. We must get out of here. I'm afraid we are in grave danger."

Hook looked about the dungeon, its ponderous stone walls, its hand-forged bars that in the past had caged so many.

"Hook," Andrea said, clutching his arm through the bars. "I smell smoke."

Hook hung his head and closed his eyes. "Fire," he said.

"Oh, God," Andrea said.

Baldwin grabbed the cell door, shaking it. "She's killing us," he yelled. "She's burning us alive."

Even as he spoke, smoke rolled down the stairwell, a black wave that dimmed the lantern light in its wake. Andrea dropped to the floor. Baldwin coughed and shook his head.

"The key," Hook said, rubbing at his eyes. "The key on the wall."

Andrea said, "It can't be reached. We've tried and tried."

"Tear strips off your skirt," Hook said.

"What?"

"Strips," he said. "Do it now. The smoke is going to snuff out our lantern any second."

Andrea stepped out of her skirt. Starting each strip with her teeth, she ripped them off one by one and pushed them through the bars to Hook.

Hook shed his shirt and pulled off his prosthesis. He knotted the strips together and threaded one end through the prosthesis, the opposite end to the cell bars.

Baldwin now lay on the floor, gasping for air, mucus dripping from his nose. Andrea covered her face with her hands. The caustic smoke had deepened about them in an ominous black cloud.

Hook squinted the tears from his eyes and pitched the prosthesis at the ring on the wall. It fell short. Gathering it up, he pitched it again, this time knocking the ring from its mooring. But even as it clattered onto the floor, the lamplight fluttered and went out.

40

Hook DROPPED TO his knees and peered into the blackness. The key could be anywhere. He could hear Baldwin wheezing on the floor next to him.

"Hook," Andrea said. "I can't breathe."

"Hang in there," Hook said, carefully pulling in the prosthesis. "I think I have the key."

When it clanked against the bars, he reached through and felt along the floor. His lungs were aflame, and sweat trickled down his neck.

"I've got it," he said.

Working the key into the lock, he heard it click, and the door gave way. He slipped his prosthesis back on, and within moments he'd freed Andrea and Baldwin. They groped their way up the stairwell, the smoke growing warmer and thicker as they climbed.

Mixer met them at the top of the stairs, his tail thumping.

"Go get the others," Hook said to Andrea. "Call the police and the fire department."

"Where are you going?" she asked, holding on to him.

"There are men trapped up there."

"But those men are dangerous."

"Hurry, Andrea," he said.

"Hook," she said. "She might be waiting."

"Andrea, we don't have much time."

"I'll go with you," Baldwin said to Hook.

"I'll need you both down here when we come out," Hook said. "Now go, and take Mixer with you."

Andrea squeezed Hook's arm and turned for the door.

When they'd gone, Hook crawled up the stairs, keeping beneath the heat and smoke. He ran his hand over the door, warm but not yet hot. He took out his handkerchief, covered his face, and opened the door.

At the far end of the cell block, flames licked up the walls, crackling and hissing as they consumed the aging structure. The inmates howled from their cells. Some hid behind their mattresses. Others lay under the bunks to escape the scorching smoke that drifted down the hallway. Hook could hear the wail of sirens coming from somewhere in the distance.

When he spotted Shorty sprawled on the floor, Hook knelt at his side and turned him over. Brain matter oozed from the wound in his head, and his eyes stared off into space. By the looks of things, Helms had turned Shorty's axe handle against him with fatal results.

He took the keys from Shorty's belt and opened the cells. He pointed to the exit, motioning for each inmate to keep as low as possible. On another day, any one of them could have killed him, but even madness could not bear the flames that now raged about them.

Only then did Hook see Van Diefendorf in the last cell. He sat on his bunk, his hands folded in his lap. Flames lapped up about him, a gathering inferno, its belly blue with heat, its flames crackling and churning up the walls.

Hook edged toward Van Diefendorf, but the heat drove him back, the stink of scorched hair and flesh. Van Diefendorf looked out from the heart of the firestorm, his features melting like wax, and he smiled.

When Hook exited the guardhouse, a cheer rose up from the crowd that had gathered. The staff took charge of the inmates, and Andrea rushed forward to hold him. The fire chief waited and then stepped forward.

"Anyone else in there?" he asked.

"Not alive," Hook said.

Hook looked back at the guardhouse. Embers lifted into the night, and the old building creaked and moaned as it surrendered to the flames.

"Hook," Andrea said, pointing to where the firelight gave way to the darkness. "Out there."

Hook turned to see Helms watching the fire from the shadows of the fort cemetery. She stood naked, her arms wrapped about herself against the morning chill.

41

HOOK AND ANDREA sat on the steps of the caboose and watched the birds bank in the rising sun. A train whistle rose and fell in the distance, and Andrea leaned her head on Hook's shoulder.

"Doctor Baldwin should be back from Helms's preliminary hearing by now," she said.

"In a way, he can't let her go," Hook said. "They've been together a long time when you think about it."

"I'm going to miss you," Andrea said.

"You could still come along," he said.

"They need me now more than ever," she said.

Black smoke from Frenchy's engine broke on the horizon, and the thud of its drivers rode down the rails. Within minutes, Frenchy brought her in, the brakes screeching, the heat of the boiler quivering off into the morning cool.

Frenchy leaned out of the cab, rolling his cigar into the corner of his mouth.

"There's a reefer icing in Waynoka. She's headed south. We might catch her if we don't wait too goddang long."

"Thought you were going to retire?" Hook said over the chug of the engine.

"Someone's got to look out for you," Frenchy said, grinning.

"Bring her in, Frenchy, and don't scatter my books all over hell."

"Look who's coming," Andrea said.

Roy, Santos, Oatney, and Doctor Baldwin were all walking down the tracks toward them. Behind them were Lucy, Ruth, Anna, and Bertha. They were waving with large swings of their arms like schoolgirls.

Hook realized how fond he had grown of all of them. The world had left them behind because they didn't fit the mold. He, too, had come to their aid reluctantly, with doubts and fears of his own. He'd dismissed them as nutty and looney and smiled knowingly at their antics. But in the course of things, something had changed. He'd gotten to know them, as had Roy, Santos, and Oatney, to know their names, their desires, and their fears.

Now he understood Andrea's dedication to them, as people to care for and to protect. The world had failed them. It should have been there to mourn when those boys were sent, anonymous and abandoned, into a mass grave.

The group gathered behind the caboose. Oatney pulled Ruth's skirt down and slipped her arm over her shoulder.

"You might be needing this," Roy said, handing Hook's sidearm up to him. "They found it where Doctor Helms had been hiding."

"Who's running the shop?" Hook asked, dropping his sidearm into its holster.

"We're letting the new folks have a go at it," Roy said. "Figured the worst that they could do is burn the place down."

"Seth called," Oatney said. "Tulsa turned out."

Doctor Baldwin came around and reached up to shake Hook's hand.

"Many lives were saved," he said. "We've been given a second chance here in this place."

Frenchy signaled with three short blasts of the whistle. Andrea looked up at Hook, her eyes filling. He kissed her and lowered her off the steps.

Steam shot out of the sides of the bullgine as Frenchy took up the coupler slack.

Hook turned to Doctor Baldwin. "About Helms's charges?"

"Premeditated murder," he said.

The caboose lurched and edged forward, picking up speed. Hook leaned out on the grab iron.

"How'd she plea?"

As the train pulled away, Baldwin cupped his mouth with his hands.

"Innocent," he said, shouting over the din of the engine. "By reason of insanity."